THE DRAGON TREE

JULIA IBBOTSON

ARCHBURY BOOKS

CONTENTS

Prologue	1
Chapter 1	3
Chapter 2	21
Chapter 3	39
Chapter 4	55
Chapter 5	68
Chapter 6	82
Chapter 7	90
Chapter 8	105
Chapter 9	116
Chapter 10	127
Chapter 11	134
Chapter 12	142
Chapter 13	151
Chapter 14	161
Chapter 15	169
Chapter 16	180
Chapter 17	194
Chapter 18	207
Chapter 19	217
Chapter 20	228
Chapter 21	240
Chapter 22	249
Chapter 23	264
Chapter 24	275
Chapter 25	286
Chapter 26	302
Chapter 27	309

Chapter 28	320
Chapter 29	327
Chapter 30	339
Chapter 31	351
Chapter 32	361
Chapter 33	372
Epilogue	381
Afterword	385
Acknowledgments	393
Also by Julia Ibbotson	395

Copyright © Julia Helene Ibbotson 2021

All rights reserved

The Dragon Tree: published by Archbury Books

ISBN 978-1-7398877-1-1

The right of Julia Helene Ibbotson to be identified as the author of this work has been asserted by her in accordance with the Copyright, Designs and Patents Act 1988

This story and any parts thereof may not be reproduced or used in any manner whatsoever without the written consent of the author. This is a work of fiction.

The characters and events in this novel are entirely fictional and in no way reflect or represent any real events nor persons living or dead.

Cover design by Lisa Firth at *www.fullybookeddesign.co.uk*

PROLOGUE

5 million years ago

It begins with a rumbling far beneath the ocean waters, a boiling deep below the waves.

The ocean floor tenses and strains to breaking, buckled with the magnitude of the forces within itself, and finally gives way to the turbulent might of the earth.

As the tumult rises four thousand metres to the surface, the seas become a mass of fiery explosions, a curtain of flames and all is clouded with plumes of steam and ash. The seas themselves are boiling across the blue-grey, it seems. Huge waves crash against each other, as fire rises and rages to the heavens, churning red and orange and black. The earth below the seas spews forth torrents of gas and fissural eruptions of basalt rocks. And embedded there amongst them are tiny creatures, encased in death in unyielding rock.

At length, after unimaginable time, the explosions gradually calm and the earth cools. The lava flows settle themselves into unsteady forms, into chimneys and columns and prisms. The leaking magma slows to a crust on the underwater edifice, pushing its way upwards seven thousand metres above the seabed to the surface. And on upwards, mountainous rocks of basalt and limestone and pumice, reaching up towards the sky.

And there within the crevices of the towering cliffs in the north and the east, begin the tiny possibilities of life: the minute organisms, trilobites and brachiopods, crustaceans leaking calcium to grow coral reefs. The rich fertile volcanic sand at the base of the cliffs gives shelter to the first vegetation, and the holes in the pumice stone of the causeways where the gases had exploded give rest to huge seabirds and protection for their nests.

But one ammonite, from the beginning of time itself, is flung far from the core, down the mountain and into the valley where it comes to rest, finally, not far from the ocean where it began. It clings to the cliff base, and there it is covered with rock and debris and ash until it is at last found and its power finally discovered ...

CHAPTER 1

VIV

The present day

Viv rubbed her fingertips over the roughness of the ancient ammonite in her left hand, trying to get her head around what Rory just said. She shrugged his hand off her shoulder and took another slug of red wine. A little splashed on to her ivory silk top. But she didn't care.

"What? Rory! Fly off to a volcanic island somewhere in the Atlantic for a year? No way! How would that help?" She slammed her glass onto the side table next to the French windows of the old rectory. This time the splashes hit the antique Indian carpet. Rory stared at it for a moment, then took a deep breath.

"Hey, it's not some desert island away from civilisation, darling. It's Madeira." Rory's voice was quiet, strained, and she could detect the suppressed frustration in his voice, the disappointment. She could almost feel the tightness in his chest, the air between them was so tense. He ran his fingers round his stark-white clerical collar as though it was suddenly too tight. "But it's your decision."

She drew in her ragged breath and looked down, frowning, and noticed that her gel nails, blood red against the fossil stone, were already beginning to chip. Surely it had only been a week? Or maybe two? Oh God, they looked so tatty, so ugly. And she'd only just been able to face getting her hair and nails done again, after what had happened. Only just pulled herself up, pushed herself out of bed in the mornings, forced herself out of the house.

OK, so she'd let herself go. Unsurprisingly – surely she could forgive herself that much. And yet she'd always been so careful to be groomed, professional, her trademark amongst some of her more casual, even scruffy, faculty colleagues. Well, after all, it was her armour, her defence against her self-doubt. That imposter syndrome she felt about her academic work. How had she managed to convince the university that she should have that senior role? Yes, she knew she was clever ... but *that* clever? She really wasn't sure any more.

Now she couldn't even keep her gel intact for a week. That couldn't be right. The emerald-green-haired girl at the new nail bar had said it would last

THE DRAGON TREE

two or even three weeks. She'd go in to complain tomorrow. If she could summon up the strength.

The brain fog drifted across her mind. Try to refocus. Away from that niggling little voice in her head. So ... Rory's announcement.

"You're expecting me to make a big life-decision, Rory! For God's sake! I can't even manage to decide what I fancy to eat next, let alone decide to make a new home somewhere."

"Viv, darling, wait a minute, it's not exactly a new home, it's just for a year, not a lifetime ..." his hand clutching her arm, the other running fingers over the dark stubble on his chin as she turned away, "calm down, please, let's just think about it as a possibility ... an opportunity, even. For us both. Not just me. A rest in the sun for you, away from work, maybe a place to start to heal. I reckon it could help, right now ..."

In her dry mouth, she could still sense the bitter after-taste of the headache pills she'd been grabbing as he landed this new bombshell on her. She wondered if she'd have been wiser to have taken the pink Migraleve that would have fended off yet another migraine attack. She seemed to have been getting a lot these days, since it happened anyway. Her vision was wobbly, and she was waiting for that warning sign: the zigzags blotting out half the sight in her right eye.

She pressed the small hard stone into her palm and welcomed the pain as its sharp edges pierced her skin. She remembered it all, every horrible moment.

Nauseous, she shivered, truly not wanting to relive it. But this had brought it all back.

"It won't help. Why do you always have to do that – trying to make it all OK again. It'll never be OK." She didn't *want* it to be OK. You can't blot something like this out, forget and move on. "How could you even suggest such a thing!" Ana was worth more than that.

And why did Rory always have to be so calm and rational, when she was churning inside, guts swirling with that constant sinking sensation.

"Darling, I understand, really I do. I know you don't believe me, but I do feel the same. I just want the best for us now – in the circumstances."

She was so tired. She'd hardly slept for weeks, living in a dream world, agonising about how to repair her torn body and broken heart. And unable to do anything about it. She couldn't even think straight. She could hardly string a sentence together, let alone consider a proposition for their future. Ana consumed all her thoughts; there was no room for a future without her.

"But Rory, I can't leave her." Her voice sounded feeble even in her own ears. "I can't fly off to Funchal and leave her all alone here, in that God-awful place."

He raised his eyebrows. "God-awful place?"

But she was trembling now, waves of apprehension rising through her. How many weeks had it been now? Oh, of course she knew *exactly* how many.

"What's happening to me? Oh, God, Rory, I hardly

know myself any more. I can't think straight. I have to keep reminding myself I am actually Dr Viv DuLac. What a travesty. Seems like another world."

Medievalist, academic. That life hardly seemed real any more. It was like someone else's life. Someone who was always strong and capable. She bit her lip, her flesh chewed and raw. Running her tongue around inside her lips, she could feel the sore tenderness of the abrasions.

Viv turned away from him, towards the glazed outer doors of the rectory. God, she was a wreck, such a jumble of emotions.

Rory's patient breath was warm, but it prickled the back of her neck as he nestled in to her back. She shrugged. He didn't seem to feel her try to push him away, because his arms slid around her waist, folding across the buckle of her jeans belt.

Standing there at the French windows closed tight against the March storms, Rory pressed against her back, Viv stared at the cold Derbyshire rain lashing against the glass. The great spreading trees, horse chestnut, copper beech and the English oaks that had been there since ancient times, dripped, branches weighted down, cowering. The rain had not stopped for a month and the rectory lawn was sodden, the terrace flagstones shiny and black.

Her left hand slid down to her belly, still a little swollen, and she gently stroked the contours although there was no longer any life inside her to caress.

Pregnant with life stirring, then kicking, squirming, for five months ... Rory caught her hand and held it, and she sensed that he was determined to send his comfort and love into her being, so she allowed him the moment. She felt the warmth of his muscular body against her back and his tentative kiss below her ear. What had happened to that heat which used to suffuse her body at Rory's touch? She still loved him, of course, the hot priest she'd fallen for a couple of years ago ... but ...

She wanted to push him away.

Yet, she wanted to bury herself in him.

She had no idea what she wanted any more.

Everything outside of her now seemed hollow, echoing, misshapen, as though she saw it all from under water. A watcher. A distant observer. She was submerged, still barely capable of processing the drifting dark ship-wreck shapes around her, the shapes of normal mundane objects of domestic life she had loved and that had been so familiar. Things that had seemed so solid, so ready to welcome a child's touch. Upstairs, the nursery they'd decorated so lovingly together not so long ago, the empty cot, the pristine changing mat on the white painted cupboard.

"It's OK, Viv. You're still grieving." Rory paused. "*We're* still grieving. It'll take time for us to surface." He hugged her closer to him. "That cliché, time heals, isn't right, you know. It doesn't. But the pain *will* get easier to bear."

Easier? Easier! Viv swivelled round, trying to quell her annoyance, to bury her cheeks into his old prickly sweater, and inhale the fusty smell of the church vestry, dank and dusty. To find herself again. "Oh God, don't you go starting a sermon with me, Reverend Netherbridge!"

She stopped her urge to beat his strong broad chest in frustration and hurt. It wasn't his fault. She knew he was only trying to be kind. To be empathetic. But somehow it angered her that he was so objective, distant, while she was torn apart. That he was so ... so *vicar-like*, when she was so frail and flawed.

"Sorry." He stroked her back. "I didn't mean to sound like, well, pulpit-moralising, patronising. I just ..." He moved his hand from her to rake his fingers through his thick dark hair. "Look, Viv, I just don't know how to reach you. I don't know what to say any more." She heard his deep breath draw in and the almost imperceptible tremble at his ribs as his breath caught. "I just ... I do love you, you know."

She heard his hope reaching for the surface, and she couldn't help but respond with a press of her lips, a wisp of a motion, into his chest, and felt his answering sigh into the crown of her head, nestling his kiss into her thick auburn hair. She knew exactly what he was thinking, she always did, that this was the first time in weeks that she had shown even a glimmer of the young wife he knew. He wanted her to be the teasing, happy girl he fell for, as though none of this had happened. Yet she didn't want to pretend it away. They each responded to it all so differently. She couldn't 'switch off' and act a part.

Suddenly he pulled away, clutching his stomach as if he had been stabbed. "Ouch. Good grief, Viv, what on earth have you got in your hand, woman?"

For a moment she'd lost her awareness of the stone. Shocked, she opened her fist and stared at the fossil in her palm, and the dark spots of blood that oozed around it, seeping slowly into the rough limestone, reflecting the red of her nails.

"Oh God, I'm sorry. It's ..." She looked up at Rory's surprised eyes. A sharp point must have pierced him as he held her close. "It's the fossil ammonite that I found ages ago in my mother's memory box, the one that she brought back from that archaeological dig." She jerked her head back. "Well, that's ironic. It was a dig in Madeira, I'm sure it was! D'you remember me going through that box, finally, before ..." She frowned and bit her lip. Again. That'd be bleeding soon as well. "Oh lord, have I hurt you?"

Rory shuddered and shook his head. "No, it's OK. I think I'll live," but he winced. He raised the hem of his sweater, pulling the shirt beneath it out from his jeans waistband. He peered at his taut upper abdomen, toned from his morning runs around the peaceful narrow lanes of the sleepy Derbyshire parish. "No, there's nothing, no mark at all. How odd. For a moment, I was sure it had pierced through my skin." He shrugged. "Ah well. Good."

But his voice was soft, undulating in a way that wasn't his, echoing from far away. She seemed to hear it through a mist as if she wasn't really there. Was it the migraine coming?

Viv glanced down at her own palm with its torn skin and bloodied marks. She caught her breath. A wisp of a memory. The room around her seemed to draw in its breath too, and she felt the uneven wooden floor with its covering of worn carpet judder beneath her feet.

She was drifting, muzzy, so light-headed that all her thoughts flickered away and disappeared, leaving her with only feelings, sensations.

Nauseous, she sensed unfamiliar silver-green laurel trees outside in the garden moving barely perceptibly, just a slight dipping and readjustment of their roots buried deep in the wet soil. And just there, a strangely shaped tree, like a dragon, dark with outstretched branches, weeping purple blood. She felt the swish of a warm breeze on her bare skin and smelt the salty tang of the sea. Murmurings, movements, and the gentle thud of a soft footfall on the baked red earth. The brushing of a cloak on the grass. Noises swirling around her head, growing louder, reverberating through her consciousness. The sweep of a robe through the trees, the flash of frightened eyes, for a moment holding hers in a silent plea ... Then a memory of water. Great waves crashing around her, breaking on the timbers of the hull; the horrendous sound of the mast creaking to splitting point. Someone screaming, hand outstretched towards jagged cliffs towering above ... Then deeper, deeper, falling, her brain splitting and crashing, she saw turbulent boiling seas, and fire, red and black, raging in its angry path towards her, molten magma blasting to the skies, mountains forcing their might through the waves, flinging boulders away from their rage ...

Viv shrank back, covering her face with her hands, yet compelled to look through her shaking fingers, seeing the frightened eyes, the silent plea, the outstretched hand, opening ... and in it a small lump of rock embedded with a calcified creature curled in horrified terror.

She could hear Rory saying something ... at first from a long way away, but gently coming closer to her, his voice clearing away her visions, soothing her thoughts, words becoming more comprehensible. His hand was stroking her shoulder. Dizzy, she turned to the French windows. As they came into focus again, her mind processed the trees, strong solid English oak, beech, and chestnut. No silver-green laurels or a dark tree weeping blood, here in this village as far as it could be from the coast; her garden not caressed by warm sea breezes but buffeted in the cold beating English rain.

She turned and saw Rory's white face and startled eyes. "Oh God," she spluttered. "It's happening again."

~

Rory released her from his hug, guided her onto the battered sofa, and rose to fetch fresh glasses and a new bottle of wine. He carefully pressed a large goblet into her trembling hand, a wedding present, the one with her true name etched into the glass, and smiled ruefully. He poured the rich red wine right to the brim. The shock of the last hour had blasted her brain back to reality. She clutched the arm of the old worn sofa as her brain shifted gear to a flicker of the old Viv. A ghost of a smile.

"I hope it's not that expensive communion wine you're sloshing around," she said, hearing the slight tremor still in her voice.

He grinned tentatively, eyes fixed on her, and adopted a comic sonorous voice reminiscent of the bishop's. "'Tut tut, Mrs Netherbridge, or Doctor Whatever-you-call-yourself.'" He'd got the bishop's slightly impatient derisory confusion down to a tee. "Ahem. 'After over a year as a vicar's wife, I think you know that communion wine is certainly not Beaujolais nouveau, my dear.' Huh." Rory snorted. "Mind you, Viv, it might as well be vin de primeur the ridiculous cost of it at the church suppliers. No, not something we could drink at home!"

"Well, frankly, I really don't understand why on earth you have to buy it from one particular suppliers. If it was up to me, I'd just grab cheap plonk from the supermarket. People only have a tiny sip at communion anyway. Nobody'd know the difference."

"Good God, Viv! Cheap Aldi plonk?" Rory pulled an exaggeratedly mock-shocked expression. "It has to be the real deal! And properly blessed." He winked, but Viv caught the jerkiness, the hesitation as he assessed her mood.

"Well, I hope you've blessed this one, Rory, cheap plonk or not. And us," she added raising the glass to him with a sheepish smile. A heartbeat. "Especially after these past few weeks."

He grimaced and sipped his wine thoughtfully as he sat across from her on the old leather wing chair, his face lit by the flicker of the roaring log burner. She remembered how she used to feel her heart stop when she looked at him: his deep dark eyes that crinkled at the corners, his devastatingly intimate smile that bore into her soul. But goodness, it felt like a long time ago, before they were married, yet it was really no time at all. Yet now her heart felt numb.

She thought about how they met. It seemed like a whole other time and place. And in a way it was. She was still a little shivery from the visions, but she remembered how it had been that last time, the time she had first met Rory, the time they had reached out to each other across the centuries. That was when she had found out about her antecedents and the truth about her mother, Dr Elaine DuLac, descended from an ancestral line with special powers of insight into past lives. And discovered that she could never change her name, not even after marriage, because of that weird connection to the medieval Lady of the Lake, Nymue DuLac. And, even more weird, that Rory also, like her, somehow had the power to touch other past worlds. Because of the spiritual nature of his job, he said. He was never as knocked out by it all as she was. More accepting of whatever befell them. Well, whatever ... the point was that they had worked together to save Lady Vivianne and Sir Roland and their kingdom, retrieved their artefacts and managed to retain their own lives in the present day.

How extraordinary was that? It still felt unbelievable, dream-like, to her. And yet, what was it that had just happened? Rory had always told her that she was somehow inherently sensitive, vulnerable, to other-worldly echoes. She touched the mound of her stomach. And, goodness knows, she felt fragile now.

Pulling her legs up onto the sofa and tucking her feet beneath her, snuggling up, careful of her still tender belly and of her glass of wine, she reached over to the fossil that lay, innocent now, on the cushion beside her. Was it her imagination, or had it really curled more tightly in on itself? She stroked it as if it was soft and not hard and rough-surfaced. She'd treasured it ever since her beloved archaeologist parents had brought back the fossil ammonite from their excavations in a place called Machico. One of their last digs before their plane was blown out of the sky. She was sure that was in Madeira. She must google it.

She had a hazy memory of the delight she had as a young child as she stroked the rock with the curled shape inside. They had said that they'd brought it back from a distant land, a volcanic island in the Atlantic, and they had told her it was millions of years old. At the time she could barely understand what that meant. But it was special, a treasure. They said it was "magical". And now, a precious reminder of them and their explorations. She had nestled it carefully and respectfully back in the memory box after she was told that her parents were no longer coming back home to her. In times of trouble over the years, she had taken it out again and found comfort from it. And now, dear God, Rory was suggesting taking up a secondment to Madeira.

Well, maybe there was some kind of symmetry in it.

Her heart-beat stilling a little as she felt Rory's gaze on her, and looked across to him, sprawled in his armchair, long legs stretching across the rug, the heat of the fire glowing on his olive-skinned face. He smiled that sexy lopsided smile and raked his hand through his dark, curly hair, and ... goodness, was that a flicker of the familiar heart-flutter? She probably didn't deserve this strong, clever, thoughtful man who smiled at her now with such love, did she, when she felt so flawed and lost. She drew in a long thin wisp of a breath.

"Oh God, I'm sorry, Rory. For how I reacted to your news. I'm just so mixed up at the moment ..."

He shook his head, a dismissive gesture with his hand underlining his words. "You don't need to apologise. It's alright. I understand. It's early days and everything is still raw. It's come at a bad time. I shouldn't have thrown it at you like that. Look, it's entirely up to you. Your decision. But whichever way you decide, ... well, they need an answer pretty quickly. And I guess it won't be offered again. I had to tell you about it, didn't I?"

"Well, yes, but it was a surprise, it's so difficult at the moment. But then having that ... that *episode* again. After so long." She exhaled and closed her eyes. A flicker of crashing waves, a weird tree, an outstretched hand, opening to reveal a curled stone creature.

"Are you feeling a bit better now, Viv?"

She snapped her eyes open again and looked down at her glass, seeing that it was half empty, yet she had no recollection of drinking any of it. Just like that last time. She took a deep breath.

"Yes, I'm OK. It was just a ... I don't know what it was!"

"Not a full-blown slip, then?"

"No." She began to tell him about her...what was it? – a haunting, a vision? She was so glad that he understood her weird episodes. Of course he did; he had shared in them in some way, before, and for him as a priest, she guessed the other-worldly nature of life was not so great a leap of comprehension. He listened to her quietly, without interrupting, and then, in his usual calm way, smiled, a little sadly, and nodded.

"I'm sure it's the result of the distress at losing the baby, Viv. I mean, at five months pregnancy it's a traumatic miscarriage, and it's bound to have consequences. Having to go through with the birth, knowing …" He hesitated. "Darling, I do wish you'd go back to that counsellor. I'm sure it was helping."

"Well, frankly, no, I don't think so. I just didn't want to keep going through it all, over and over, analysing my feelings. How many different ways can you explain it? I need to find my own way, take control myself." She sighed.

This decision about Madeira. What to do? In many ways she longed to get away from the feelings of loss, and of failure. But at the same time, she dreaded leaving Ana behind. And yet she was torn; objectively she knew that her feelings were illogical and probably unfair to Rory, and to their partnership. Intellectually she knew perfectly well that it would take time and that she needed to begin the process of regaining her emotional strength, whatever her heart was whispering to her. It was just so hard. She didn't know why his announcement was such a shock, why she was so frightened of it. It wouldn't have been like that, before. She would have shared the excitement, the adventure. She really needed to start to get back to her old self again.

And maybe it was the shock of the new that she needed to have, to feel alive again.

"The counsellor suggested that you could be suffering from post-traumatic stress, Viv. Not surprising. So maybe distancing from the place, the associations, could help you recover from it. What do you think?"

She took a deep breath. "Well, Rory, actually I think, I don't know, maybe you're right. I think ..." She needed to say it before she lost her nerve, because once she'd said it she couldn't take it back. "... yes, I'm thinking maybe we ought to take up that secondment. You're right, it *is* only a year. Hmm, an interregnum in Madeira for you, a bit of a rest for me. Maybe this is a sign." Rory was looking across at her, frowning. "I mean a sign we should go." She touched her belly, stroking the emptiness, the remembered soreness. "Perhaps it's the right time. Maybe it's a Godsend, in more ways than one." She grimaced ruefully, knowing that he was well aware of her religious scepticism. "Ha, a divine intervention." She snorted with self-mockery. He smiled gently, making the corners of this eyes crinkle. She remembered the fluttering of her breath as she used to look at him. She nodded. "Yes, we should take this opportunity. That's my decision. Let's go."

"The baby ..." he began, stopping as Viv caught his

eye, "*Ana*. She isn't in an awful place, you know, darling. She's at peace in that lovely little corner of our churchyard. And we can plant a flowering shrub there before we go, and when we get back it'll be in full bloom. It's not for that long."

"I know. It isn't awful at all, really. It's death that's awful. And the cold earth on top of her." She shuddered. "I was just suddenly so frightened that she'd think we'd left her, forgotten her, there under the earth. That probably sounds stupid for a five-month pregnancy."

Rory moved across to her, took her glass from her, and rested it on the floor, and enfolded her in his arms. "Not at all. She's a real person. She was starting to stir, to kick. Even though she didn't get to take a breath in the world. She knows, I'm convinced of it, that we haven't forgotten her or abandoned her. Thoughts and prayers cross the boundaries of life and death and time. We won't ever forget our firstborn." He stroked Viv's back as her tears tracked down her face.

Keeping her cheek pressed against his chest, she silently reached out for the fossil from the cushion behind him, and traced the curled shape within it, and shivered.

CHAPTER 2

VIV

A few weeks later

The wings of the plane looked as though they were about to touch the Madeiran cliffs as Viv turned her head tentatively to the right, muscles tensed, and watched the land below. She felt the judder of the aircraft descending. Oh God, surely it was approaching too fast? Although she had travelled widely, especially for international conferences for the university, she never liked the flying itself. Especially after she had lost her parents in that air crash when she was only a child. Flying always gave her that echoing sense of doom.

She'd drifted off to sleep for most of the flight, having slept little the night before in anticipation of the early start that morning. She now felt groggy as she pulled herself from her dreams and the recurring nightmare of Ana's birth. She'd relived that drugged horror so many times since: the flashbacks of ripping and emptiness. Seeing herself as if from outside, a couple of metres above that sweat-damp, bloody hospital bed. Struggling to breathe, struggling to focus, despairing. Resisting the young nurse's gentle kindly-meant proposal to take the tiny swaddled body away to be 'disposed of' by the hospital. Good God, what *was* she thinking? Then later, relief, as the hospital chaplain, taking in the clerical collar on Rory who had been rushed away from evensong by the verger, softly suggesting a proper church burial and hesitantly asking Rory if he would prefer him to officiate. What a lovely sweet man, stilling her frantic heart. Rory nodding in silent gratitude. The chaplain asking the baby's name. *Ana*. A beautiful name, he'd smiled. A real person, though still and pale and lifeless in Viv's arms, asleep forever. The name they'd chosen, from a distant ancestor of Viv's late mother. *Ana*: with one 'n'. Where on earth had that memory come from? Viv had no idea why that name above all others had sprung into her mind and fixed itself there, but it was somehow right.

Now, she gripped the arms of her plastic seat, anchoring herself as the plane manoeuvred between sea and rocky cliffs. It was also right (she hoped so, anyway) that they went away to a different context for a while, to refocus, regroup. Hopefully, the Funchal assignment would help them to take a breath and move forwards, somehow, to find themselves again, in a new location, find their marriage again. Well, what else was there, after all? Not forgetting, but somehow coping, step by slow step.

Viv drew in a deep breath and stared intently at the seat in front, with its pocket of in-flight magazines, duty-free merchandise leaflet, sick bag and safety information card. She had squeezed her bottle of still mineral water behind the webbing as well, and she reached forward to lever it out and take a sip.

Rory leaned across her and she inhaled the bergamot fragrance of his cologne. And with it she inhaled the memory of their first meeting. "That's Machico down there," he said. "Where the Portuguese explorers Zarco and Teixeira first landed in their ships in the fifteenth century." He smiled at her, winking teasingly, pre-empting any murmur about 'mansplaining'. She shook her head and flicked her eyes up to the control panel above her.

She slid her glance warily to the window and recoiled at the angle of the plane and the nearness of the waves below. Rory touched her arm and drew her attention back to him. "As I told you, I came here as a child with mum and dad, the year before dad died. And of course it's where your parents found the fossil. Or, as I call it, the dangerous weapon!" He grinned and mimed an exaggerated howl as he clutched his abdomen.

Viv replaced the bottle and snorted indulgently, rubbing the scar on her right palm that still refused to heal. "Hmmm. And it's here in my bag if I ever need it to get rid of an interminably cheerful husband."

Rory leaned back in his seat. "Not so cheerful right now, actually. More cramped. Ou - ch. Goodness, I'll be glad to get off this plane, even though it's only been three and a half hours." He tried in vain to stretch his long legs, but only succeeded in banging his knees hard against the seat in front. Its occupant swivelled round. "I'm so sorry." The lady melted at Rory's smile. He glanced at Viv and she raised her eyebrows. For goodness sake! "We should have come first class scheduled, not charter economy."

"Not on the diocese money, the so-called travel allowance. Or on your salary. Not with my basically unpaid leave from the university. I feel very odd, being a kept woman this year."

"Er, not entirely 'kept' or 'unpaid'. You have actually got to do some research that you're getting paid for."

The university had been good, in all honesty. They had kept her job open, although she'd only been promoted to head of medieval studies two years ago, and she'd only been on the full promoted salary grade for a year since her probationary year in the faculty senior management team. Now she was on half-pay for six months anyway, following her late miscarriage and illness. But the Dean had amazingly found her a private desk-research project to do while she was in Madeira which provided a year's additional income. It would give her a focus while Rory was covering for the chaplain at Holy Trinity until a new permanent incumbent was found. And, truth be told, she was glad of time away from the teaching part of her job, being in the firing line, feeling vulnerable. Documentary research, she knew she could do well.

The last few weeks had revived her energy as she had prepared for the year that stretched out in front of her, and a little of her old motivation had crept back as she tackled the tasks systematically, planning and packing.

But all she really knew at the moment about their year ahead was that the church and the 'grace and favour' apartment where they would be staying were up a steep hill from the centre of Funchal. She hoped it would be easier to maintain than their charming but draughty old rectory back in Derbyshire.

She'd never visited Madeira, not wanting to see where her parents enacted one of the last events of their careers, but she'd researched the climate and knew that they were certainly leaving behind the chilly wet April weather of England for heat and sunshine, much more like an unusually good British summer, fine, dry, with lots of sun and mid-twenties consistently every day. The real heat, though, would come later, in July and August when the temperatures could easily rise well into the thirties.

Even now, as she peered cautiously again out of the cabin window, she could see the sharp golden light on the sparkling deep blue sea and could almost feel the heat haze rising from the rugged cliffs that appeared to climb steeply up from the edge of the water. She could make out the white painted houses with red tiled roofs clustered closely up every gorge, clinging to the very edge of the radiating ravines that slashed through the towering mountains up into the clouds and the heart of the volcano.

"*Woa*!" Viv clutched the armrests on either side again, gripping tightly as the aircraft suddenly tipped sideways and manoeuvred, sweeping back out to sea.

"It's OK," said Rory. "They have to swing round and approach from the west. I know the wings seem to be almost touching the waves. They really aren't. If you see a landing from the ground, you can see how high up it actually is." He covered her hand with his and stroked it gently with his thumb. He was always able to soothe her, body and soul, before. "When I came here as a boy, it was onto the short old runway, built on stilts over the sea. It was like something from a wartime movie, the way the pilot had to manoeuvre to hit head on and force it into reverse throttle, it was so tight."

Viv glanced sideways at him with a frown. "You tell me this, now?"

"I looked it up before we came," he grinned sheepishly. "So I knew it was OK now. It's a new airport and the runway's been extended for the large jets that come here these days. All the package holidays."

Viv shook her head but when she turned again to the window, she saw that they were already coming quite gently down onto the runway, steam rising from the concrete.

∼

"Well, it's good that you could make it," said John, one of the two church wardens who had sent the taxi to the airport to pick them up and had met them at the church. He sounded less than enthusiastic, but he seemed courteous, albeit serious and unsmiling, and perhaps a little agitated as his fingernails tapped the railing at the side of the steps that led up to the apartment above the church meeting rooms.

Viv was surprised to see that John was wearing a dark formal suit, shirt and tie, despite the heat, and carried a large tan briefcase that bulged with documents. Perhaps he was off back to work after greeting them. She noticed his fair, slightly ginger buzz cut, merging into the rough skin of his face, English paleness reddened by the sun. She wondered idly how long he had lived here, and what he did for a living: a bank clerk maybe, or an office manager?

John coughed, a rather nervous high-pitched bark, which made Viv glance quickly at him, as he directed the local taxi driver with an imperious wave of the hand to carry their luggage up to the apartment.

Viv turned to the other church warden in the 'welcome party'. She was a tall slim woman not much older than herself, but elegant and graceful in her tight white jeans and prettily draping dusky-pink top. She introduced herself as Georgina, "church warden by default", as she shook hands with Viv and gave her a rueful, intimate smile. She guessed she was English, but the coverage of her smooth light tan suggested a long residency on Madeira. Viv took in her skilfully applied make-up and glossy smooth blonde bob, and felt herself sticky and unkempt by comparison, stale from the journey, curly auburn-brown hair pulled carelessly back into a ponytail. She couldn't help but notice Georgina's beautifully manicured nails, polished with perfect red gel.

She also noticed the swift appreciative glance Georgina sent in Rory's direction. She was only too aware that women never failed to flutter at his athletic body and sexy lop-sided smile. She turned away, raising her eyebrows and grimacing to herself. She knew she should be used to it by now.

"Well, the church certainly looks imposing," Viv said as she looked across the lawns at the building standing four-square before her in the glaring sunshine, its pairs of Doric-style columns on the steps either side of the great wooden doors. She could make out a dome rising from the roof and thought it was rather an austere façade.

She must have sounded critical because John frowned, and Georgina raised a quizzical eyebrow. Rory glanced over at her and shook his head.

"But the garden is ..." She breathed in the scent and serenity of the extensive tropical gardens around them, the bright bougainvillea spreading across the walls at the entrance to the drive, the pretty hibiscus, tall thin fragrant eucalyptus, and the jacaranda trees. She couldn't help but feel the peace of this place, the sunshine warming her back, her limbs, and, in time, she hoped, maybe even her heart, "... like an oasis, hiding a tropical mystery."

John stared at her for a moment with a curious expression, then turned sharply away, ushering Rory up the steps to the apartment. "Come, come."

Viv turned to Georgina. "It's lovely," she added, although she could hear the flatness of her voice. John and Rory were already deep in conversation. She didn't think that John was the kind of man to include the clergy wives in serious matters of church affairs. Probably thought they were only good for providing parish tea and cake. She frowned. Oh God, since when had she become so cynical? Since always, Rory would say of course.

"I do hope you like it here, Viv," said Georgina, catching Viv's expression. "I'm sure that the heat and humidity will take a bit of getting used to after an English winter. The island's nearer to Africa than Portugal of course, off the west coast of Africa in fact, but it's not really too hot and at least with the Atlantic breezes the nights are comfortable. And of course, you've got decent air-con in the apartment," Georgina smiled, hooking her arm into Viv's and gesturing Viv towards the steps up to the apartment which would be their home for the next year. "I'm so pleased to have a young couple here. To be honest, Viv," Georgina leaned in and whispered as they walked, "I'm not exactly what you might call church warden material, but we've been having a few ... er ... 'issues' here, so I'm lending a hand." She waggled her fingers to indicate the inverted commas. She wrinkled her nose. "Tell you about them over a gin later." She stopped a moment on the steps, glanced up at Rory's retreating back, and squeezed Viv's arm. "I do hope you stay. The others didn't last long."

∼

No sooner had they had finished unpacking and made a reviving pot of English tea from the welcome pack left for them in the kitchen, than Rory said that he needed to sort out a few things in the study.

"Good God, Rory! We've barely walked in through the door, barely explored the apartment! I wanted to discover our new temporary home *together*. Haven't you even got a *few* minutes first?" she said, picking up the empty mugs.

"I'm sorry, darling, but I really need to do some stuff, after what John's just told me." Rory smiled apologetically and with a shrug, turned from her. He shut the study door and she was left staring at it. So soon, so quickly had he moved away from her and settled in to his new role! So much for sharing the healing together! She thrust the mugs into the dishwasher. Well, OK, she had her own things to do. The heat and the clarity of the light was reviving her, and she felt lighter than she had done for some time.

Viv left him to it, pulling on her shorts and trainers to explore down in the town. She probably should still be resting after the miscarriage, and she was certainly tired and disorientated, but, goodness, she was stiff from the flight and needed to stretch her limbs and get some fresh sea air. She thought she'd make herself useful, instead of moping, and find a supermarket to buy their first provisions. Rory was clearly not thinking about *that*. She'd treat herself to a taxi to bring any shopping bags back up the hill. She still had to be careful about heavy lifting.

Georgina had said she'd pop back around six and bring a bottle for a pre-dinner G and T, but Viv wanted to see that she had some drinks and snacks in to be hospitable. She also wanted to start stocking the fridge freezer, and get some fresh fruit and vegetables. Oh God, she grimaced to herself, she was behaving exactly as John might expect of a clergy wife. But, tough, she liked being in control.

She left the Holy Trinity gardens through the tall gates onto the street, and wandered in the heat of the afternoon sun, down the dangerously steep Rua do Quebra Costas, slowly picking her way over the shiny slippery cobbles with their grey mosaic patterns, cautious of falling in her still-fragile state. It was strange, this new physical hesitation; she'd never felt so feeble before, so wobbly.

At the bottom of the steepest part of the hill, she took the road labelled Rua Carreira, drinking in the old shabby buildings on either side. Two and three storeys high, the pastel houses had large casement windows, green louvred shutters, and twisted iron balconies. To her eyes, even the dilapidated ramshackle houses had that wonderful historic beauty of age.

From the dark interiors she could hear music and shouting. A torrent of angry Portuguese; then laughter. Other people's lives. Surprised, she realised that she was actually smiling to herself. Well, she guessed, somehow life went on, didn't it? At least, for other people ... She found a street named after the explorer Zarco that she could see ran downhill and followed it to a small square dominated by his statue. By the time she reached the sea front the sweat was trickling down between her breasts.

So it was refreshing to walk along by the sea,

THE DRAGON TREE

feeling the gentle warm breezes, breathing in the fresh salty air, and watching the blue fishing boats drifting lazily beyond the rocky shore. She thought of the vastness of time and space: the way she had reached out before, across the centuries, touching other lives, other times.

"*Hey, lady!*" The shout awoke Viv's senses in the present and, quickly sidestepping a motorbike that swerved around her, she leapt back onto the pavement.

Viv had retreated so much into her own world that she realised she had wandered off the main promenade into a little street lined with squashed street cafes, all vying for attention, their posters and menus jostling with each other, all apparently offering the identical espada fish, salads, traditional skewered beef espatada, the same beer, coffee and bolo de mel cake.

She had clearly wandered into the Old Town, to the tiny medieval fishermen's cottages, many now remodelled as bars. Waiters, hovering outside, one after the other called to her, gesturing, inviting her to their fresh-linen draped tables nestling on the pavement. She smiled, shaking her head, tentatively murmuring, "*não muito obrigada*" as she weaved her way through the noise, glad that she'd learned a few guide-book phrases.

Finally, she found herself in a quaint enclosed square, bordered with a long row of little houses, no more than cabins really, packed together, quiet but for the gentle warm breeze rustling through the leaves of the silver-green laurels and the spreading jacaranda. At the centre of the square a dark strangely-shaped tree reached out its branches like claws. A brief wisp of déjà vu trailed across her mind, and then was gone. She glanced desperately around her, trying to catch it, but it was gone.

She was standing in front of a small white stone church. The wooden notice by the gate outside told her that it was the Capela do Corpo Santo. It had the plain simple look of a tiny medieval chapel that had served the local people, the fishermen, for many years, solid and reassuring in the midst of their dangerous lives. She stood for a moment, calming herself and reading the board. It said that this 'chapel of the body of Christ', dating from possibly the early fifteenth century was the oldest surviving church in Funchal.

She looked up to its roof, breathing in its history. The bell in the simple, undecorated tower above the wooden door stood silent, presiding over the cobbled square as it had done for centuries, waiting. Maybe it had rung out to warn of disaster and danger, or to celebrate a marriage or birth. It made her think of the many fishing folk who had passed by here, entering the chapel with hope, or maybe despair, in their hearts. She could feel them around her, brushing past to disappear into the darkness of the interior. A cold shiver slowly rose up her spine. The air drifted over her, thick, suffocating, as the words on the board blurred and juddered.

A silent formless presence at her back seemed to push her through the iron gate. The wooden church doors were standing open under their gothic style architrave and she moved onwards into the dimness of the chapel. It was chilly inside and she shuddered, aware that it was not only the physical cold that numbed her body so.

The walls of the simple wooden nave closed in upon her. Highly decorated across the floors and up the height of the walls with those Moorish azure blue and white tiles she'd seen pictures of in the guides, they pressed the breath from her chest. Frescos and ceiling paintings between the heavy dark beams felt oppressive. Her eyes were drawn to the altar: above it was a huge medieval mural of Christ, or maybe a saint; it was hard to tell as he seemed to be dressed in peasant clothes, although with a glowing gilded halo. Beside him was a local fisherman in what she guessed was a traditional tunic and cap, hauling a large net, and, in the background, a Portuguese cog with its distinctive square rigging. It was oddly beautiful yet somehow a shiver of apprehension brushed the length of her spine.

She anchored herself on the edge of a rough wooden pew. The chapel was deserted, and she slipped onto the hard seat for a moment to steady her breath.

Light-headed, she sat there losing all sense of time,

letting the silence of the church enfold her. But gradually she felt a colder chill drift around her, and something seemed to be drawing her back to the cog. Her vision blurred and she rubbed her eyes. As she looked across the nave, a mist seemed to swirl around her, the chancel swayed dizzily and, alarmed, she blinked furiously, trying to clear her mind. But the dizzy patterns of the Moorish tiles seemed to clash and struggle with each other, a migraine across the walls and floor. The framed paintings and plaster icons seemed to stretch out towards her. An anguished Madonna caught her eye with a wretched plea.

Viv realised she was holding her breath and heard her own heart thrumming in her chest.

Desperately, she swung around, searching for something stable, solid. But something was pulling her back again and again to the mural of the cog. Her brain seemed to have shifted gear, her head hurting, and thoughts jumbled, scrambled.

The air around her stilled, waiting.

The waves on the painting seeming to grow higher, rougher, breaking onto the deck as she watched. She clutched the back of the pew in front, trying to steady herself as the ship seemed to heave in the storm and biting rain lashed her face as lightning struck the mast, sending it crashing down as it rent in two. The awful echo of splintering wood and rush of water reverberated through the chapel as the sea battered the craft, smashing and pounding the timbers.

"Oh God, no, this isn't happening!" she gasped out loud, banging the pew with her fists. "Not again!" She tightened her grip on the wooden rail, grasping for reality, for 'now' to return. Slowly, she felt again the tiled floor beneath her feet, saw the plastered walls at her side, the mural recede, a painting once more. Viv drew in a long unsteady breath, ragged air burning her chest, her throat.

She looked round. She was alone in the chapel.

She had to get out. She needed air.

Faint and nauseous, Viv pushed herself up on shaky legs, grabbed hold of her bag, and, stumbling, ran out of the door. The dusty heat and noisy bustle of the street slammed into her consciousness. For a moment she pulled in ragged breaths, then, dodging the startled waiters and tourists, she ran.

She didn't stop until she reached the seafront again. Clutching on to the sea wall she gasped for breath. Her hand on her throat, she glanced round. Nobody was following her; nobody was even looking back at her. The sea stretched out in front of her, deep blue, vast and angry.

Although the sun was bright, a strong hot wind had arisen, and it seemed to be high tide. How long had she been inside the chapel? Viv concentrated on breathing as deeply and as calmly as she could, leaning on the concrete wall and watching the power of the waves crashing onto the rocks beyond her. The sea so assailed her senses that she felt everything else around her blotted out by its roaring, sucking and breaking. And suddenly she was thinking again about Ana, her naming of her, and wondering if that terrible void – yes, a void even though she had Rory - would ever be filled. She shuddered and pulled on the jacket she had squashed in her bag, wrapping it tightly around her as she trembled. How could you miss a five-month pregnancy? *But, Ana, I do miss you so ...*

CHAPTER 3

ANA D'ARAFET

1344

But, Ana, I do miss you so ... A quiet soft unrecognised voice swirled around her head from far off and made her frown. A voice on the wind, above the waves that reached and grasped at the rocks before her on the shore. Ana d'Arafet shuddered and wrapped her tattered mantle more tightly around her body, still gaunt and unsteady after the terrifying journey across the seas in the frail craft. Its timbers had creaked and strained against the buffeting of the tempest, and then lately smashed and pounded against the might of the ocean until the cog, built for the English channel, not to be swept off course into the violent Atlantic storms, could take no more.

She fought away the memories of the broken mast, the rush of the sea over the deck, the cries of horrified men. She pushed away the visions of her own cold terror as she had clung fast to the cabin bunk, squeezing her thin body to the beams, the crashing of the waves and the splintering timbers resounding in her head over the rolling thunder. She had prayed and cried until she could pray and cry no more. Until she screamed to God one minute to save them and the next to let her die, not knowing which she wanted. She felt the sickness and the fever still, the trembling faintness that racked her body even now on dry land.

Now, she watched and listened as the ocean, rough at high tide, roared and sucked at the rocks of the bay where she stood. She smelled the thickness and power of the sea, and she saw the gaunt black skeletal shapes of their wrecked ship out in the bay amongst the jagged bulk of rocks fallen from the cliffs. The storm had abated, thank God, but the tide had yet to calm. She had no idea where they had been washed up. An island, perhaps, but far from France where they had been headed.

That voice. Did someone really miss her? Surely not her father. He would not miss her after what she had done. A gentle voice yet full of anguish. A woman's voice. Her nurse or maid, perhaps, back at home in England?

"My love," called Robert, startling her as he came up behind her and wrapped his arms around her shivering body. "Come inside the shelter before you catch the chills."

Her hand slipped to her belly and she stroked the beginnings of life within. She had first felt the stirring as their cog, the Welfayre, was caught in the beginnings of the storm - although of course she had suspected as much before they left from England – and it had somehow clung on inside her through all the tumult.

She thought about her father, Sir Henri, remembering him shouting angrily at her in the great hall of their manor house not far from the bustling, noisy, smelly town of London.

"How dare you, Ana! You have lain with ... with *him* ..." he had spat out the word without condescending to utter the name, "in my house, the enemy of my king! You dare to debase yourself and bring shame upon us!"

"Robert is not an enemy to the king!" she had protested, clutching her skirts with trembling hands.

"Pah! He did not flatter and bow to my king as a courtier should! And *you* – you were sworn to *Sir Thomas*! Not some jumped-up sailor, tupping the daughter of a nobleman!" her father had retorted.

"He didn't and he's not a ...!" Ana had begun, but her father had swept out of her chamber, his heavy cloak knocking her mother's precious casket from the little table as he went, smelling of his rage and sweat, and the cheap musky scent of his latest mistress on his flailing hands. Her mother's jewels and treasures, gold and blue and white, shattered and scattered across the floor. She knelt, sobbing, desperately trying to gather them up in her shaking hands, precious stones and strange little fragments of tiles, fragments of her sweet dead mother.

"He didn't, he didn't ..." she cried quietly to the empty room. But she knew that she could never say why.

Gently she had stroked the blue and white tiles in her palm, her tears falling upon the shards as she tried to piece them together again.

Her father was always angry with her, ever since she had killed her mother in childbed fourteen years before. But he had managed well enough without his wife these years, with many a village woman, and sometimes a court lady if he was minded to be gentle when they entertained Edward the king on his summer progress through his royal domains.

But there was nothing debased about her love for Robert, nor his for her. Nothing! Their eyes had caught each other's the year before, at her father's great feast for the king's visit. She was permitted to attend, with not a little reluctance, as her father's companion as she had reached her thirteenth year. She had put aside her books and sat beside him on the top table, intrigued, observant, in her new green kirtle and bejewelled overgown, feeling very grand, yet not a little nervous and confused.

And the king had spoken gently to her, although she knew that he was often brusque, and invited her to his court. He seemed smitten with her and kept touching her hand, his long fingers slipping beneath her wide sleeve and creeping up her arm. She grimaced to herself now as she remembered pulling her hand away crossly, frowning, trying to wriggle further away from him, and fiddling instead with the pouch hanging at her belt, even though he was the king and she knew that she was supposed to be pleased and willing.

And it was then that she had caught Sir Robert Machym's eye. She had glanced shyly up at him beneath her dark lashes and he had looked at her, bold but serious, with a slight embarrassed frown. They had exchanged a tentative smile, and her stomach had quivered alarmingly ... but deliciously. He was taller and broader of chest than his fellows so that he seemed to her to rise above them, and her heart fluttered. Yet, of all the king's courtiers he had gentle features she could see, earnest and pensive, and she wondered if he liked studying as much as she did.

He was certainly, she could tell, not inclined to the loud and boisterous joshing of his companions on the mid-benches, and his cotehardie was not as rich with fur, nor his chaperon as lavishly pleated. As she watched him, she thought that he looked almost out of place, as he ruffled his fair beard and shuffled slightly on his seat as if he wished to be elsewhere. As did she, then. And she had smiled with fellow feeling, and felt a warm glow suffuse her body, knowing there was indeed someone else like her in this hot noisy suffocating room.

When the king and his favourite courtiers and ladies forgot her (and even her sometime maidservant Joan, red-faced and ale-loosed-bodied, sprawled across one of the ostlers) and began their carousing, when the hall became sweaty and raucous, voices drunken and strident, she saw Sir Robert slipping away from the hall. He went with an almost imperceptible backward glance at her and she excused herself to her uninterested neighbours and boldly followed him.

They talked in the shadows of the garden throughout the distant echoes of merry-making that night, almost until the sun rose again, and for many nights after that, whenever Robert could get away from court. Their secret whispers whenever her father was distracted told her that his family were minor noblemen and ship-owners from Bristol.

She remembered how she had clapped her hands together with delight. To her, Bristol, with its trading ships and exotic cargo, seemed like something from the books she read. She longed to go with him to his family where she might have a better welcome than at home with her father and his series of mistresses who glared at her or tossed their heads and swept away with a sneer.

But that was before she was sent away to court, to Edward the king, and before she was betrothed to another.

She would not think of that, and of what happened, no, she would not. No, it could not have really happened, or else Robert would not love her.

Yet Robert had called her his wife, and they were hand-fasted as soon as they boarded his ship for France, with Joan (bless her that she had fled with her and away from her ostler boy) and the captain as witnesses, not waiting for the priest. She did not know whether she was to be named for him, Machym, although Robert said it was so.

And now, here in the present, on the wild shore, pushing away her past, she heard the crunching of the shingle behind her as he shifted his position to hold her. "Come inside," Robert whispered now into her hair, all wild and red and unbound in the wind. How horrified her father would have been that she was not neat in her coif or her new crespine, even though she had only recently been allowed to wear anything on her braids as befitted womanhood. Robert lifted her as he had done those long hours before when he had carried her, weak and sick from the tempest on the seas, through the shallows onto the solid rocky ground of this strange bay.

In his arms, she touched the leather pouch at her waist-belt, feeling there her magic treasure, the hard sharp rock she had found the day they had staggered together up the shingles to the shelter of the overhanging cliffs. It was precious because she found it at the entrance to the cave which had given them refuge from the tempest and their shattered cog. She knew that it was holy because inside it there was a curled creature, reminding her of Robert and herself and their crew, hiding safe from the storm, and also of the curled life nestling inside her.

Robert gently lowered her to the ground under the canopy of the cave, straightened her mantle around her body, and caressed her cheek. He opened his mouth as if to speak, but instead he turned thoughtfully to regard the sea, now so much quieter than when they were first wrecked here, yet still dangerous, rough, and loud. The roaring of the waves echoed against the rocky walls of the cave and seemed to press in to her. Ana steadied herself with a hand on the rock. For a moment she watched Robert's tall broad-shouldered figure silhouetted against the light, his arms raised so that the sleeves of his thick woollen cloak resembled the wings of an eagle.

She reached into her pouch, her fingers finding the magic stone creature, and she took it out to place it carefully by the tiny jagged shard of pretty azul blue and white patterned tile she had almost tripped over that first sunrise. The colours on the tile, although it was only a sliver, reminded her of her mother's precious fragments and jewels that had spilled from her little casket when her father knocked it off her table back home at Darbey Hall. Already she had discovered a niche in the rock of the cave where she

THE DRAGON TREE

could keep her little collection of treasures, just as she had done in her mother's casket at home.

Ana kissed her precious objects, like rosary beads, and covered them gently with the bedraggled fragment of ermine trim that had been torn off her cloak as they had staggered ashore. She knelt awkwardly and crossed herself, murmuring her prayer of gratitude for their safety and that of most of their crew from the Welfayre. They had lost but two men, and although she grieved for them, men she barely knew, she also knew it could have been a great deal worse, as Robert had said, telling her to dry her tears. She shivered. It had all been so terrible. But they had come through it and were on dry land once more, and the storm had abated over a night and a day. In desperation, she had prayed directly to God to keep them safe, not through the Madonna Maria, and somehow He had heard her prayers.

"*Kyrie Eleison,*" she murmured, thinking back to the daily mass in the chapel back home at the hall. Lord have mercy. She struggled to recall the words of the liturgical prayer since they seemed alien in this wild untamed place, even though they should have been so familiar to her. But home was far away, and the rituals broken.

"*Agnus Dei, qui tollis peccata mundi, miserere nobis,*" she whispered as the words tumbled back into her mind. Lamb of God who takes away the sins of the world, have mercy on us, "*Agnus Dei, qui tollis peccata mundi, dona nobis pacem.*" Give us your peace. She paused. Was that right? Would God hear her this time if she got it wrong?

Robert turned to her, and she caught his frown before his expression softened. "Oh Ana, my love, what have we done? Is it indeed our sins that have brought us here to this God-forsaken place? What have I done? Taken you from your rightful position, your comfortable home, with only one maidservant here to tend you ... endangered you and the life within you!"

"No, Robert dearest. It was not so. I could not have stayed there, with my father as he was. Nor at court with Edward the king. Nor betrothed to his advisor Sir Thomas ..."

"But Sir Thomas was rich and favoured at court and he could have given you far more than I," he sighed. "I, a minor nobleman with few connections, and consigned to the lower tables, well below the salt. A detractor of the king. Or at least one who failed to fawn and grovel as I should have done. And all I can give you is a ..." he shook his head, "a cave!"

Ana pushed herself up from her knees and brushed the folds of her tattered gown. One hand rested on her belly, the other cross-fingered behind her back. She took a deep breath against her fears. "You have given me this."

Robert grinned ruefully. "Well, Sir Thomas could have done that too."

"No, he could not, not as we do!" Ana stamped her

foot, but she did not meet Robert's eyes. "I could never have lain with him ... *like that*, like us ... I hate him. He is old and ugly and fat. He is cunning and cruel. God knows, I could never, ever lie with him *in that way* ... as his wife!"

Robert smiled, raising his eyebrows, and inclined his head. He opened his arms as he stepped towards her and enfolded her body into his. "Oh, my dear little Ana." He kissed the top of her head, burying his lips into her mass of red curls. "We have indeed loved as God intended husband and wife and this is the blessing from it." He glanced down at her belly. "Ana, I love you with all my heart, simple and lowly as it might be."

Ana leaned in to his warm broad chest and gently released the breath she had been holding. She could hear the tide retreating and felt the heat of the sun slowly becoming stronger. She did feel safe, as safe as she could be, here, with him, although she had no idea how they would build the more comfortable shelter that Robert had promised her. And she had no idea how they would find better food than the strange-tasting vegetable they had eaten, which Robert called 'the fennel' because he knew it from trading in Portugal – and those unknown animals and odd-looking fish they had roasted over the simple fire the men had built on the rocks. As she snuggled into Robert's body, Ana could hear the shouts of his crew as they cut and stacked branches of laurel and began the task of clearing the trees that ringed the beach. She trusted him. She had to.

"I must leave you a moment." Robert pushed her gently away from him. "Now that the storms have abated, I want the men to help me wade out to the wreck of the cog and rescue whatever we can. Timbers, clothes, and blankets. They could dry out now that the sun and warmth are returning. Any provisions that may be still edible, tools, whichever chickens and goats that have survived ..." He turned from her and stepped outside the cave to direct the men, and she heard him calling to them.

Ana watched his figure bounding steadily over the slippery rocks and knew that her future and that of her unborn baby depended totally on him. A small frisson of fear threatened to rise in her breast, but she took a deep breath and forced it down. Still it niggled at her. Maybe he was right. Maybe she should have stayed to be an obedient daughter.

Could she have agreed to be with Sir Thomas, forced herself to accept her fate as most of her sex did, stayed at court in Queen Philippa's retinue, as her father so desired?

But yet she loved Robert so, and wanted him. And that was everything, was it not?

One hand on the rock of the cave wall to steady herself, she knelt again at her little niche and lifted the ermine trim. She reached in to touch the stone and caressed the tiny curled creature within it. Was it really

THE DRAGON TREE

some kind of holy relic? And how did come to be here, on this beach of black sand? As her fingers stroked the sharp rough rock, she felt it pierce her skin and turned her palm to see tiny dark beads of blood on her finger tips and on the inner surface of her hand, piercing her life-lines. It did not hurt but she frowned and bit her lip. There was something ... a shifting ... a drifting, a swaying. The sounds of the men outside on the shore, the voice of Robert, the chopping and cutting, it all seemed to be echoing, growing distant and faint, as if through a sea mist. The earth beneath her knees and the rock wall at her hand seemed to shake, her vision was clouding, and her head dizzying.

She was falling, deeper and deeper, splitting and crashing, into turbulent boiling seas, and fire, red and black, raging in its angry path towards her, molten magma blasting to the skies, mountains forcing their might through the waves, flinging boulders away from their rage ... a curled creature, horrified, flung away and coming to rest. A hand, another palm with torn skin and bloodied marks. But a golden hand, not white like hers, a hand that did things, not a hand that directed servants. A hand that rested on a belly, but empty, not full like hers. And tears. She lifted her hand to brush them away, but her palm found soft skin, wet cheeks, not her own, a woman's face before her eyes, close to hers. A great overwhelming sadness filled her.

The woman's face faded and as Ana looked up to the cave entrance arching in front and above her, she thought she saw a great silver bird-like creature in the sky, monstrous with outspread wings roaring almost touching the cliffs themselves. Dark, it blotted out the sun and circled, swooping round across the bay, then flew off to the west. She closed her eyes against it. A voice, clear and soft, but frightened: "*woa*!"

A wisp of memory.

"Ana!" Robert's voice cutting through the dreams. "I heard you shout!" She felt his shadow across her tightly closed eyes and cautiously she opened them. She struggled to stand, catching her foot in her robe. Robert reached out to hold her.

She shook her head. "Oh. I think I felt a little faint," she stuttered. "Maybe with kneeling down."

Robert helped her upright. She glanced down at her hands. There was no blood, there were no marks. "You must lie down a while," he said. "Here, on the pallet. Let me fold your cloak properly over you."

"I am quite well now, thank you, Robert."

"No, stay there. Until your head clears, my love. Let me fetch Joan."

"Do not disturb Joan," Ana held a restraining palm towards him. She knew full well where Joan was, and it was certainly not storing her herbs and potions in the dry, nor counting her rosary.

She sighed and allowed herself to rest. She had never felt so fragile before. If this is what it was like to bear a child, she was not sure she wanted to do it again. Yet she knew she would have no choice; it could not be prevented. But the prospect of loving this child was so comforting to her, especially now that she had no family but Robert. The love they had together was so beautiful and good. Maybe that love would result in another child ... if only the love did not always have to result in such fragility and faintness. She knew she must try to be strong, and after all, she had her maidservant to tend her: Joan was well versed in childbed, having born three of her own with no husband or attendant, and birthed countless other infants, a goodly number of them surviving.

Robert settled her, fussing with her cloak, then turned back to watch his men wading under the weight of cargo through the water to hand their burden to the chain of men ready to pile the goods on the top of the beach safe from the sea. "We have been able to rescue many valuable things from the cog, Ana. I mean valuable for us to survive here a while, not treasure." He smiled. "We will manage."

"I was thinking, Robert. Should we build a fire, a beacon, my dearest, so that a ship might see and know that we are here?" Ana struggled to raise herself up on her elbows. "And take us on to France where we should be?"

Robert swivelled round to face her and laughed. "Well. You are right and the cleverest wife I have!"

"Your only wife, I trust!"

"Indeed. I had thought no further than rescuing what we could from the cog. But you are correct and now that we have the possibility of survival here awhile, in the meantime we must turn our minds to escape, back to civilisation." He leaned his hand on the cave wall and stared out to sea.

"I wonder what this place is," he murmured, his tall sturdy figure blocking the sunlight at the entrance to the cave and plunging her into darkness. "My sailors only know it as a fearful island far from our intended course to France. Yet there is the fennel growing and rich soil, and a profusion of laurel trees, fish in the waters of the bay and the streams, and strange little wild animals to eat." He paused to turn to Ana and smile. "It is a blessed relief from the storm for us, my love. And I will refer to it by our name of Machym and call it Machyco. What think you, my love?"

CHAPTER 4

ANA

Ana's dreams were garish that night. Robert had stuffed soft leaves into a fold of a dry cloak the men had rescued from the cog and she was able to lie upon it in reasonable comfort so that, wrapped in her overgown and fur lined mantle, snuggling into Robert's arms, she was able to sleep for the first time in many nights. No longer tossed and battered, sick and terrified, in the tiny cabin as the storm raged, nor spine-pierced on the rock of the cave floor, she was able to rest and give way to her nightmares.

The familiar memory of water. Great waves crashing around her, breaking on the timbers of the hull; the horrendous sound of the mast creaking to splitting point. In the darkness she cried out and half-felt Robert pull her closer.

Then the waves and the roaring gave way to a bright

light drawing closer towards her and gaining intensity, glaring into her eyes. And she thought that she was somewhere very white, stark, and intense. Somewhere she did not recognise. Somewhere she felt frightened and also dreadfully sad. She dreamed that she was lying on a bed that was being pushed by figures in white robes and headgear, like the nuns of her father's chapel at the Hall. She heard her own urgent cries as she was pushed down a long narrow hall with white walls, bare, with no tapestries or hangings. Light flashing into her eyes, like the flames from the sconces in the hall, close to her face. Heat and sweat, trembling. Something heavy and suffocating pushed over her mouth and nose. Darkness. Nothing.

Ana! No-o-o! Please not this ... Oh God, she didn't even get to take a breath in the world ... we won't ever forget our firstborn.

Ana woke with a start and found that she was trembling and feverish. Her hand slipped into her cloak and rested on her belly.

She became aware that Robert was staring at her. She felt the warmth of the sun that was rising and warming the rocks that surrounded her. As she blinked in the light, she shuddered.

"Oh, my lord. Such a night terror that pervaded my dreams, Robert. I am pleased and thankful to be awake now and safe."

Robert stroked her arm and wrapped his woollen cloak further around them both. "It is not surprising, after all we have endured. But, Ana, I will keep you safe. You must never fear. And you are strong of body and mind. We will be warm and well fed here and as soon as we can alert a ship, will be sailing on calm seas to France. And then our son will be born."

Ana smiled. "It may be a daughter, Robert. Perhaps to be named for me, as I was for my mother. Have you considered that?"

"Of course, and if God wills it, then I know she will be as beautiful and strong and wilful as her mother!"

"Wilful?" Ana reached across and thumped his chest. "I think not! Only that I know my own mind."

"Indeed," murmured Robert. "And I dare not gainsay such a lady!"

He kissed her gently and then rose, careful not to disturb her coverings. "I hear the men rising and I must see that the shelters are completed today."

Ana watched him go and lay back, listening to the men's shouts as they worked. He was always busy, often distracted. But of course she knew that he had much on his mind, and much to take care of, not least herself in her condition, and the baby growing in her belly.

She was not sure how long she had lain there when one of the crew called at the entrance to their cave that Sir Robert had sent him to bring her some refreshment. She recognised the high reedy, still child-like voice. Will? She sat up, pulling the cover higher over her bosom, though it was clothed, and told him to enter.

Yes, it was indeed the fair young deck hand called

Will, but he hesitated on the threshold, unsure again as he had been the morning before.

"May I come inside with this, my lady?" He stared at her with a rueful grin. "This does not feel right. It should be your maid of the chamber who brings this. But she is ... she is..."

He blushed and bent to lay a goblet and bowl beside her makeshift bed, careful to keep as much distance as could be had between them. She liked Will. He did not have her dear Robert's seriousness and sense of responsibility, of course, but he had a mischievous smile and a quick wit. She liked that, especially in these circumstances; it cheered her. Sometimes Robert was perhaps a little too ... no, she mustn't think like that ...

"Of course, Will, do not fear, and thank you for serving me." Ana gave him an encouraging nod of her head and realised that her hair was escaping from her cap. She tucked the strands back under the cloth.

"My lady," Will grinned more confidently now, straightening up his youthful body. "This is some kind of four-legged animal, like a squirrel or a rat, but it is well roasted to break your fast." He indicated the bowl and sniffed. "It is cooked a second time, to make sure, in a broth of the fennel and also roots. And salty sea water. Hmm, and at least you can wash it down with some good red wine we rescued from the ship."

"Thank you, Will," Ana nodded. "And as soon as

we are on dry land in a civilised place, I will search books to find out what the creature might be."

Will stepped back and Ana was sure she saw him wink. "You may not wish to find out, Lady Ana. Best not to know."

She stifled a giggle with her hand.

He turned to go, then paused, fumbling over his words. "Oh, and, my lady, Mistress Joan said to tell you she would attend you presently to help you with your ... er toilet ... er to dress." In truth, there was little toiletry or dressing to be done here, shipwrecked on a forsaken island, but if Joan ever attended her station on time, she could at least assist her to tidy herself and to find a secluded place for a privy moment.

Ana privately wondered on the slackness Joan was now displaying, ever since they had embarked at Bristol. But truth to tell, she had never been as conscientious as she should have been, her mind more focused on the hose and braies of the stable-lads.

"Well, tell her that I shall need her shortly, if you please."

As Will bowed and left her, she reached across to the bowl, and she was suddenly overcome with hunger. Having eaten little on the terrible journey and the day or so since, and having vomited up most of any morsel she had attempted to take, she now felt ravenous. The meaty broth was in fact quite delicious, rich and tasty, and suited her very well to break her fast. The wine was certainly a good one, and reminded her of her father's feasting hall, wine full-bodied and thick from the monastery vines.

Sated, she rose, pulled off her cap, twisted her red hair into a thick braid and brushed down her kirtle, aware that her torn linen shift beneath did not smell sweet. In fact, as she moved, she was only too aware of the odour of her body, especially that secret place beneath her skirts, back home so well perfumed by the servants of the bed chamber. The oblivion of the past days fell from her and suddenly her senses were once more awake.

Impatient, she could not wait for Joan, she must go in search of fragranced plants to crush for oil for her face and privy cloths. For the first time in days she knew her own stink and untidiness. She touched her braided hair and made herself smell her fingers, wrinkling her nose. Perhaps she could fashion a caul or crespine of some sort for her hair, out of strong stemmed plants and fragrant flowerheads if she could find any. She must not sink. Despite the night's dreams, she felt stronger and more hopeful this new day.

As quickly as they had arisen, the storms had ceased as if they had never been, and the sun was already high and hot. Ana looked up, shielding her eyes against the sun, and then around her, over the beach and the cliffs that surrounded the bay, and beyond, rising above the dense woodlands, the towering mountains in the heart of the island, reaching up towards the sky, mystical and magical, wreathed in cloud.

Drawing a deep smiling breath and feeling remarkably lithe and not yet too cumbersome with child, Ana slowly and cautiously clambered over the rocks of the bay, steadying herself with her hand on the overhang. She kept close to the under-cliffs for safety and well within the sound of the men's voices as they strove to build simple shelters in the lee of the great craggy escarpment.

Ana marvelled at the skills of these men, more used to handling the sea than huge branches, at the way they were able to visualise how the trunks would stack and how the leafy branches would bend. She guessed the way they worked together as a crew on the cog helped them to work together here, striving for a different task.

As she turned around, carefully so as not to slip on the wet rocks, she caught sight of Robert, taller than the rest and clearly the leader, directing his men to their work. How she wished that she could lead, like him. She adored his strength of mind, body and spirit, and she was glad that, just now in their difficult circumstances, she had such a man. In her physical weakness now, she relied on him to look after her. But she knew that when they were back in civilisation, in a home that would be theirs, together, with their servants, she would direct the household and she would look after him, in her own way, the way that women of her rank did.

She thought of those strange visions she had that night, those night terrors, when she felt that she was wracked with pain and sweating and crying out for her 'firstborn'. She knew, although it seemed like a different world, that this was her lot in life, the lot of every woman who ever breathed, throughout time. Yet she did not want to be only this. Of course, she would be mistress of her own household in time and she would rule her court as she had been raised to do. But her reading, her study, even secretly behind her father's back, taught her that women could be strong leaders in their own right. She had snuggled behind the tapestries on the casement seat at Darbey Hall, reading about Boudicca, and Isabella, Edward the king's mother regent. And she had felt her heart fill with yearning and determination.

And then, of course, that day her eyes had met Robert's. Her heart had juddered and then it had all come to this.

Ana's foot slipped on the rocks and she stumbled, grasping a jutting crag. She looked down and saw that she had slithered on an outcrop of wet foliage. The pressure of her foot had released a pungent scent. She breathed in the peppery spicy smell, quite pleasantly reminiscent of the flowers of purple thyme in the herb garden at her father's hall.

Her back tugged oddly as she bent to pick the

THE DRAGON TREE

delicate deep pink blossoms and pull up part of the plant at the root, too, so that she might replant it nearer to their shelters. She held the bunch up to her nose and inhaled. It was not unlike the earthy smell of the feathery leaves of the fennel plant that Robert's men had found, recognising it from their trading trips to Portugal and France. She slipped as much as she could into the pouch at her belt, fixed a sprig into her braid, and surveyed the under-cliffs for more useful vegetation.

She must ask Robert to bring her books from the cog, so that she could dry them by the fire, especially the one about the using of herbs and the making of potions and salves. She had poured over that book, reading the receipts out to Joan, who clucked and nodded in recognition. Her forebears, Joan maintained, had long had knowledge of healing and magic. Although Ana thought that there was a great deal more of the latter – and paid well for it they were too.

The sun, rising high and naked in the cloudless sky, was hot on her uncovered head, and it was beginning to make her feel dizzy. She should turn back. The sheer rocks that surrounded her, jagged edges sharply focused, seemed to judder. She slipped again, nearly losing her footing. The stones beneath her feet skittered away. This was becoming dangerous. As her eyes darted around her, seeking out a flat stable rock to regain her balance for a moment, Ana could feel her heart thrumming in her chest. Her eyes misted. She cursed her impulsive nature. If she had waited for Joan, she would have had assistance. Although, truth to tell, Joan would probably have dissuaded her from such an adventure.

Then, as her eyes cleared, something came into focus a few paces away from her, almost hidden by the overhang, and it took her breath away. A strange gap in the crags. The rock on either side looked to her as though at some time it had been hewn to form an entrance, a passageway. And in a fraction of a moment, all her senses were focused on the rock. She frowned. How could this be? No animal had done this. Someone had fashioned this with some kind of tool. Who? And why? The island was deserted, and Robert and the men had declared it an unknown land, not showing on their own portolan nor their written portolani that they had brought from their trading travels to Pisa and Genoa. They were the first to step here, so Robert had said.

She herself had begun to study the chart at the start of their journey out of Bristol and south east round the cape towards France. Although she had not been trained to interpret the chart, Robert with all his seafaring experience had explained some of it. The web of intersecting rhumb lines had begun to make some sense; but she still could not make out but faint uncertain lines south into the wide seas beyond England. She knew that Robert was adding lines himself from the compass bearings; perhaps he would add this island. She would like to name it: island of woods, maybe, or island of the fennel? For no man before them had set his foot on this land. Robert had said so and therefore clearly it must be true.

And yet ...

Puzzled, she picked her way towards the cliffside, and stood and stared at it. She reached out and touched the rough-hewn sides to the gap in the rocks. An entrance to a cave? – no, there was a glimmer of daylight beyond the jagged narrow slip of rock – an open space? She ran her fingers across the opening and felt the sharp edges where an axe – surely an axe - had splintered the stone. The gap was not very wide, just enough for a man to push through, someone with tools in his hand or on his back. Who could it have been? She turned back towards the sea and thought that someone surely must have been here before and that maybe this entrance was to protect someone, or something, from the sea storms and winds.

She slipped through.

What she saw there caught her breath.

It was a cultivated patch, with rows of unidentifiable vegetation, overgrown from many years of neglect. She could make out amidst the jutting tree roots and the fallen rocks, juniper and hawthorn that she knew, and a strangely shaped tree. It seemed to her like a frozen witches' curse, weeping its purple blood, its claws reaching out to her. And amidst all this, a raised platform of rock and, scattered around it, shards that looked so much like the bleached bones of unknown creatures.

Like a holy shrine.

She could not tell whether she heard the sound outside of her body or whether it was her pounding heart and blood that filled her ears. But it sounded to her like the murmurings, moanings, incantations of priests and the low songs of ceremonies, filling her head.

Something behind her. She whipped round, nearly losing her balance, and her foot struck something hard and sharp on the earth. A blue and white tile, like the tiny shard she found at the entrance to their cave, but with strange brown and purple markings like letters or symbols, a tile whole and perfect. Above her head stretched the branches of the strangely shaped tree and from this angle she saw that it looked like a dragon and that its purple blood had dripped onto the tile.

She bent and picked it up so that she could study the intricate pattern upon it and she stroked her hand gently across its smooth raised markings. On one side of the glazed upper surface were curious symbols she had never seen before, curved and straight and dots, but on the other were the letters IHS which she knew to be ancient Christian symbols. She knew with certainty that this was, like her fragment in the cave, a holy relic. Her heart filled with calm and she knew above all else that this was a symbol of peace and prosperity, a talisman that would bring hope and safety after their travails. And this place, whoever had made it, whatever was its intended purpose, whomsoever's God it reached out to, it was now her own special place, and she would come back to it as her own altar, her own prie-dieu.

A distant shout startled her, and Ana realised that the shadows were lengthening in the bright sun, and the day was speeding on to noontime. It was getting late and she needed to return. She thrust the tile into her pouch and turned back to the beach.

CHAPTER 5

VIV

The present day

*V*iv blinked as if she was struggling to emerge from a dream. But it was not the lingering fear she had experienced at the Capela do Corpo Santo, of the cog and the tempest that still flooded her head, but another image altogether, one of a rocky clearing, a shrine, and of herself bending down, grasping a tile. She tried to shake the strange image of the oddly patterned tile from her mind, although it lingered there like the after-image of the sun, with those angular markings and IHS imprinted on it, and above her that dragon-shaped tree with its purple sap.

She glanced at her wrist-watch and made herself focus on its rose-gold face. Slowly the images drifted away from her. She frowned and shifted her brain into the present and into gear.

It was already getting late and she still had the shopping to do. Georgina had said that she was coming round at six o' clock for a G and T. Oh God, why couldn't she concentrate on what she was supposed to be doing? Her mind was all over the place these days. She never used to be like this. Before. And she wasn't keen on the cold empty distracted shell she'd become. She took a deep breath in and squared her shoulders. Right. Focus.

The wind had abated, and the sunlight was golden. She picked up her bag and turned to the steep street that ran at right angles to the sea front, towards the shopping mall.

An hour later, by the time Viv had extricated her carrier bags from the taxi boot, paid, and begun to heft them up the concrete steps to the apartment, she was hot and sweaty again and saw that it was heading towards six.

She could hear Rory, oblivious, on the phone in his study as she unpacked her goodies. He'd clearly hardly registered that she'd gone, let alone that she'd returned safely. The nerve endings in her hand prickled and as a box of eggs slipped from her grip, she felt a frisson of frustration with him. It would have been nice, the least he could do, if he'd emerged from his lair to help her unpack the food shopping. Then she immediately felt annoyed with herself for acting like a martyr when she knew, really, that it was her own choice.

She quickly put out bottles of Bombay Sapphire gin, Indian tonic, and vino verde on the table, sliced the lemons, and arranged some mini pastel de nata on a plate, then emptied a packet of mixed nuts into a bowl. In her haste, she managed to spray half of them onto the counter top. Scooping them up, she hoped that Georgina was a little late, and, if she was absolutely honest, regretting that she was coming over at all. She dashed into the bathroom for a quick shower and changed with relief out of her sticky shorts and top into a light dress and sandals.

As she brushed her dark auburn hair, pulling it up off her neck into a gold clip, and repaired her eye make-up and lipstick, Viv heard the doorbell and Rory greeting Georgina.

Viv was aware of how coolly elegant Georgina had looked and felt herself rushed and messy again. She hadn't had time to shampoo her hair under the shower; it would have taken too long to dry, so it still felt sticky. She could hear the two of them, voices muffled as though heads were bent close, laughing at some shared exchange, and then as she walked into the kitchen area, saw them step apart. But Rory turned to her as she came through and smiled quickly.

"Goodness, Viv, you know you shouldn't have done all this shopping on your own. I'd have done it tomorrow." He gestured to the bread, salmon, and runner beans on the counter top.

"Er," Viv shook her head, but not wanting to be too cutting in front of Georgina, "We needed dinner for tonight and breakfast for tomorrow morning, Rory! Not to mention pre-dinner drinks with our guest."

Rory grimaced and looked a little shame-faced, at which Viv immediately felt guilty - he had been working right through the afternoon, after all. "Yes, of course. Sorry. I just had to get up to date with things ahead of the parochial church council meeting tomorrow morning." But Viv couldn't fail to catch the glance he made to Georgina.

"Oh, I'm so sorry if I've caused a problem coming over," said Georgina, turning to Viv.

Dear God, she'd put her foot in it, again. Heat rose to her cheeks and she tried to compose herself, counting to three. She didn't want to leave too much of a silent pause in case Rory jumped in. "Not at all, Georgina. Lovely to see you and thanks for coming. I'm sorry. It was my fault. I got a little distracted in town. So ... what can I get you to drink?" She gestured to the table. "We can take it out onto the balcony if you like. There's a bit of shade there."

"Oh, how lovely. I popped over this afternoon while you were in town, actually, and we sat on the balcony then, didn't we, Rory? It was nice and cool." She smiled over at Rory.

"Oh?" Viv frowned, biting back her impulse to say she thought Rory was working hard all afternoon. She didn't want any more awkwardness. It could wait till later. She glanced at her husband, but he just shrugged and raised his eyebrows.

Georgina waved a bottle of what Viv recognised as expensive gin in the air and then added it to the cluster of bottles on the table. "My contribution." Georgina leaned in to Viv and kissed her on both cheeks. "But, honestly, sweetie, you didn't need to go shopping as far as I'm concerned."

"Well, OK, I'll leave you girls to it, then." Rory raked his fingers through his thick hair and then grinned ruefully over at Georgina. "There are still a few things to do in the study. I had a bit of trouble setting up the internet connection."

"Ha, yes, it's not always great here!" Georgina smiled back. "I shouldn't bother too much about tomorrow's parish council meeting, though, Rory. Honestly. It'll mainly be John banging on about the concert season and the other three sighing."

"Concert season?" asked Viv as she poured the drinks and watched Rory, with apologies to Georgina, taking his vino verde and a pastel de nata back into the study. Maybe this was how it was going to be here, Rory absent in his study. But of course it was often like that at home: Rory in his room and she either out at the university or in her own study. It was really no different here, except that she wasn't working full time, hectically rushing from computer to lecture theatre. And except that in the past few weeks she had been largely at home, recovering, and it had all seemed so different. It's just that it would have been nice to start off life here together, not in separate bubbles.

Georgina took the balloon of gin from Viv and sighed.

"Yes. A couple of years ago we started a season of hiring out the church premises to various groups and solo artists on Wednesdays and Fridays. All carefully vetted of course. But it makes a little income for the church upkeep." She added tonic from the large bottle on the table.

Viv carried her own glass and juggled the nibbles out to the balcony table. Earlier, she had softened the white wrought iron chairs with large cushions she had found in a cupboard, and she gestured Georgina to sit.

"This is so brilliant, Viv." Georgina's gaze swept the vista, over the gardens to the red pantiled rooftops below and away to the ocean. "What a wonderful view this is."

Viv sank into a chair and took a grateful sip of her G and T. Actually, she realised that she was glad of Georgina's company, now that she could relax and have a few moments of peace, especially with Rory ensconced in his study. It had been a long day, with the journeys, unpacking and shopping, not to say the incident in the chapel. She took a deep breath, drank in the view, and felt the irritations and tensions begin to drift from her. She needed to get focused and organised again, fill her mind with her work, with positives. With things she could feel passionate about again. Get her life back on track.

From the vantage point of the first floor balcony, the gardens did look lush with their tropical palms and bright jewel-coloured flowers: the flame trees, the frangipani and clumps of blue African lilies jostling between tall elegant Australian ferns and the straight narrow trunks of the date palms. She'd planned on making a start on her research tomorrow, but she must make time, she decided, to identify the unfamiliar plants and to explore the little stony paths that wound around the large shrubberies and under the pergola at the side.

"That strangely shaped tree over there," Viv pointed. "It's like something out of Lord of the Rings or A Game of Thrones. An almost fantastical shape. Do you know what it is?"

Georgina peered over the balcony railing. "Oh, that's called a dragon tree. It's supposed to look like a dragon. Not sure myself, but that's what they say. It has purple sap and I think it was highly prized by the early settlers as a dye. You know, purple was the colour of royalty or nobility, or something?"

"Oh right. That rings a bell. I think I read

somewhere about Madeira being named the purple isles. So maybe that's the reason. Hmm. Interesting."

"You need to visit the museum down in the town. It's by the cable car that goes up to Monte. It has all the stuff about the history of the island."

"I will do." Viv settled back against her cushion. "Mmm, yes, this view is certainly lovely. I think this will become a favourite spot. I'm rather taken with sitting out here to do my work."

A flicker of surprise crossed Georgina's face. "Oh, you're going to work over here? And what work do you do, then?"

She told Georgina briefly about her main research project on the dark ages circa fifth to seventh century AD for the medieval studies department of the university.

"So, is that your ... er ... 'specialist field'?" Georgina curled her fingers in the air to denote the quotation marks. For a moment Viv wondered if there was a hint of humour there, or slight mockery. But Georgina smiled broadly, revealing bright white even teeth, and touched Viv's arm affectionately, and Viv felt mean.

"Mainly, yes. And I've just published a new translation of Beowulf, before ... well, a few months ago ... But actually, because a colleague left suddenly and we've all had to 'muck in' to cover his students, my supervision areas have had to widen to later in the Middle English period." She paused seeing Georgina's puzzled frown. "I mean further into the medieval period, around the fourteenth century onwards, from the reign of Edward III. So I've been assigned a review of published research into various aspects of his reign while I'm over here, to support my colleagues back in the UK." She hesitated again, embarrassed. "Sorry, I'm being boring!"

"Not at all. Medieval history's not my subject really. Ha ha – well, I haven't got a subject at all! I don't work. Thankfully, I don't have to." She steepled her fingertips with their long beautifully manicured gel nails. "I just dabble with things. Interior design. Painting. And taking the odd photo. But history is so fascinating, although I don't know much about Edward III, except that … hmm, something rings a bell. Oh, wasn't he the one who introduced the English parliament and laws?"

Viv raised her eyebrows. "Something like that. Although arguably Alfred the Great started that some five centuries before."

"Wow, you must be really clever. Rory said you'd got a doctorate and that you two met while he was also having time out of vicar-ing … is there such a word, what's the verb from vicar, I don't know!" She flicked her long fingernails and they glinted like blood in the sun. "Anyway, he said he was on secondment at the university studying for a PhD, and you were lecturing in the same department. Clever pair!"

Viv smiled but didn't open up about how they really met. How do you explain to someone that you both have a weird ability to touch other ages, other centuries? To time-slip, in their case, into the fifth century. Herself in the greatest intensity because of her ancestors, a skill inherited from her mother, Elaine DuLac, and going back through the maternal line to the Lady of the Lake, Lady Vivianne. And possibly, for all she knew, even further back.

No, you didn't tell someone about that when you first met them. She would think they were quite mad, or fantasists, not people who found themselves blessed, or maybe cursed, with a peculiar connection across time and space. Rory had held on to a scientific explanation of quantum mechanics, the Einstein-Rosen Bridge theory. She herself just knew what she was experiencing, whatever the theory. For her it was about emotions and feeling. And something really quite mind-bending.

And so for a while, they chatted about life on Madeira island and what Viv might like to explore. It was a gentle companiable hour in which Viv hardly thought about Ana at all. But then her mind drifted to what Georgina had said to her earlier that day.

"Georgina, to change the subject ... you said you'd update me on the issues here." Viv chewed her lip, then stopped herself and rubbed her forefinger round the rim of her glass. "I got the impression there were problems. I must confess I feel a little concerned if, as you were saying, people don't last long here. Why?" Some annoying internal politics, maybe? She really couldn't be bothered with that – there was enough of that back at the university.

"Well." Georgina sighed. "The concert season brought it all to a head. Some of us were very keen on the whole idea as a community project, plus the fact that the church really needs the money." She leaned forward towards Viv. "But *certain people* were very much opposed. To the extent that there was ... well, I can only call it sabotage. But weird."

"Sabotage? Goodness, that sounds melodramatic. Is this some kind of joke?"

"Believe me, it's no joke. Of course it all goes back to before the concert season was mooted. Your predecessors began to complain about being ... how can I put it ... spiritually disturbed ... discombobulated. Oh, go on ... I'll say it straight ... haunted."

Viv jolted. "Haunted? What do you mean?"

"The last two only lasted here a couple of months. I'm talking about the chaplains on secondment to cover the interregnum, like your lovely husband, not the permanent priest. *He* was Canon Jeffries – tootled off back home to Cornwall for a promotion. No, I mean the temporaries, here until we can find the right permanent replacement. They said that odd incidents kept occurring, like odd sightings of a something, someone, a womanly figure ... and azulejo falling off the vestry walls when they'd only just been fixed." Viv murmured confusion. "Oh, you know, those blue and white Moorish tiles. Azulejo they call them."

"Azulejo? Is that what they're called. I saw them at the Capela do Corpo Santo today in the old town."

Georgina waved her hand impatiently. "Yes, yes, sweetie, they're all over the island. In all the churches and public buildings. Apparently they have historical and religious significance. Anyway, then John Waller, the other church warden you met today, who I'm afraid wasn't happy about the concerts being held in the church itself, cancelled one of the events at the last minute because he said the electrics weren't safe."

"Well, maybe they weren't." And maybe Georgina was making a fuss over nothing. Was she a bit of a drama queen? Viv was feeling increasingly bewildered by the story and by Georgina. For someone so sophisticated, she was coming across as someone not a little unhinged. She was unsure what to make of it all. And yet, what, she wondered would Georgina make of her own weird experiences of touching the past? She tried to be logical. "I mean, you've got to be incredibly careful of health and safety these days when you're putting on a public event. Goodness, the trouble we had at the university! I know fire risks do have to be monitored thoroughly. Back in England it's quite a nightmare of bureaucracy. But it's just not worth risking anything if people could be hurt."

"Yes, yes, I know all that," said Georgina, frowning. "But the electrics had only just been redone and retested. John came into the church to do some last-minute fiddling, as he does – well, you'll find out what he's like! – and apparently there was an explosion. And although at the time I suspected John was exaggerating because he didn't want the concerts, it was strange because he said the mother board and the sockets were drenched with water. Yet there was no water source anywhere near. He showed me a part of it. And the funny thing was, it was salty ... it was sea water."

"Sea water? Odd." Viv took a sip of her gin and frowned. "But why was John opposed to the concerts?"

"He maintains that we shouldn't hold any 'light' entertainment events in the nave and near the chancel. He says it's sacrilegious. I mean, he's entitled to his own opinion, of course, but he gets quite, well ... aggressive about it. Trouble is, he objects to all fund-raising activities, and, frankly, I think he doesn't really like people milling around the church at all. But we have no choice but to throw it open for events as much as we can. We just don't get enough funding or income from central sources to cope with building repairs and maintenance, let alone the things we should be doing for the community."

"Sorry ... er what are you saying? That John is deliberately spoiling the fun?"

"Well, yes, in a way. But it's more than that, Viv." She put her glass down on the table. "Look, I feel bad 'grassing' on someone – or whatever it is the gangsters say! *Is* that what they say?" Her bright smile dropped.

"But I just feel you ought to know what you're up against."

"Oh, surely it can't be as bad as that?" Viv flicked a fallen twig off the table.

Georgina leaned back, crossing one slim tanned leg over the other, her silky skirt pooling down her calf.

"Well. The last chaplain nearly died."

CHAPTER 6

VIV

"That's ridiculous," said Rory that night as they lay in bed, air con roaring. He raised his arm above his head and slapped the pillow, unusually irritable. "What on earth are you suggesting?"

"Rory, for a start it isn't me who's saying it, it's Georgina. I'm just repeating to you what she said this afternoon and trying to make sense of it all. I tried to quiz her about what she meant about the previous chaplains not lasting long and the last one nearly dying, but it seemed very vague and confused." Viv shuffled to find a more comfortable spot and pushed the duvet away although it wasn't as humid and sticky as she had anticipated. She tried to stroke away the pains in her stomach and the muscle aches in her thighs. "It was almost as if she was trying to put me off, warn me about something."

She really felt the exhaustion of the day now, the travelling, the shopping, the strangeness of it all. She yawned, wanting to clear her mind of the agitated buzz she had been feeling since Georgina left. "I think she's got some sort of obsession with the atmosphere in the church. Peculiar goings-on!"

Rory laughed. "Really? It seems a perfectly pleasant atmosphere to me. I had a good look around earlier and everything seemed totally normal and in order. Look, I think you've got the wrong impression entirely of Georgina. Maybe you misinterpreted what she was saying. She seems an eminently sensible woman to me ... and very charming."

"Hmm, maybe you can't see beyond those charms!"

"Viv, darling, I'm sorry but I really need to sleep. My head's full of all these anomalies I've found in the church records. We'll talk tomorrow. But just now I'm shattered." He lay back, frowning.

Viv was aware that she hadn't yet told Rory about her experience in the Capela do Corpus Santo. She'd been waiting for the right time, but after Georgina's disturbing comments there hadn't been a right time. Over supper, Rory's sole concern had been the PCC meeting the next day and what he'd found out about the state of the church finances and record-keeping. Then he'd disappeared into his study again. Frustrating, but the chapel would keep until tomorrow.

Time was when they had talked about everything,

and nothing had to wait. Now it was different. Yet she really needed to reach out to him.

But he had kicked his side of the duvet away and flopped on top of it. She turned on her side and ran her hands over Rory's torso and felt it toned from the routine of gym work and a run down the country lanes every morning back home. Yet he just touched her arm absently and resumed his frowning. She sighed, turning to lie flat on her back, a gap between them.

She too frowned in the darkness and bit her lip. Oh dear, she really must stop that habit; her mouth was getting raw. She was aware of the physical distance between them, that she had somehow moved away from his body. What was happening to them?

Or maybe it was *her*. Perhaps she *was* too suggestible. She had tried to question Georgina, to remain objective. Maybe it *was* just all about rumours getting out of hand … She felt Rory's presence next to her, his heat, his unease, and immediately a flood of guilt washed over her. She was obviously getting too sensitive, too quick to jump to conclusions. He was hurting too. He was simply better at hiding it.

She grimaced and drew in her breath.

"I'm sorry, Rory." She turned fully and closed the gap between them, snuggling onto Rory's broad chest, kissing his hot skin. In spite of the strange content of their conversation and the lateness of the hour, she was aware that it had been some time since they had felt close. It was as though the closeness, the intimacy, had been broken by the events around losing Ana. Had they retreated into their own shells for protection? She realised how much she wanted to bring that intimacy back again.

He exhaled deeply and slowly moved his arm to enfold her. "Viv darling, do you think ..." he said gently, "that things are just a little ... emotional at the moment?"

"You mean you think I'm taking this stuff too much to heart? No, I'm just telling you what Georgina told me. I don't know what to make of it. But we both know that there is more in heaven and earth, etc, etc ... It's all a bit weird ..." She felt Rory turn his head to hers and kiss her hair, "... and, OK, maybe I'm a bit unnerved."

"I wish you hadn't had that kind of conversation with Georgina as soon as we arrived. You ... *we* can do without this." He stroked her arm and bent to kiss her mouth.

"Mmm. I know but I guess she was only warning us. What about, I'm not yet sure."

Viv liked Georgina, well, in some ways anyway, her vivaciousness, her warmth, but she was also aware that her new-found friend was extremely attractive and glamorous and that she herself felt dowdy in comparison. No, she actually *was* dowdy these days, ever since the trauma of Ana. The name was in her heart now. And maybe her heart was too broken to return to that happy, glowing, attractive person she knew she used to be.

She was very aware of Rory beside her, the heat of his body and his need. His arm pulled her closer to him.

"Look, let's just forget it all for tonight at least. We've both had an exhausting day." Rory turned further to lean in to her.

Viv held a restraining hand on his chest. "Rory?"

"Mmm?"

"What was Georgina doing here this afternoon? What was that all about?"

Rory paused - a little too long Viv thought - and held her upturned gaze. "Nothing much. Just updating me about a few things. We got on well. She seems a nice woman. She'd be a good friend for you while we're here." He smiled ruefully. "As long as she doesn't keep putting disturbing ideas into your head." He planted a tender kiss on her mouth and whispered. "Love you. Thank you for agreeing to come here with me. Although I sincerely hope it turns out to be a good idea! You know?" he murmured, his voice soft, "Perhaps sleep can wait a few minutes."

Then he pushed himself up on his right arm, lowered himself slowly upon her and her mind went blank as she wound her arms around his broad muscular back. She inhaled the woody fragrance of the bergamot cologne he always wore, and it reminded her of when they met and the scent that followed her through the centuries from another world. They had shared so much. Exhausted, numbed or not, she needed him.

~

BUT VIV'S DREAMS WERE DISTURBING THAT NIGHT.

Again, she seemed to be watching the ocean as towering waves rose up and a tumult of roaring molten rock seethed up to the surface of the sea. She felt the burning heat fill her body, and heard the deafening fiery explosions, the sea a boiling mass of flame and smoke. Clouds of steam and ash engulfed her, and she smelt the sulphur and death, and she knew the rage and was filled with terror. Behind her eyes, darkened with the blackness of the smoke and debris, there flashed the colours of a migraine, blood red and orange, and she saw the churning ocean spewing out explosive gases and rocks and tiny creatures, and the air was filled with fear.

Then she startled to find herself standing in blinding sun, on craggy shingle, sand, and rocks, under towering cliffs, and saw in her hands a curled ammonite, and at her feet a painted square of pottery, bright blue and white. A quick stab of pain made her press a hand against her rounded belly, and she felt a kick against her palm. A momentary rush of joy quickly overcome by dread. A drawing back to separate herself from the woman standing there before her.

She was that person and yet she was outside of her, observing, unable to help. An almost overwhelming desire to enfold the woman and give her comfort, yet knowing with certainty that she could not. Viv saw the woman turn towards her and for a moment they stared into each other's eyes. A searing pain passed between them. Viv gasped then dropped her head in her hands, unable to look at the distress so clear in the other woman's eyes. She recognised it: the pain, the loss, the emptiness.

And when she looked up again, she saw the frantic puckering of the brow, the terror in the eyes, the movement of the lips.

"Help me, help me."

⁓

Viv woke with a start, echoes of a scream searing her brain, aware that it was the middle of the night, yet still seeing bright sunlight and migraine flashes of colour. For a few moments she couldn't locate herself. The bedroom wasn't hers. The darkness rushing now through her head and forming itself into the shapes and shadows of curtains and furniture, confusing her semi-consciousness. She was staring at something, an indistinct form across the room, near the door, hands raised in supplication. And then it was gone, the dream, the vision, the fear. Viv drew in her ragged breath and realised that her fists were bunched on the edge of the duvet, pulling it up to her chin.

She pushed the duvet away from her damp body, and slowed her breathing, calming her racing heart.

Rory stirred beside her and her thoughts drifted to what she hadn't told Georgina about the way they had met ...

But now, Rory flung his arm out and murmured in his sleep. Viv frowned for a while at the empty space by the door, then turned to him and snuggled up against his body, blotting out the dark.

CHAPTER 7

VIV

Amazingly, after such a disturbed night, when Viv awoke she did not feel particularly tired, just aware that Rory's side of the bed was empty and the bedroom door ajar. In fact her head felt unusually light and she lay there pondering the clarity of the birdsong in the garden and the sounds of the town awakening, the deep boom of the Porto Santo ferry's horn in the bay, the rumble of distant cars, a motorbike on the hill, someone shouting at a barking dog.

The anxieties of the previous day and the strange dreams that followed them, seemed more in perspective this morning. She'd been exhausted after the journey and her mind had clearly been too stressed to think straight, making her see 'ghosts' in the room. It was not surprising really.

The sun was filtering through the curtains and she thought about the day ahead. She wanted to start work on her research, knowing that Rory would be ensconced in the study or meetings all day, and she was looking forward to sitting in the warm sunshine on the balcony, peacefully searching documents on her laptop and making notes. Nothing too demanding.

She had all the time in the world. Well, nearly. There were a couple of deadlines.

She slipped out of bed, padded across the wooden floorboards to the windows, and pushed the curtains aside. The view over the garden was tranquil, bathed in the golden light of morning and heralding another gloriously hot day.

As she took in the bright flowers of the oleander and hibiscus down below in the garden, the spreading palm trees, sturdy laurel and tall narrow eucalyptus, the whole lush greenery of it all, glowing in a sharp artists' light, she felt she could breathe in the calm.

It was not the wide open view she enjoyed from their bedroom back home at their Derbyshire rectory in the middle of the English countryside, with its wide expanse of fields, trees and hedges, the smooth softness of gentle rolling hills broken by drystone walls. But here the view over the red pantile roofs of the white-washed houses with their strange little sand and blue-tiled chimneys and terracotta birds perched on the apex was beautiful. The glimpse of the glinting azure sea beyond and the towering cliffs over to the east filled her heart with a surprising and equal contentment. She was beginning to feel a glimmer of gladness that she had agreed to come here, despite the shaky start yesterday.

She pushed the window further open and leaned out, inhaling deeply the musky smell of wood smoke and the fragrance of the late spring jacaranda and mimosa mingling with the deep scent of the ocean. The clarity of the tropical light enhanced everything sharply in focus. For the first time in weeks she was beginning to feel alive again. She stroked her stomach and held the memory of Ana tightly to her.

She remembered that Georgina had mentioned a history centre and museum by the cable car that took you up to the old village of Monte in the mountains. There was so much to explore. She realised that for the first time in ages, she was becoming hungry for discovery again, for moving from the past into what lay ahead – if only she could.

She turned away from the window and lay back down on the bed again, on top of the covers, practising her deep yoga breaths. Rarely in England did she have the luxury of late lazy mornings.

Viv could hear Rory in the kitchen making coffee. Even at home he liked to rise early, saying it was the best time of day. She wouldn't be surprised if he had already been out for his morning run before the heat of the sun made it too uncomfortable. For a few moments she luxuriated in the laziness of the bed, gently doing her stretching and muscle relaxant exercises, as the physiotherapist had advised.

Sometimes she forgot, in the busy-ness of daily life of work and at the rectory, that she was still officially recuperating and not yet back to her usual full strength.

"You look rested," smiled Rory as he pushed through the door, juggling two mugs of coffee. She sat up and took one gratefully. "I didn't want to disturb you. I just slipped out for my run. I left a note in case you woke." He nodded towards the bedside table on Viv's side and she saw the piece of paper she hadn't noticed before.

"Oh, thank you. I've only just woken up. Where did you run?"

"Down the Rua Carreira and the Avenida do Zarco into town. I just ran along the seafront and then back up the hill. There was a quiet little park on the way, tucked behind the Avenida, with a pond and fountains. Lots of trees and blossoms. You should go and investigate. It looked like a good spot to sit and reflect. It comes out onto the main thoroughfare that's parallel to the promenade."

"Yes, I think I saw the edge of it yesterday. I thought I might do a bit of exploring in the afternoons for the first few weeks here. I want to get my bearings." Viv turned her face to his and closed her eyes, expecting the usual feel of his mouth on hers.

"Good idea." Rory kissed the top of her head quickly and then retreated with his coffee mug, calling back, "I'm off to have a shower."

"OK," she said to the empty doorway.

~

It was late morning when the landline in the hallway rang and Viv thrust her papers and pen onto her keyboard on the balcony table, pulled off her glasses, and hurried indoors to grab phone before it disturbed Rory in the study. He'd retreated there after the PCC meeting in the church, quiet and distracted. And he'd been quiet in there the rest of the morning apart from a couple of conversations on the phone extension on his desk. Viv had taken a mug of coffee in to him about an hour before but he'd been talking to John, frowning into the mouthpiece and shuffling spreadsheets, so she'd just put it down at his side and closed the door softly behind her. He had not looked happy at all.

Viv picked up the receiver and pressed the green button. "Hello. Priest's house." It amused her to say that, and she didn't know whether it should be 'vicarage' or 'rectory' or what; she should ask Rory. There was an awkward pause which Viv had to fill. "Er, I mean, Reverend Netherbridge. Well, not actually ... I'm his wife ..."

Then, abruptly a chortle, as though the caller had finally decided how to respond.

"Viv!" laughed a clear, refined voice. "It's Georgina."

Viv wondered why she had left that strange

unnerving pause, but before she could form the words Georgina blustered on. "Oh, Viv, so glad it was you who came to the phone. I expect the lovely Rory's busy working, after that difficult PCC? What a trouper ... I was just wondering ... ah, if you'd like to come for a light lunch in town with me." Viv was not unaware of the slight hesitation as if Georgina's brain was quickly computing an unexpected situation.

"Well ..." Viv had been hoping to get a bit more research done before stopping for lunch.

"I don't know whether you've noticed it," Georgina rushed on quickly, "but there's a lovely restaurant near the statue of Zarco on the avenida. The Golden Gate. It dates from the 1920s I think, the heyday of visitors coming over on the seaplanes to take the healing waters and healthy air. It was closed for a while, but it reopened last year. All 1920s décor. Or is it 1930s? Anyway, it's very atmospheric. I wanted to reciprocate your hospitality yesterday. I've booked a table for two for lunch. Please do say you'll come!"

Reciprocate my hospitality! She'd only given her a gin, some savoury nibbles and a pastel da nata! But, on the other hand, a lunch date in the continued absence of her husband would be welcome. "Well, I'm sure my work can wait a little. Yes, thank you. I can do with a break. I'd love to join you."

Viv was glad that she had changed from her shorts and sun-top into a smart short sleeved ivory dress as she crossed the square towards The Golden Gate. It wasn't really the sort of place for shorts.

The façade was, indeed, beautifully elegant and the building, with its white walls and wrap-around wrought iron balcony on the first floor, curved around the corner of the Avenida Arriaga and the southern pedestrianized end of the Avenida do Zarco that ran down towards the sea. She hadn't realised there were places like this on the island. She'd really only seen the church, the old town, and the supermarket, and much of it seemed to be quite shabby, even dilapidated and decaying in some parts, although, to her eyes, having its own kind of decaying beauty. Her mental image had always been of her parents on their dig, scrabbling in the earth of an undeveloped island, and although since then clearly there were many newer buildings crowded together, she hadn't expected such historic elegance and grace.

A white-uniformed, gold braided maître d' of The Golden Gate stood at the mahogany double doors on the corner and smiled at her as she approached.

"Lunch, madam?"

"Oh. Yes. Thank you. I'm meeting a friend upstairs."

"Of course." He bowed. "Please come this way."

But as she was led inside to the cool interior with its full height brown-framed louvred French windows, marble topped tables, and crystal chandeliers, she saw Georgina, chic in a softly draping little blush-pink number, at the top of the wide, curved oak staircase, one hand resting on the polished balustrade. She looked as though she was posed for a portrait.

"Viv! You made it! Wonderful!" Her voice sounded louder than usual, forced.

"I wasn't sure if we were upstairs or out at the café tables on the street."

"Oh, the street tables are nice, but it's quieter up here with the white-glove service, and anyway I'd already booked a table on the off-chance you could join me ..."

Viv wondered if that was what Georgina normally did. Maybe she often came here for lunch. Booked a table for two, and hoped she'd get someone to join her? It seemed a little odd. Especially at such a clearly expensive location.

The maître d' bowed and gestured with his arm, taking in both the sumptuous dining room and the balcony. "Would Madam Machin and her guest prefer to enjoy a table inside or outside?"

Goodness. Viv fiddled with the shoulder strap of her bag. This would be posh for Rory and her to come for dinner, let alone a 'light lunch' as Georgina had said. Yes, pricey, she had no doubt.

"Oh, let's go outside on the balcony, sweetie," said Georgina, linking arms with Viv and patting her shoulder. "It's shaded, cooler and airy. And we can watch the people on the street below passing by along the avenida ... if that's OK with you?"

The 'light lunch' choice for both of them turned out to be a seafood salad with a salmon mousse with slices of mango. Viv watched, fascinated, as the plates were laid in front of them, covered with silver salvers. The two waiters needed for the 'show' paused dramatically for a moment until they were synchronised, and then in a coordinated movement lifted the salvers, beaming with pride.

Viv felt as though she had slipped into a bygone era of elegance and sophistication. Goodness, what would Rory say about this when she got back to the apartment? Probably something along the lines of: "don't get too used to that, not on a vicar's salary."

"What are you thinking, Viv?" Viv started, nearly spilling her prosecco. Georgina was looking intently at her over her mousse. "You know, I bet Rory would love this."

Viv frowned. Why would she assume that? How would she know what he would love or not love, after such a short acquaintance?

"Oh. Well, I was just thinking that this would be a great place for us to come for a birthday dinner. Or an anniversary. A posh evening meal."

Georgina smiled. "So, is he hard at work ensconced in his study?"

"Mmm." She wasn't sure how the conversation had

turned so quickly to Rory. Viv took a forkful of the mango and light fruity sauce. Back at home she would have served a savoury sauce with salmon, parsley maybe, or sometimes onion or cheese. But this was very tasty and tropical. "This sauce is delicious." She rested her cutlery on the edge of her plate and looked up. "But, Georgina, the things you said yesterday. They're preying on my mind. What is going on at the church?"

"Oh, really – no, don't worry about all that just now. Maybe I spoke out of turn. I expect Rory will tell me off. Just forget I said anything. Honestly."

Viv sensed a wariness, a drawing back. She could see that Georgina's expression was closed and knew that she would get nothing more from her for the moment. She picked up her knife and fork again. "Right. OK. Um, so, Georgina, I don't even know about you. Are you married ... is there a family?"

Viv couldn't help but catch the flicker that crossed Georgina's face, before she composed her expression back into a smile. "Sadly, no longer. And no children. We came out here some years ago for my husband's job, but ... well, I've been on my own for a couple of years now."

"Oh, I'm sorry." Viv grimaced across the table at Georgina, but she had turned abruptly and was waving enthusiastically over the balcony railing to a couple with a baby in a papoose, down below on the avenida. The man waved back, nudging his partner to look up at Georgina and wave too. Then they strolled on under the trees.

Georgina watched the couple walk away and turned her attention back to Viv.

"Before we came to Funchal, we divided our time between the UK and Portugal, but mainly Portugal. I'm from London, but my parents have both passed away and I don't have any brothers or sisters. My husband was from near Lisbon. A large seafaring family. Well, at least, they owned a number of trading ships."

"Goodness."

"So, I haven't really got ties back in the UK and I don't really have a base except for here. And I suppose I've made this my home now and can't face starting again somewhere else, not on my own." She paused. "And it's not viable for me to live in the UK any more."

Viv wondered why. She tried to read Georgina's face but all she could see was calm confidence. "No, I can understand that. You put down roots and then nothing else compares." She rested her cutlery on her plate and sat back. "I think your own familiar 'base' is important. Back home in Derbyshire, I even kept my apartment when I moved in to the rectory with Rory. He calls it my 'bachelor bolt hole'! But, you know, I can retreat there if things get too much. Like trying to be the good clergy wife, and all that." She'd loved that apartment from first sight, and her associations of it with her previous partner, Pete, had shrunk into the dimmer recesses of her mind. After all, his awful behaviour had led indirectly to her meeting Rory, hadn't it? And now the charming converted stable mews was a welcome escape, not from Rory but from being what she feared she wasn't and could never be.

∽

AFTER LUNCH AND WHEN VIV AND GEORGINA HAD KISSED on both cheeks and parted, Georgina off to do some clothes shopping, Viv wandered down the avenida in the direction of the Sé, feeling oddly uneasy and unwilling to head back to the apartment and her work. She liked Georgina in many ways, very much; she was warm-hearted but there was somehow a frisson of discomfort which Viv couldn't quite place. She felt drawn to the cool solace of the cathedral.

The Sé was closed, so she took the narrow passageway to the side of the cathedral walls and followed the maze of little cobbled streets behind. The sun beat on her back and as she tried to work out the direction she needed to emerge into the wide promenade, she felt flushed, aware of the sweat trickling down her spine and pooling in the hollow of her back. She glanced round and realised that there was nobody else on the street; the noise and busy-ness of the avenida and the cathedral quarter had morphed into an eerie quiet.

Reaching out her hand she touched the cool solidity of the aged peeling wall beside her, reassuringly real. But the dingy battered stone frontages seemed to press in on her, shadowy alleyways between the silent buildings seemed to hide a secret menace, and she heard her breath loud in her ears and her heart beat faster.

The narrow street turned a sharp corner and she found herself with only one way to go: up a flight of concrete steps, a graffitied wall in front of her obscuring any view of her route ahead. Perhaps she should turn round and retrace her footsteps, but heavy footfall behind her made her continue quickly to the top of the steps. She stopped and looked back, but there was nobody in sight. Yet as she moved on the footfall reverberated from the concrete walls and paused at her back. She shivered, her heart thrumming. Something, or someone, was pushing her on. But the narrow passageway was empty. Except for herself.

Ahead, she could see that there was a cramped pathway alongside the wall, but it appeared to open out at the end and, panicked, she forced herself onwards. She could make out jacaranda trees ahead, so she squeezed on through.

Where the wall ended there was another short flight of steps downwards and with great relief she saw a car passing by on a street not far beyond. She stopped at the top of the steps to regain her breath, but just as she had felt in the capela, her eye was drawn to the graffiti on the wall at her side. She stared as the drawing slipped in and out of focus.

The imprint on her brain was a simple representation of a sailing ship and beside it a square bearing the distinctive geometric Moorish design. Azulejo, Georgina had called it. It looked as though at one time in the past it had been coloured in. There were faint traces of brown, purple and blue in the outlines. But it was the drawing of the ship that made her bend closely to look more easily. The ship was sketched as if the sail was being buffeted by the wind, and on the deck, standing out clearly from the many indistinguishable figures, were a man and a woman richly clothed in lavish fur-lined cloaks, staring out to the waves that lashed the hull. Basic as the drawing of the lady was, Viv felt a shudder of recognition.

It was the lady who haunted her dreams. She was sure of it. Names and faces drifted across her mind. Sir Robert. Joan, the maid servant. Lady Ana.

"*Ana?*"

A car screeched by on the street below, skidding off down the hill. In its wake, a nervous, high pitched bark of a cough. Viv looked up and saw a familiar figure staring up at her. For a strange unnerving moment her world fragmented like a spilled jigsaw. Then it configured itself again.

A charcoal suit, even in this heat, a tan leather briefcase in his hand, emerging from a doorway, a frightened expression on his face, fingers to his throat, as he caught her eye. John? The church warden? As she stared back, he thrust something into his jacket pocket and scurried away. Viv wondered what he was hiding.

As he disappeared, she ran down the steps and onto the street below. He was nowhere in sight. But where he had been standing looking up at her, she saw a narrow door and a brass plaque. She peered at it and read: Jorges da Freitas, private investigator.

CHAPTER 8

VIV

"You must have been mistaken," Rory grunted, not looking up, eyes fixed on the computer screen, fingers tapping rapidly on the keyboard, as Viv stood leaning against the jamb of the door to the study. "Why would he be frightened to see you there? He's our church warden, Viv. And why would he be visiting a private investigator? He was most probably just standing in the doorway for a moment."

Viv looked at Rory's hair, dark and curly, thick tendrils around his ears. Her breath felt thin, insubstantial. "Rory, he looked guilty, as though I'd caught him at something. And I'm sure that he was coming out of that office."

Rory looked up at her and shook his head. "Viv, I'm sure that was not the case at all." She noted the slight impatience in his voice, as though she were an imaginative child, inventing oddnesses where there weren't any.

"It was just so weird. Creepy." But even as she said it, she was not sure at all. Was she going crazy, her imagination running away with her?

"Oh, Viv, *please*! I really don't think that the extremely staid John would be doing something strange or weird or creepy. For goodness sake! Just forget it. Please." She'd never seen him so irritable before. He turned back to his computer so that she had to speak to the back of his head.

"But I do know what I saw."

"Mmm," murmured Rory, eyes fixed back on the screen, attention distracted.

Viv felt so oddly uneasy, even disoriented, that she could hear her heart beating too fast, her pulse throbbing too rapidly. She drew in a ragged breath. What was wrong with her? Why was she so disturbed at the moment? Because of what …seeing a church warden in town, doing what? Nothing, really. A silly thing. And the lunch with Georgina, wondering about her and what she was up to … Rory's distraction, his sudden distance from her since they had been in Funchal?

She knew when she had felt a bit like this before. A couple of years previously, when she met Rory, *how* she met Rory in fact, and perhaps for a while afterwards, when she had experienced that extraordinary episode and the world as she had known it had shifted on its

THE DRAGON TREE

axis. That wobbliness of slipping time. Those shivery visions, the fragile faintness of her new realities that he had called 'quantum mechanics', the Einstein - Rosen Bridge theory, traversable worm-holes, touching another time and place. Was it all coming back? And where would it lead this time? She shuddered.

As she turned quietly away from him, leaving him to focus on his work in his study, and returned to the balcony overlooking the lush tropical garden, she knew that the past had come back again to haunt her. The frightening episode she had thought was firmly in the past, was not finished with her yet.

She gripped the balcony rail and took a deep breath, making herself drink in the beauty of the jewel-bright bougainvillea below and the rich deep greens of the thick foliage of palm and eucalyptus. Biting her lip yet again, she forced herself to think of the wonderful positives that had come out of those events. She'd met Rory, she'd found the peace and refuge of the Derbyshire rectory, the hope and delight of the early months of her pregnancy.

She watched as a seagull swooped over the jacaranda trees, shrieking, and refocused to the balcony rail she was leaning on. Her eyes followed a tiny golden lizard as it flicked its head towards her hand, then scuttled off down the wall, oblivious to her fears. She believed that since her marriage to Rory and her pregnancy she had shaken off the other-worldly heritage from her mother and their ancient antecedents. Hoped that she'd escaped that weird and unsettling gift she hadn't known she possessed until her worlds, past and present, had collided two years ago. Before that episode, and since it, she believed that she was firmly rooted in the reality of the present world, that she was a normal ordinary *logical* person. That she was objective and practical.

But ... maybe she wasn't. Maybe she would never be quite the same again. Maybe it was all destined to recur throughout her life now that she'd touched that other world.

And, truth be known, she had felt a bit isolated before they came out to Funchal, ever since the miscarriage. Nothing like a trauma to make you feel alone, screwed up inside yourself. Compounded by Rory's preoccupation out here. Understandable, but it still made her feel empty.

Well, blow him. So, she'd just have to do her own thing. She needed to focus on her own interests, her work, her research. Her own concrete reality.

For the next few weeks she settled into a routine of spending all morning working on her research on the balcony overlooking the garden, absorbed with her work, only from time to time looking up to watch the geckos running up the walls or following the flight path of the gulls overhead.

Occasionally her eyes would rise up to the mountains where it rained every day and filled the water courses, the levadas, to bring precious water down the steep slopes to the coast. The mountains, wreathed in cloud, that looked so magical and mysterious, that reached up above the town to hide the bowl-core of the volcano at their heart never ceased to amaze her. She never tired of watching them; they looked different every day: clear and sharp, or dark and brooding, or misty and surreal. She was beginning to love those mornings on the balcony.

In the afternoons, when she wasn't resting on top of their bed, she explored the town and even took a cable car up to the quiet little village of Monte perched high on the mountainside above Funchal. But all the time she kept thinking how much nicer it would have been if Rory had shared it with her. He didn't seem to be seeing the island at all, except for meetings in town with John or the auditor or some higher official of the church. She had a niggling feeling that Georgina had been there too at some of the meetings, but he didn't mention her.

She really must get him away from his work. She'd hardly seen him, except over dinner, and then he was often quiet and somehow absent. To be fair, he did often share in making the evening meal, but it would be good to *do* things together, like they used to. And he really needed to take a break, however difficult it might be sorting out the church affairs. OK, he had his daily early morning run through the town, but that wasn't quite the same thing, was it? A walk along the levadas together would be a good and maybe they could hire a car to explore the volcano and the lava fields. And Machico – she'd like to see where her parents had worked on their dig. OK, Rory didn't have a 'normal' weekend because of his services on Sundays and prep for them on Saturdays, but back at home he had usually managed to take Mondays and Tuesdays off in lieu.

That day had started a little cloudy but by early afternoon the sun was again hot and glaring in the deep blue sky above her head. Viv pushed back from her laptop, stretching and arching her spine. She blinked rapidly to clear the blur from the screen.

A scraping noise from down in the garden caught her attention and she squinted over the balcony railing, pulling off her reading glasses. There was a movement in the bushes to the side near the wall. Members of the church community often came to tend the garden or sit reflectively in the peace of the palms and tropical plants, but there was something odd about the way the shrubs were moving that made her stare. As she watched, John Waller crept out from the undergrowth, spade in hand, and looked rapidly around him.

Viv drew back, not sure why she needed to hide from his view, but she could still see him through the railing from her vantage point. He hurried out of her sight, presumably off down the drive. He was probably just doing some weeding or tidying in the shrubbery, yet he seemed surreptitious. Odd. But then he often did have that guilty look about him. He was a strange fellow. She turned back to her laptop and peered again at the website she had been engrossed in.

She had looked up the period of the cog that she had seen in the capela and behind the Sé and found to her surprise that it had been in common use during the time of Edward III, the period she was researching for the university. The screen image of the fourteenth century Edward III shifted and refocused. For a moment the print seemed to scorch her eyeballs. She knew that she should have stopped earlier for a coffee and lunch but she had been too engaged with material on the politics of the king's marriage at sixteen to the young French Philippa of Hainault to want to break her concentration. She would need to email a paper back to her colleagues within the next couple of weeks.

She stared at the regal image, all rich robes and ermine-trimmed cloak, the pointed facial features, high forehead, sharp cheekbones and staring eyes, and wondered how accurate the artist's portrayal of the king could be. He was well into adulthood by the time the portrait was done. Clearly the role of the painter was to flatter, but the eyes in the image somehow looked to her to reveal a cruel stare, a harshness. Yet Edward was reportedly popular in his own time, and his marriage loving and certainly unusually long with at least six surviving children. But she had also found other papers that argued for a difficult and temperamental king. What was he really like? The creator of the origins of our modern parliament and the duchy of Cornwall, ruthless warring adventurer, owing his crown to his treacherous, husband-killing mother and her lover Mortimer, yet destroyer of their liaison – a man of many parts and conflicts. Viv was drawn to those eyes in the portrait and the realisation that there was some kind of connection between him and the weird experiences she'd been having, however coincidental, brought a shiver to her body.

Viv was pondering the conflicting arguments in her research as she made herself a late lunch, then shoved some washing into the machine and prepared a casserole to put in the oven for that evening. It wasn't really her turn, but Rory was out all day and wouldn't be back until later, so she'd volunteered cooking duty.

It was now impossible for her to settle back to her work although it was barely three o' clock. Her mind was all over the place. She needed to clear her head. And, after all, she had promised herself to use the afternoons exploring. Maybe the history centre and museum by the cable car was still open. She gathered her papers together and closed her laptop, bringing everything indoors in case it rained, although she knew it never did, not down here on the coast. She didn't bother to change out of her shorts but replaced her flip flops with flat sturdy sandals that were better for walking down the steep cobbled streets.

She felt for the hardness of the fossil nestled comfortingly in her pocket. She no longer went anywhere without it.

∽

VIV DECIDED SHE MUST BE GETTING USED TO THE HEAT now as she took a short cut through the narrow side lanes between the strange cramped shops away from the main streets, feeling quite comfortable as she wound her way downhill towards the promenade and the cable car terminus on the edge of the old town.

She realised she'd overshot a little too far when she dropped down onto the Rua de Santa Maria above the square where she had found the Capela do Corpo Santo. She needed to turn left downhill back towards the cable car to find the museum, but it was a charming detour as she passed the painted doors of the old town streets with their fascinating murals of fishermen and pop-art abstracts. Viv noticed that some were depicting the specialism of the shop they fronted or the profession of the services within: a glorious hat shop with an array of glamorous fascinators; a huge eye emerging from spectacles at a tiny optician's office. She stopped to take a few photos on her iphone, peering at the images through her screen, moving from one door to another without looking up, hitting the button, click, click, intrigued.

Then one image zoomed into focus. It was of a mountain rising above the waves of the ocean, fire spewing from its peak, plumes of gases clouding the boiling seas below. She shivered and peered more closely into her camera. She could see rocks flung away from the central mass. And there, amidst the fiery explosions, a fragment of rock, a fossil ammonite, like her precious memento of her parents. Like the vision she had had in their rectory drawing room that wet wild March day before they came to Funchal. She swiped the camera image on her phone to enlarge and focus on a close up of the crustacean, glowing as it was flung away from the lava.

The world swayed. Viv's hand reached out behind her to touch the wall of the house at her back, yet she still stared at the image on her phone. She clicked, eyes reluctant to draw away from the vision, but forcing herself to look up and across the little narrow street. The door she stood opposite was decorated with an image of fishermen dragging their nets over the shingle. Not a volcano. Not a fossil ammonite. Wildly she turned. Where was it? But the doors showed no ocean, no explosions of magma. She felt her breath quickening, her pulse pounding.

Fingers trembling, Viv scrolled through the pictures on her phone: the hat shop, the fishermen, the opticians. But no mountain, no fossil. She took a deep breath and steadied herself. She was aware that passers-by, tourists also snapping the murals on the doors, were staring at her, frowning. She stretched a smile and slipped her phone into her bag, drawing in her ragged breath. Automatically her hand reached down to her pocket and she stroked the roughness of the fossil that lay there.

CHAPTER 9

ANA

"*L*ady Ana!" Joan's shrill voice resonated through the cave where Ana sat stroking the strange blue tile with its raised brown and purple markings, her slim fingers questioning the IHS letters, her mind full of the holy shrine further along the shore where she had come upon it so surprisingly.

Quickly she thrust it back into her pouch where she could feel its hardness against her stomach. She shifted slightly on the rock that served as her stool, so that the sharp corners of the tile did not prick her swelling belly.

"Joan! Where have you been?"

Ana's maidservant, promoted, unavoidably but rather unwisely, to that position from the back kitchens of Darbey Hall, failed to look in the least bit sheepish. She tossed her head and exhaled sharply, huffing her displeasure. "'Sakes, more to the point, lady, where have *you* been all morning?"

Ana frowned and flicked invisible sand from her kirtle. She took a deep breath and settled her voice to sound severe. "Joan. We have spoken of this matter before. I have been where I needed to be. You, on the other hand, have not. I was obliged to attend to my own toilet this morning."

Joan opened her fleshy mouth in retort but, concluding that discretion was the better part of valour, sighed loudly, her lips quivering into a confidential smirk. She glanced at the space on the rock beside her mistress, then grimaced and instead squatted in front of her lady, legs wide apart to accommodate her stomach. "Well. There be a tale." She winked, rested her thick forearms on her haunches and grinned lasciviously, revealing her black uneven teeth stumps. "Oh, my, oh my, Lady Ana! Mercy me, such carousing we had last night! It was like being back at your dear Hall! The wine seemed to go straight to my head. We told stories of the old court and laughed – oh such a laugh we had!" She leaned in towards Ana who shrank back from the stink of sour breath and the spray of spittle and lowered her voice. "I laughed till I wet my underskirt ..." Joan paused for breath, flapping her skirts up, but seeing Lady Ana's horrified face and quite possibly noticing it for the first time, pressed her lips together and looked round behind her as if seeking someone else who had spoken.

"For goodness sakes, Joan. You forget yourself. I do not wish to know." Ana's mouth had dropped open and she wriggled a little further back from the stench of urine and the words that thundered around her head. She thought there were always undignified smells about her maidservant, especially around her nether regions, and she wondered if it was the same for herself too. She so wished that she were able to clean herself properly and change her kirtle. Was it come to this? But of course it had. There was no privy here, only corners of the caves and behind the rocks and trees, and no chamber-servants to help Joan to fetch buckets of sea water to cleanse away the smells that must cling to them all.

She was sure that Joan would not have spoken to her like that back at Darbey Hall, and, indeed, if she had, her father would have dismissed her straightway. But on the sea passage many vulgar and coarse words had drifted to her ears, however Robert might have tried to protect her from the sailors' talk, she and Joan being the only females present. And here, in a cave, herself with tattered robes and sitting on a rock instead of a sumptuous Italian upholstered chair …

Joan huffed loudly and struggled to push her bulk up to standing, jowls wobbling. She tossed her head, greasy locks falling loose from her grubby cap. "Well. There be a thing. So, what does my lady have need of me just now? Braid her hair for the feasting dinner maybe? Or lay out her many rich gowns on the bed for her to choose?" She set her mouth in a hard line and her eyes glittered with annoyance.

"Joan ..." Ana frowned. Her father would have sent her maidservant from his sight for such insolence. But here there was nowhere to go. And yet ... Why wouldn't the right words come to her? She recalled those times on the passage, times that Joan had cared for her on her sickbed despite her own fever, held her head as she vomited with each crashing wave; the tender way Joan had raised her head from the pillow to sip some soothing herbal brew that would ease her sore ravaged belly.

"Joan," she began again, biting her lip with the effort of making her voice low and steady. "I am sure you do not mean ... It is so hard here. And in many ways we are all reduced to ... Well. I am sorry to speak sharply to you. I am sure you mean well. I hope you do. But do you not think it is important that we keep some semblance of, well, civilisation, yes civilisation, even while we are trapped in this place? I know that life at the moment is, hmm, basic to say the least. And that it was so even on our ship, with the seasickness and the turbulence. But," Ana drew in a sharp breath and straightened her back, lifting her chin, although her fingers clenched around a fold of her gown. "But we must try to be as we were at home, at the Hall. As much as it is possible. And remember who we are." She softened her tone. "Do you not think?"

Joan tipped her head to one side, mouth twisted, considering. Ana could imagine what was going on in her mind: there was little she, Ana, could do, whatever her status and wealth back in England, if a maidservant or any of Sir Robert's crew behaved in a way that was unacceptable at home. Yet they were all in the same perilous situation here on this God-forsaken island, and all dependent upon each other for survival. Surely Joan was canny enough to realise that. She and Joan were the only women there, the only ones who could keep a semblance of normality. The only ones who could maintain the dignity and ways of home. But for a few moments her heart trembled in her chest and her hand shook against her overgown as she tried to compose her expression.

Joan did not speak, but then, abruptly, she exhaled sharply, muttered to herself, then squeezed herself around behind Ana and began to busy herself with the back of her mistress's hair, re-braiding and pinning. She began to hum the tune they used to sing at Darbey Hall. Ana gently exhaled the breath she had been holding, and presently Joan fell silent. Ana could feel her stubby fingers carefully twisting and stroking, concentrating on her task.

Ana listened to the quietness, disturbed only by the murmur of the sea on the shingles and the distant shouts of the men as they worked on building shelters, and after a while Joan moved round to stand before her. She gestured for Ana to stand, frowned and grimaced, gazing critically at her mistress, her eyes travelling up and down, head to one side. She reached out and brushed Ana's stained gown with her hand, fussing with the folds, arranging the drape as if she were dressing her for court dinner.

"Well, my lady. Here be a thing. I do believe that the men have rescued a few pieces of clothing from the ship. I will attend to them and bring them to you so that you can change from these rags." She sniffed her nose in the air and tossed her head, but as she turned away Ana caught her wiping her nose on her sleeve and heard her belching a low rumbling cough. "Hmph. My lady, they are not befitting."

Ana smiled to herself.

~

LATER, AS THE AFTERNOON SUN BEGAN TO FADE, ANA smoothed the clean gown over her knees and bent to shake the grains of black sand that clung to her hems. She had rested a while earlier but still rubbed her stomach where pains lingered. Perhaps her stumble on the shore and her discovery of the shrine in the clearing had tired her more than she expected. This growing of a baby inside her was so strange and hostile to her body. She knew very little about it all, only the few strange things that Joan had hinted at, or that she had overheard from the servants.

She sighed, wishing that her mother had been with her still and could have told her what to expect. But she had never known her mother, and her other women relatives were not intimate and had been reluctant to speak of such matters to her. There was only greedy and boorish Lady Maria, her father's sister, who lived with them at Darbey Hall and who was supposed to be tasked with her comforts, but she was old and sour and had never married or birthed a child, and did her best to remain sitting scowling over her needlework in the corner by the fire, sucking sweetmeats all day.

If only she had been blessed with friendships but there were few girls of her own age that she was allowed to spend time with. The only girls she ever saw were the kitchen maids and the scullery servants.

Ana remembered hiding behind the tapestries one day when the maids were setting the table, overhearing them talking about Megs who had been dismissed by her father for falling pregnant, apparently by one of the ostlers. They had been quite graphic in their tales of the act in the stables, her father's angry dispatching of the girl back to her village, and of her suffering in childbirth, leaving her with a dead child and herself crippled for life. Although it was strange ... the way they looked at each other out of the corners of their eyes, mouths turned down as they mentioned the ostler, as if they did not believe the tale. And she did wonder why her father paid Megs's family such a large dowry to marry the ostler when he was so furious with her.

But as to the growing of a baby, a new real human being, getting it ready to be birthed, and the birth itself, she knew almost nothing. She had tried one time, desperately, to broach the subject with Alys, her maid of the chamber at the Hall, purely for academic interest because there was nothing in the books she was allowed from her father's library. But she had been so embarrassed the words did not come and her maid had retired with a puzzled frown. Ana was glad that it was Joan from the back kitchens, unofficial midwife and healer, who had overheard their plans and had been persuaded to flee the court with her, and she would always be grateful to her for that. Although she was quite sure that Robert had given Joan a fat purse to do so – and also that her target was, in truth, Roger the giant of a quartermaster in Robert's pay.

Another sharp pain swept her belly and she wondered if it was a bout of gripe from eating the unfamiliar meat that Will had brought her. As she winced, Joan reappeared, ducking into the entrance to the cave.

"Oh, my lady, are you unwell?" Joan quickly made the sign of the cross and bustled inside, wiping her red meaty hands on her skirts. She frowned at Ana.

"I am a little ... there is a pain, just here." Ana

indicated her lower abdomen. "I expect I am tired from my walk this morning."

"That was indeed unwise," chided Joan, picking up Ana's cloak and wrapping it around her lady's shoulders, as though that would make her pains better. She clucked and shook her head. "You need to be careful. After all that knocking and blundering on the sea passage as well! I told you!"

"Yes, yes, the sea storms were dreadful. But I am not an invalid so ..." Ana stopped as she saw Joan stand before her, arms folded across her bosom, mouth tightly stretched. "You see ..." she hesitated. "I do not know what to expect, what is usual and what is not."

Joan looked at her for a few moments, head to one side, considering.

"No. All your book learning and you do not know the most basic things of life." She shook her head and grinned. "Well, you clearly know one basic thing, the act that made the babe within your belly, eh?" She began to laugh in a ribald fashion. But she paused as she caught sight of Ana's face. "Will you let me instruct you, my lady? I have birthed a few in my time. And chosen potions and ointments for all the difficulties of carrying a child."

"I wish you would, Joan," nodded Ana eagerly. "I know it is early yet, but I want to be prepared and warned of what is to come. I felt so ill on the passage and in the storms that I had no care for what caused my discomfort, only to reach the safety of firm land.

But, please, instruction would be of great comfort to me."

"Well then. Do not be afeared, but I will tell you everything."

And she did.

Ana listened agape, only interrupting to gasp and grimace, rubbing her stomach with its small fragile bump.

"And I will feel all these things? And the child will come out ... like that ... and I will live?"

Joan guffawed, hands on hips, rocking to and fro with mirth. "The Gods above! Well, it is too late now!"

Ana dropped her head into her cupped hands, screwed up her eyes and took a deep breath, long and slow. "So you must help me, Joan. When my time comes, but also before. And even now," her voice muffled by the darkness behind her hands. "The potion for this pain, you will prepare it and I will take it, though you say it is foul-tasting and may make me dizzy. And the soothing balms, the camomile leaves and ginger, I will take it all so that I may be strong enough to live through these days and when my time is come. You say you still have these dried potions safe that you brought on the cog?"

She looked up at Joan, standing there, large and comforting, with her knowledge of healing and magic. An idea started to germinate in her mind. Something she could do, not only for herself now, but also to make herself a strong mistress when she could run her own household properly. When she held her own court in the manor that she knew Robert would provide for them all when they arrived in France at last.

Joan nodded firmly. "I may be a fool for the men and the drink. But I know what I know."

"Oh, and I can learn more of your skill and your learning, so that I may direct our household staff when we get to France!" Ana began to smile, holding herself straight-backed, head high, a new hope filling her soul. She had her book learning on herbs but no practical experience to confirm it. "Do you not agree, Joan?"

"Lord, yes. There be a thing. I'm sure you can learn it from me, my lady," and she puffed out her chest although she frowned. "But you will have your own court, remember, and should not stoop so low as to mess with being a healer."

"Well, we shall see." Ana stood and rubbed her lower back to ease the stiffness there, although her belly was not great as yet and there was little weight there to hurt her back. "Bring me your pain potions and soothing balms, and you can give me my first lesson tonight."

CHAPTER 10

ANA

"Joan?" Ana looked up from her grinding of the mixture of leaves in the mortar that was balanced on her lap, wondering how much of the "goodness" was left in their dryness after the squally sea passage. But Joan had been instructing her well in the practice and she felt much more confident than when she first started learning the potions.

The hot sun beat upon her head as she sat outside the cave mouth, and she screwed her eyes up to the intense light and rubbed the ache that had started to sever her temples.

"Yes, my lady?" Joan raised her eyebrows and rested her hand a while on the edge of the bowl. The wooden pestle, fashioned from laurel by "young Will", still in her fist, she brushed wayward strands of greasy hair from her forehead with the back of her wrist. She puffed. "It would have been better if we had been able to do this in the shade of the cave."

Unfortunately, Robert was resting there that day, having eaten something that made his belly roil with a liquid turbulence. The mint water that Joan had given him had yet to take its course and they were preparing more camomile and ginger infusions for Ana out on the rocky beach while he slept in the cool shade.

"Joan, I need to speak of this ...the secret is like an ant irritating at my skin. But first, you must promise me on your life that you will not tell any living soul." Ana glared at her maidservant as furiously as she could muster.

"On my life." Joan's eyes glinted greedily, ready for some scandal. "What in God's truth is it that ails you so?" She leaned forward towards Ana, the bowl gripped between her knees, pestle abandoned inside it.

Ana lifted her mortar and placed it carefully on the rock beside her. She smoothed her overgown across her knees. "I need to go ... somewhere ... to a hidden secret place, but I dare not go alone in case, God forbid, I fall on the rocks. I am more fragile than I was when I first found the place." Joan was staring at her, wide eyed.

"Where on God's earth do you mean? Where have you been without assistance?"

"A while ago I found a place, holy I believe. In a clearing behind the cliff rocks. Near where I pulled the fennel that I brought back and planted in the black mud back there. But there was a tree that wept purple blood like a dragon, and something in the manner of a shrine ... Joan, do not look so!"

"My lady! How can that be holy? And how can there be a shrine when no man has stepped upon this island until we came here, wrecked ashore?" She crossed herself quickly. "Are there spirits? Is there magic here? Or evil things?"

Ana thrust her hand into her pouch and pulled out the strange coloured tile she had found at the shrine. "Look. I found this too." She held it out to Joan who peered closer. "These markings here. IHS. My book learning tells me that they are from the Greek letters, iota eta sigma. IHΣ. They mean in Latin Jesu Hominum Salvator. Jesus Our Saviour. It is a Christian symbol. And very ancient."

"Oh, my Lord!" Joan shrank back, hands flying to her throat. "How can that be?"

"And I *think* ... I think that these patterns just here," she touched them carefully, "are not Christian but Moorish. Arabic. I have struggled to remember where I saw this pattern before. And then in my dreams last night I recalled. It was a picture in an old manuscript in the library at Darbey Hall."

Ana watched Joan recoiling from the tile that she held out, shaking her head, confusion distorting her features.

"Joan, I have to go back to that shrine."

Never before had Ana seen a mouth drop open so far and eyes so frightened and confused.

"No, no, my lady. It is magic, the spirits of the dead, the work of the devil himself ..."

"I think not. I believe it is something magical, yes, but good and holy. It is of peoples coming together. But at least I need to find out more. I need to return to that place and see again, feel it again ..." She reached out and touched Joan's hands that were gripped together and shaking.

"But Moorish, my lady? Arabic words? Oooh, but there is danger and unholy matter in that."

"Joan, do not be so foolish. I need you to come with me."

"I will not. No, no."

"It is drawing me to it. Whatever it is. I am going." She looked sternly at Joan, mouth set tight. "But if I fall on the way and lose the baby, what will Sir Robert say to you, my maid ...?"

Joan bit her lip. She looked Ana up and down, frowning. "Well. If you are determined to go, I will accompany you across the rocks to see you safe, but I will not go inside any unholy place. Not for you, nor for anyone, upon my mortal soul."

∽

When the sun rose again and Robert still slept, not restlessly any more but soundly, soothing the exhaustion that had swept through him, his belly calmed by the mint infusions that Ana had urged him to swallow through the night, she kissed him gently. Then she and Joan crept across the rocks to the undercliff.

All the way over the rocky shore, Joan kept reaching out and clutching on to Ana's gown until she had to stop and tell her to desist; it was making a fall more likely. When they reached the site, Ana, although grateful that she had another person at her side in case of an accident, was glad to flick her maid's hand from her skirts and proceed alone.

"Oh, my Lord," breathed Joan, clutching at her throat.

Ana could sense her maid peering after her as she squeezed through the entrance into the clearing. She wondered if Joan could also see the flattened platform and white shards like bleached bones and a ghostly tree that looked like the dragons she had seen on the tapestries at Darbey Hall. Joan's duty was only to accompany her over the rocks to ensure her safety where it was an easy matter to slip. Ana had told her not to follow her into the clearing but to wait on the rocks a short distance away. She had warned her that it was a strange and magical place, but she knew that Joan's natural curiosity, despite her fear, would not let her turn her eyes away.

A surreptitious glance back told her that, despite her warnings, Joan had not been able to help herself from following and peering through the rocky gateway into this strange place. She hadn't dared to enter, though, but Ana felt Joan's eyes searing into her back, watching, curious, and yet most probably greatly afeared at this place and desperate to know what captivated her lady so much.

Ana stood beneath the dragon tree and looked up through its branches as if in a trance. It felt as though something was guiding her beyond her will. Hardly aware of what she was doing, she was bending and picking at stones, casting some away, pocketing others in her pouch, peering closely at the things that looked like bleached bones beneath the raised platform. She knew now that they were not bones, but what they were, she could not tell: strange shells or stones like the one she had found with the curled creature within. Then she stood very still and quiet for a moment before sinking awkwardly to her knees and pressing her palms together in prayer. It was a prayer for Robert, for the baby inside her, for Joan and all the crew, for their safety and for their rescue.

And it was a prayer for all those who she was now certain had been here before.

She heard a gasp and looked up and back to see Joan making a quick obeisance, crossing herself deftly. She shook her head, driving away the will that had consumed her a moment ago. Enough. She rose and turned to the narrow entrance.

As Ana squeezed out of the clearing again, she saw

Joan, white-faced and clutching her hands to her heart, and knew that she had seen her praying there and would not understand.

"Do not be afeared, Joan," she said, "this place is holy to me, just as it was to those who came before, be they other Christians or Moors or whosoever. It is magical but a place of goodness and safety and peace."

"That is as may be," Joan grunted. "But I do not like it. It is not good to pound our religion with others like the pestle in the mortar, my lady. It is an unholy magic."

People sometimes called Joan's potions 'magic', but Ana knew that they were not. They were just the herbs that grew around the Hall and often ones in the herb garden beyond the kitchens, the ones that were picked for the food.

But this kind of 'magic' - Ana was aware that this was a very different matter for Joan. She reached out her hand and patted Joan on her arm in reassurance.

"But yet, Joan," Ana smiled, "You ... *we* ... make *your* sort of magic with herbs."

"But that is for good, for healing!"

"Indeed, we think so, but others do not. Think on that, Joan." And she turned on her heel and swept off across the rocks, as Joan scampered behind, calling out "take care, my lady!"

CHAPTER 11

VIV

The museum was right opposite the cable car terminus and almost beneath its continuous line of carriages climbing up towards Monte. By the time Viv reached it she had controlled her breathing again and cleared her head. There was a school party ahead of her in the queue for admission and she was glad of the normality of their excited chattering and the teacher's attempts to herd her charges into a crocodile line.

Whatever had happened on the Rua de Santa Maria was, after all, most likely a moment of her wild imagination getting the better of her. Or was 'it' happening all over again? Was she really, again, going to find herself inhabiting the body of another woman centuries ago, set on a quest to solve a mystery, as she had done before? With a flickering heart, she realised that it looked very much like it.

It was cool inside the centre and a beaming attendant gave her a ticket, indicating that she should proceed through black 'stage flats' into a dark area of low echoing background sounds that crescendoed into crashing and roaring. The information boards around the walls described the volcanic origins of the island and a glowing red 'fire' beneath her feet breached the geological model of the eruption creating the mountains that rose above the surface of the ocean. It was like the door painting she thought she had seen and yet she felt no dizziness or panic as she explored the plastic models and fake painted lava flows.

The plaques told her that twenty million years ago tectonic plates on the ocean floor at the geological fault-line would tense and buckle, leaking magma and a series of underwater eruptions would begin on the seabed, so great that a volcanic mass formed and slowly rose to the surface finally breaking out of the water some five million years ago. It was mind-blowing. So absorbed was she in reading the information that she hardly noticed that the group of school children had moved on out of sight through the museum and a quietness had descended. Quiet, except for the artificial recordings of the volcanic rumblings issuing from the hidden speakers behind the exhibits.

How amazing that the explosive pyroclasts of basalt, ashes, lapilli, and solid rugged bombs of rock, so violently expelled from the rising mountain of magma and the emission of lava should cool and form the dykes, seams, peaks and valleys of an island. Yet there were the models, there were the real examples of basalt and tufa and scoriae for her to reach out and touch.

It was beyond imagining, and yet she could imagine it only too well. Because she had seen it. She shuddered: that day at the rectory when she had realised that she was capable of slipping again, that it wasn't all over, when she had felt herself falling deeper, deeper, her brain splitting and crashing, when she had seen turbulent boiling seas, and fire, red and black, raging in its angry path towards her, molten magma blasting to the skies, mountains forcing their might through the waves, flinging boulders away from their rage …

That was the beginning. Then the capela, that night with her disturbing dreams and the hazy vision of someone in the room, the passageway behind the Sé and just now on the Rua de Santa Maria. It was becoming more intensive, whatever it was. Something was reaching out to her.

Or someone.

Her breathing seemed to stop and for a moment she held everything tight, incapable of moving, incapable of thinking. Around her the museum, in semi-darkness and reverberating with the dim rumblings of synthetic volcanic activity, swayed and echoed in waves of dizziness.

The excited scream of a child and the answering

reprimand of the teacher jolted her back into the present. She took a deep breath, realising that she had screwed her eyes tightly shut. For a moment Viv concentrated on slowing her breathing and focusing on the model island before her, realigning herself. Shaken, she dragged herself away and moved on through the museum, away from the darkness of the presentation and towards the more brightly lit area that depicted the discovery of the Madeira archipelago.

One or two stragglers from the school group were trying to clamber up onto the large dais where lifesized, and pretty realistic, static models of the first fifteenth century Portuguese explorers were grouped in a tableau, frozen in time, pouring over maps. At first glance they looked so real, Viv thought they might be like the living tableaux at the Jorvik museum in York, and that one was about to move and speak to her. On closer look, she saw clearly that they were cleverly made from some kind of plastic material complete with facial wrinkles and frowns, scarred skin, and bushy eyebrows. The children had succeeded in squeezing onto the dais and were stroking the long heavy fur-lined robes of the figures, and having failed to reach high enough up to touch the voluminous velvet headgear, were now trying to wrest the scrolled maps from their fixed position on a wooden box. Their teacher arrived in time to pull one child away from the astrolabe and hustled them away with angry remonstrations.

The information board told Viv that the figures represented Zarco, Teixeira and Perestrello in 1419, adventurer captains sent by the Infante Dom Henrique, Prince Henry 'the Navigator', supposedly intent on spreading Christianity to Moorish North Africa.

Hmm, possibly more importantly to drive the Moors from control of the valuable desert trading routes and gain foothold themselves! She turned to the glass case beside the tableau and inspected the model ships, a reconstruction of an early fifteenth century Portuguese caravel modelled on Arab vessels with its three masts, triangular rigged. And beside it something that stopped her in her tracks.

A square-rigged clinker-built cog, with its tall sturdy mast and wrap-round crow's nest, its raised deck at the aft and cabin area beneath stopped her breath. A frisson of recognition shivered through her body. It was the image of the ship on the altar mural in the capela and on the painted tiles on the wall behind the Sé, the cog of her strange visions.

Disturbed, Viv moved to the glazed display case containing maps, centuries old, ancient portolans with rudimentary mappings and written navigational instructions scrawled across them. The plaque said that these were Italian and Catalan charts and on one of them she could just make out the archipelago of Madeira marked faintly. She leaned over the case, slipped on her glasses, and peered more closely, making out the locations of ports and indications of the courses to be steered, the wind roses and rhumb lines, so different from the modern maps familiar to Viv with their longitude and latitude grids and coordinates. But these were dated in the fourteenth century, long before Zarco arrived and 'discovered' the island in 1419. And here was a page from a Catalan Atlas dated 1378 with its little illustrations of battle tents and ships, like the illustrated manuscripts Viv had studied for her research back at the university. Indistinct but just visible was an inscription '*Insula de Legname*', which Viv knew was the original name given to Madeira island. Island of woods.

So surely that suggested that the island and its location had been known long before the official discovery by the three famous Portuguese explorers? And why was it named island of woods unless someone had landed there, or at the very least, sailed so close that they could see the forests?

Viv pulled out her iphone from her bag and logged in to the museum wi-fi. She surfed the internet for some time before she found an obscure academic site that gave a reference to the Medici Atlas of 1351 indicating the Atlantic islands located "at the western edge of the known world". Scrolling back, she almost missed a short passage citing an event in 1147. According to this source, a group of runaways from Lisbon had landed on "an island populated by cattle", thought to be Madeira.

Fascinated, Viv scrolled even further back to yet another reference, this time to Pliny the Elder, who had apparently mentioned 'purple isles' in the Atlantic off the coast of north Africa which was taken by some scholars to signify the so-called 'dragon trees' abundant on the island and which were treasured for their purple sap used for precious regal dyes. Georgina had mentioned something like that. And hadn't she read or seen or heard something somewhere about a dragon tree weeping its 'purple blood'?

She frowned. What should she make of all this? She clicked through to Pliny the Elder and saw that he had died in 79 AD. So detailed references to this island went way back, if these were to be believed, long before the reputed 'discovery' by the Iberian captains who annexed Madeira for their Portuguese prince. She knew from her extensive research experience as an academic that sources needed to be treated with caution and may well have been written long after the event. But she made a mental note for herself to conduct a more rigorous search when she got back to her computer.

But before she clicked off the site, she noticed another reference, this one to a possible Moorish map indicating that the Arabs from the Iberian Peninsula might have navigated the area hundreds of years before the recorded exploration by Prince Henry's men. She closed down the web and stared at her home screen with its array of little square app icons.

The sound of the school group excitedly leaving the area and making for the exit pulled her back to the present, and she realised that it was getting late. She'd have to come back again to investigate the rest of the museum another day.

Then as she turned, she caught a glimpse of a small information board and the heading 'Legend'.

Just below it was the name '*Ana*'.

CHAPTER 12

VIV

She felt her breath catch and her body go cold. The air around her seemed to shift and stir, and the floor beneath her feet shuddered.

Shifting her bag further on to her shoulder, and straightening her glasses, she began to read the legend of Lady Ana d'Arafet and her lover Sir Robert Machym, a minor nobleman in the court of Edward III. Here he was again! The legend told the tale of their elopement when they supposedly fled together from England in 1344 in his cog The Welfayre and were shipwrecked on Madeira. She knew these names. But not from reading them. From hearing them spoken – and hearing them speak. It all seemed so familiar and a heart-trembling feeling of déjà vu shivered through her.

Scanning the information board further down, she read that the bay of Machico which was where they were shipwrecked – and which of course was also where her parents had excavated years ago – was said to be named after Robert Machym, sometimes known as Machin. Why did that echo somewhere else in her memory?

The words on the board trembled and shifted out of focus, and through them, as they grew fainter, she saw the image of a lady she somehow knew to be Ana, the woman of her strange dreams, bending down to pick up a piece of azulejo, turning it over in her hands. Was it Ana? Or herself? She could feel the warm ocean breezes stirring her long skirts of her robe, could sense the rustling of laurel leaves, the pungent scent of eucalyptus. The smell of the purple sap of the dragon tree above her head, dripping its blood upon the tile in her right hand. She let her left hand slip downwards over her smooth heavy dress and let it rest on her swollen belly.

But she was not that woman. This was the lady of her visions, she knew it.

Wrenching herself back to the present and the museum, Viv willed the text to come in to focus again and knew with certainty that these people were real and had lived, had found themselves on this island many centuries ago. Ana d'Arafet and Robert Machym. Forgotten but for a vague half-remembered legend.

And what connection had made Viv name her lost daughter Ana? Some supposed distant ancestor of her mother's? She only recalled that the name had come back to her, unbidden, that day as she stroked the fossil ammonite and thought of the parents she had so violently lost in the plane crash.

Viv clicked on the camera icon on her iphone and took an image of the board about Lady Ana d'Arafet, hoping that it was OK to photograph items in the museum. She hadn't seen any notice prohibiting it. Then she delved in to her bag and pulled out her reporter's notebook and her pen, beginning to scribble spidergram notes on the research she had discovered from the internet and the museum information boards. She frowned as she attempted to link the different elements together, trying to create some kind of sense of it all.

"Interesting, hmm?" A deep male voice behind her made her swing round. He was tall, slim yet well-built, muscular, and tanned with dark hair and olive skin, not unlike Rory's. Smart in a dark designer suit, open collar, no tie. A little older than Rory. Late thirties, early forties perhaps? Suave. Attractive. Viv flushed, feeling as though she had been caught doing something wrong. She quickly pulled off her glasses.

"Oh, I'm sorry if ..." She held up her phone and notebook.

He waved his hand in dismissal. "No, not at all. It is permissible." She could hear his accent, although his English was clearly fluent and efficient. Not Portuguese, maybe French? "I am glad you are finding the exhibits of interest and noting research. Unlike many of our visitors, welcome as they are, of course, who just wander through, unseeing, not taking in any of the information." He smiled, the smile travelling to his teasing eyes, and his gaze sweeping her appreciatively. She felt a connection, as though they had met before, and yet she knew for certain that they had not. She couldn't help noting how good looking he was and flushed again. Yes, he did look to be in his thirties, perhaps slightly younger than she had thought at first, with the most gorgeous blue eyes, the sort of eyes you could dive into ... and drown. Her heart juddered, like it did when she first saw Rory. She took a slow calming breath.

"Are ... er, are you one of the staff?" Although his elegant suit, his pristine white shirt, and his authoritative bearing indicated otherwise.

"No. I am not staff." He shook his head slightly and smiled as if the idea amused him. "But I think the museum will close shortly, so perhaps you need to make your final notes for today."

Viv glanced at her watch. "Goodness. I hadn't realised how late it was. I was rather too engrossed in all this."

"I see you are interested in the early history of the island, its making."

"Yes, right back to the volcanic eruption that created the island – back there on the first display. Then the discoverers and the early settlers. It's fascinating." An image flashed through her mind, of the Lady Ana reaching for a piece of blue tile. "And I'm interested in the azulejo too. The Moors. How it all fits together."

She almost missed the look that passed briefly across his eyes. But then he smiled, and it was gone.

"Well. We have a few minutes left. Come. I will show you the azulejo display and then maybe you should come on another day to make some more research?"

"Oh, right, thank you." Viv pushed her pen through the spiral binding of her notebook and thrust it with her phone and glasses back into her bag as she followed the man on round the corner to further displays. It was quiet in the museum now and she guessed that most of the visitors had left. She felt a little awkward. She had no idea who this man was. But she knew that there must be staff around, and the reception desk at the front must be staffed. So she followed him round to the next area of the exhibition.

He stopped in front of an extensive display of tiles and turned to her. She had that sensation again of his eyes drawing her into their depths, and she felt the shiver run through her body. She hadn't felt like that for a long time.

"I am Bértrand, by the way." He looked over Viv's shoulder. "Oh, Carlos ..." Viv twisted round to see the beaming ticket attendant from the front desk. "Carlos, five minutes please, if you do not mind. I am just showing Miss ...?"

"Doctor." Viv smiled. "Dr Viv DuLac."

"...Dr DuLac ... I am showing her the azulejo exhibits."

"Of course, sir. Monsieur Montluc." Carlos gave a slight deferential bow and slipped away.

"So, you are a doctor?"

"An academic doctor, not a medical one."

"Ah, a real doctor, then!"

"Well, one who does research for the university, anyway. Normally early medieval, but at the moment I'm finding out more about a later medieval period, the English king Edward III onwards."

He raised his eyebrows. "Really? I see ..."

"I'm finding it all intriguing. And," she hesitated, "I love these Madeiran azulejo."

"You are an expert?" There was an eagerness in his voice.

"I guess, an expert in the medieval period – at least, more than the average person. But I'd like to know more about the azulejo in particular. I'm looking at how it fits into ... er ... aspects of my research."

"Ah." He loosened his collar a little. "So, you will see the azulejo all around the island. As you will see on this information board, the name derives from the Arabic word 'al-zulaich' which means a small polished stone. They were produced by the Portuguese around the fourteenth and fifteenth century, but it is believed that the Moors made these ceramic decorations much earlier. You see these here?"

He pointed to a board of single colour patterned tiles and Viv leaned in to peer at the inscription indicating that they were introduced to the Iberian peninsula during the thirteenth century or before.

A wisp of memory drifted across Viv's mind as she saw, like a dream, her lady - Lady Ana d'Arafet? - puzzling over the shrine and the Moorish azulejo. But not a single colour, a tile of four colours, blue, white, brown and that deep purple. And another image focused itself in her mind clearly: that Christian IHS symbol signifying Christ amidst the Arabic patterns. Something on the information board in front of her about a legend of a lost azulejo tile bearing both Christian and Arabic symbols intertwined ...

She heard Bértrand's voice as if from far off talking about how mosaics were cut with pliers and based on a single colour glazed clay.

"And so, in the fourteenth century ... Dr DuLac?"

Viv started. "Oh, sorry. I was miles away for a moment." She leaned in to the information board again, searching for the bit about the intertwined symbols, wondering what that would mean for the history of the island and its discovery. Would that turn the whole thing on its head? Question the accepted version in a much more concrete way than little shapes on ancient maps?

But she couldn't now find the words there on the board. Perhaps it was another board. There were several. She scoured them.

"Are you OK?"

Viv shook her head, puzzled. "Yes, thank you. I just ... I thought I saw something about the legend of the lost azulejo ..."

Bértrand took hold of her elbow, firmly, commandingly, and she was surprised how much she liked his touch, although normally she would shy away from a stranger touching her. She hoped that he couldn't feel the heat that suffused her. "No, no, nothing like that." His voice sounded sharp as he guided her towards the exit. "Please." He gestured to Carlos at the front desk. "Carlos, please give Dr DuLac a free pass for future visits to the museum. She is doing research here."

"Of course, Monsieur Montluc."

Carlos produced a ticket and stamped it, handing it to Viv.

Bértrand still held her elbow as they passed through the exit and back in to the dusty heat of the street. He stopped and turned to her, eyes twinkling again. "Perhaps you would like to take a coffee with me?" His smile was open, trust-worthy. "To talk about your research into the discovery of this beautiful island? I may be able to help." He must have seen the hesitation in her face. "Oh, forgive me. I apologise. I should have introduced myself properly. I am an historian, chair of the board of advisors who helped to create the museum, and I guess, one of its benefactors. I too am fascinated by the beginnings of this island, and perhaps I could help you with your research?"

"Well ... er ... I have to be back home soon."

"Your husband is waiting?" His eyes were glittering, amused. "It is fine. I too have to go home soon." She felt irritated to have made any assumptions and for him to find it amusing. He turned his wrist to look at his watch. An expensive gold Patik Philippe, Viv guessed. "I have half an hour. And there is a good coffee place just a couple of doors down on this road. I come when I am working at the museum." He looked rueful but a self-mocking expression flickered across his face. "I promise I will not behave badly." He smiled and bent a tight bow.

Although in any other circumstances she would have felt awkward at that, the direct way he said it made Viv laugh. And anyway, Rory would still be out, engrossed in his work, in something not involving her, and she saw him in her mind, distant, absorbed in something that excluded her. It would be good to chat to someone about a mutual interest for a short time. What was wrong with that? "OK. Half an hour and then I must be gone!"

And as she said that, it occurred to her that she had actually spent a stretch of time that afternoon without feeling heavy with loss.

CHAPTER 13

VIV

"So you won't come?"

"It's not that I *won't* come. It's that I can't. Not just now, anyway." Rory rinsed out his coffee cup and thrust it into the dishwasher. He ran his fingers through his hair that was still damp from his shower. "Maybe at the weekend – well, Monday?"

"Monday." Viv felt her shoulders sink.

"I've got some visits to do today. Look, things will get a bit easier soon, I'm sure. And now I've got the use of a car, it'll make things easier and hopefully soon we can get out and about." Rory reached out and held her arms, pulling her towards him. He kissed the top of her head. Viv knew that Georgina was going along to at least one of the parish visits. It seemed that Georgina was seeing a lot more of her husband than she was. She didn't know why a church warden would be involved with parish visits. She'd asked him but these days he was so vague about what was happening that she'd given up.

"Right."

"I mean, you know what it's like with a demanding job. You were the same when you were fulltime at the university. This isn't a holiday for me."

Viv pulled away. "It's not for me either."

"Look. I'm sorry. I didn't exactly mean that." He glanced quickly at his watch. "But now I must go. I'll be late."

She shrugged as she heard him close the front door. The previous week, over what had become their regular coffee chat whenever she was at the museum, Bértrand had suggested a walk along the high levada that rose towards the volcano. She had hoped that she might draw Rory away from his work to come too and explore a little and get some fresh mountain air.

Well, she'd go anyway. Bértrand had told her that you needed a guide up there on the wilder more remote levadas and he'd offered to take them both. She picked up her mobile from the counter top and clicked on Bértrand's number.

∽

Viv gripped the sides of her leather seat in Bértrand's Mercedes. At times it felt as though they were driving almost vertically up into the mountains. Every time the engine revved more loudly round another hairpin bend, she held her breath, praying that nothing was coming the opposite way.

"OK?"

She wished he wouldn't turn to her like that, smiling as if there weren't sheer precipitous drops down to the valley from the right side of the narrow road. She nodded as she gritted her teeth and stared straight ahead. On her left the land rose steeply, gnarled trees stretching their branches towards the road, gaunt bushes vying with the pink of hydrangeas and the blue balls of african lilies.

"Those trees," Bértrand flicked his head, "are remnants of the ancient laurisilva forests that used to cover the island." He swivelled towards her again. "A magical beauty, eh?"

"Oh." Oh, please stop doing that, she cried silently.

"We are not far now, and then we can park and walk the levada to the Eira do Serrado where we can see down into the curral, the heart of the volcano. It is magnificent."

He pulled the car off the road into a small parking area in front of a deserted little café bar and Viv climbed out, a little shakily, on to the, thankfully, flat stony earth. A man that Viv took to be the owner stared at her from his wooden bench by the open door as he carefully rolled a cigarette, a large beer and a pile of nuts on the table in front of him.

"Bom dia, Tiago," Bértrand called and the man raised his hand in greeting. He rattled off quick fluent

Portuguese and the man waved his hand in agreement. "Come." Bértrand took Viv's arm and guided her towards a pathway between the trees to the side of the café. "I am pleased that you took my advice and wore walking boots," he added. "It is not so easy on these high levadas. Sometimes the rain has fallen across the paths and it is slippery. Also, there are parts where the path has crumbled and there is no laurel rail for your hand."

"Oh goodness! I wish you'd told me that before. It doesn't sound very safe."

"It is fine. Where it is dangerous, I will hold you!"

She was pleased that she had brought her hiking stick too, especially when she saw the narrow rocky path alongside the levada that they were to walk. But the sun was shining, and any rainfall had stopped for the day, leaving a clear golden light picking out the red hot pokers amidst the eucalyptus trees.

"So. Tell me about your research," Bértrand smiled as he guided her over a rocky outcrop.

She began to tell him about what she was discovering about Edward III, selecting the more scandalous bits of the politics and relationships of the fourteenth century to amuse him. He was nodding, laughing at the appropriate moments, and asking encouraging questions, although she wondered if he really was interested in her work or merely being polite. But it was good to have someone taking an interest, even if superficially.

"And the azulejo?" he asked suddenly. Her brain did a quick double-take.

"Sorry?" A frisson of caution flared in her mind. She frowned. Why was he asking about that, when it was he who had been telling her about it at the museum the first time they met. Did he think she knew more about the fourteenth century history of the azelujo than she was letting on? How odd. "Oh, I really don't know any more than you about that. My reading is all about *English* history, not Portuguese." She was aware that she had spoken perhaps a little more sharply than she intended and felt flustered.

"Ah, I understand. I apologise if I offend." He turned a reassuring smile at her. "I was under the impression that ... Never mind. So. What do you think of Madeira?"

As they talked, she barely noticed that the lush greenness had given way to a more barren rocky landscape, with twisted bushes and abundant yellow gorse. They climbed away from the levada upwards through a path tangled in branches and broom, Bértrand leading, confidently striding over thick exposed roots and holding back overhanging branches for her. Viv followed more cautiously. Then almost before she knew it, they came out of the scrubland to a road and a lookout point protected by a low laurel trellis.

"Wow. That certainly is magnificent." Viv gasped at the breath-taking view of the sheer craggy mountains before her, rising up to the sky, wreathed in mist, their pinnacles jutting up from the cloud. And the tiny village that nestled in the valley way below. "Amazing!"

She was so over-awed by the almost surreal sight before her that she hardly registered Bértrand leaning in towards her.

"Look. That is Curral das Freiras. The valley of the nuns. See, down there, that green roofed building. It is a nunnery. Some say it is the safest place on the island. Maybe the safest place on earth."

"Why would ...?" Viv began but Bértrand swept both hands across the width of the valley.

"It is said that this is the crater of the volcano that made the island. But some say that the bowl shape was not the crater but a result of erosion." He shrugged. "Who knows?"

"I'd like to think it was the heart of the volcano." Viv knew that this was where her fossil had begun. She looked at the groups of houses so far below and the steep rugged cliffs of the rocks that towered over them. And it seemed that they looked menacing. What must it feel like to live down there with those crags threatening all around you? Would they feel as though they were bearing in upon you?

A jeep pulled up beside them and a group of tourists emerged, excitedly squealing and pointing their cameras.

"It is getting noisy. We can walk down to the Curral if you like?" Bértrand suggested.

"OK," she nodded although she was thinking of the steep climb back up. In normal times it wouldn't have bothered her, with her gym work and swimming and yoga classes. But at the moment, of course, she didn't feel so fit and healthy.

He gestured her towards the almost deserted pathway that wound its way downwards. She could see only a couple of hikers way down the path ahead.

The path seemed well worn although rocky. In places it had been repaired, quite recently she guessed, and there was an attempt to make steps from time to time. But in other parts it was dangerously close to a precipitous fall where rocks had crumbled and slid down the mountainside. They hiked carefully down in companionable silence for a while, listening to the birdsong, clear and soft in the trees above. Viv drank in the music and it gentled her heart.

The view, in the sharp clarity of the light, was like nothing she had ever seen before. She stopped by the side of the path and moved nearer to the edge to take a photo on her mobile, trying to capture the steepness of the valley. As she peered at the screen, ready to click, the image of the scene in front of her flickered to the picture she thought she had taken on the Rua Santa Maria the day she first went to the museum. It was the image of the door painting that had gone from her iphone photos, the one of a mountain rising above the waves of the ocean, fire spewing from its peak, plumes of gases clouding the boiling seas below, rocks flung away from the fiery explosions, and a fragment of rock, an ammonite. Her heart seemed to stop and she felt in her shorts pocket for her fossil that burrowed there, not taking her eyes away from her iphone.

But her vision clouded and she felt a waft of air behind her on the path. She sensed the presence of figures around her, trudging wearily in a long line past her down the mountainside, long thick robes brushing the rocks and the fallen branches as they pushed themselves on. She heard their voices, murmurs urgent, tired, dispirited, fearful. She felt their fear and she shuddered, tearing her eyes away from the image on her screen and swivelling wildly around. The tourists hadn't followed them down the path and nobody other than themselves was in sight now, the hiking couple long since disappeared below. It was deserted as far as she could see. And yet she could still hear their footfall, heavy further down the line as if those bringing up the rear were struggling to carry the weight of substantial burdens.

She turned to step back to the path again, but she stumbled, dizzy and light-headed, and for a moment she lost her balance as a vision of falling crashed across her brain. Bértrand's arm was instantly around her, pulling her back from the edge. He held her to his chest so tightly that she could feel the thrumming of his heart through his shirt.

"My God, I thought I had lost you there for a moment," he breathed into her hair. She inhaled the richness of his cologne. It was warm and deep and comforting. She closed her eyes. How good it would be to stay there, in his arms, blotting out all the strange things that were happening to her, all the hurt and pain ... But then she felt in the pocket of her shorts again and her fingers touched the fossil that nestled there, and across her mind swept an image, no, a feeling, a suggestion only, of Lady Ana and of someone else, robed and hooded – a priest or a monk, a nun? She drew in her breath, but it felt thin, like a wisp of air as it rose through her body.

"It's OK. For a while there, I thought I saw ..." she shook her head and pulled away from him. The sun was high overhead, but it felt oppressive now, and she felt hot and sticky even in her strappy top. She could smell the sun screen she had smothered herself in before Bértrand had picked her up at the apartment.

"Perhaps we will go down to the village in the curral another day." His forehead creased into a deep frown of concern. "It is not good to look down from such a height."

"No, probably not." Viv slipped her mobile back into her pocket against the fossil and stopped herself from looking back as they climbed the path back up to the lookout point above.

Bértrand was talking to her about the museum as they walked but she hardly heard what he was saying, so immersed in her thoughts was she, puzzling over the strange feeling on the edge of the path. Something had happened there in the long distant past, she was sure of it. Yet it didn't feel as though it was Lady Ana she sensed; there were too many people together to be Robert and the crew, and there were too many long-skirted robes, too many women to be just Ana and Joan. Someone else was slipping into the periphery of her consciousness, and she had no idea why.

CHAPTER 14

VIV

"Bom dia, Doctor DuLac," Carlos looked up from his reception desk at the entrance to the museum, beaming, and called out as he always did. She was beginning to feel at home here. "Good to see you again. Is it the maritime exhibits today, or the geology? Or perhaps," he winked, "the azulejo patterns?"

He never tired of this game.

"Hmm," Viv smiled conspiratorially. "Well, I guess today it will be ..."

A family group of tourists bustled in and Carlos attended to their tickets, nodding towards Viv, and puffing out his chest. "This is Doctor DuLac, our regular researcher," he announced to them importantly. They glanced at her with bewildered eyes and she gave a little protesting shake of her head.

"Really, Carlos, you must stop doing this," she

whispered under her breath, smiling, as the family moved into the exhibition area. "I think today I shall look at the flora and fauna upstairs. I'm interested in the dragon tree."

"Oh, and doctor," Carlos called after her as she slipped past. She paused. "Your friend Monsieur Montluc is in today, somewhere. He has a meeting with the board of directors."

Viv nodded her acknowledgement and moved on. She lingered at the legend of Ana d'Arafet and Robert Machym as she often did, for no other reason than to wonder what had become of them. She liked to let her imagination take over. What really became of them in the end? Did they reach safety in France? The stories were vague. Of course, as far as anyone else was concerned, it was only a legend.

As she stared at the information board, she sensed that Bértrand was near. She could always somehow tell when he was around. He seemed to have that kind of magnetism, a force field of his very own. She turned from the board to look for him, moving through a couple of other sections, but couldn't see him. Then, above the buzz of other voices, she heard his, but he was clearly talking to someone else, and he sounded unusually agitated. Well, she wouldn't want to interrupt an argument, although truth be told she wondered what had disturbed his normally calm authoritative demeanour.

Before she headed to the lift for the section on the

THE DRAGON TREE

dragon tree, she turned to the azulejo area. These tiles fascinated her so much for some reason and she loved studying the patterns and their meanings.

She stopped abruptly. Bértrand was by the azulejo displays, his back turned towards her. He was gesticulating towards the tiles, and as he raised his arm, she could see who he was talking to so agitatedly. It was John Waller, the church warden, red faced and sweating profusely.

She ducked out of sight. But curiosity made her listen. How did they know each other? Of course, it was a small island and it wasn't hard to imagine that they had come across each other at some point. Everyone seemed to know everyone else here. But she could only hear snatches of the conversation.

"But I cannot do that." Bértrand's voice, strained. "If you think ... why can you not ...?"

"You know why ... the church ... new priest won't ... his wife ..."

Viv caught her breath, shocked. Why on earth were they talking about them, her? Just then the family she had seen at the entrance came through, the father pointing out exhibits that might interest his grumbling children. They headed round towards the azulejo samples – "God, dad, why the hell would we be interested in a load of old tiles?" "why's the wifi not working on my mobile?"

She turned away and headed for the lift.

By the time she arrived back at the apartment, Rory was already cooking their dinner. A delicious aroma of spaghetti bolognese filled the hallway from the kitchen area.

"That smells good," she called, but not really feeling hungry. She was still disturbed by what she'd overheard in the museum.

Rory swung round as she dropped her bag onto the floor and lifted the glass of red wine that was standing on the counter top.

"Hey," he said. "That's mine! Chef's privilege."

She took a swig. "Mmm, it's a nice one."

"Get your own. There's the bottle and a glass over by the fridge. Have a good day?" He stirred the meat sauce and sipped a little from the wooden spoon.

"Yes, thanks, quite productive, one way and another. You?"

His shoulders sagged. "Well, OK, I guess. Slow progress. I don't know what the previous folks were up to – records just don't make sense. Nobody seems to know what's been happening." He shook his head. "But the parish work and services prep and sermons still have to go on. So that's where I'm focusing."

"What *is* it that's in a mess still, Rory?"

"It's just ... it's a bit of a puzzle. Pages missing. Odd appointments." He turned to her and smiled. "But I don't want to bother you, not at the moment. I'm getting it sorted."

"I don't mind!"

"No, honestly, I've gone through stuff enough today. Just let's relax tonight. I thought I'd take a break and get the meal going." He used the spaghetti fork to test the strands. "I thought you'd be back before now. Where were you off to this afternoon, then?"

"Oh, just the museum."

He swivelled around to face her, frowning. "Again? You've already been there."

"Well, yes. I like it there. It's usually fairly quiet and I'm learning a lot about the island and its history. It's fascinating. And it makes me feel comfortable and at home."

"Er ... it's a museum! Why do you want to hang around a museum?"

"Rory, I've just told you! I don't 'hang around', I've been researching. Currently Ana d'Arafet and Sir Robert ..."

"Who?"

Well, if he'd listened, he'd know. She sighed, feeling the irritation rising. "I have tried to tell you but you're always so busy!"

"Sorry, Viv, but this is my job."

"And you think this isn't mine? *This* is connected to my research, and hence *my* job, Rory!"

"OK, I'm sorry ..."

But she was in full flight mode now. "You're always

stuck in your study or in a meeting with Georgina ..."
Why did she have to say that?

"What? Rarely with Georgina ..."

"With whoever, then! You just don't seem to be interested in what I do any more. We used to talk, sit down together and discuss things, but we never do these days."

"Wait a minute ..." Rory held up his hand in a restraining gesture.

"Don't stop me when I'm in full flow, Rory!" She felt a sob rise to her throat and pulled a tissue from the box on the counter top. She couldn't stop now; it all flooded out of her, all the resentments. "You don't seem to grasp the fact that I'm basically alone here, Rory, working on my own ... I'm not in a team here. I don't have meetings to go to, people to see ..."

"Well, you could do if you ..."

"For God's sake, Rory. You don't get it, do you? I've come here, with you, for your job. OK I've contrived research to do here, and that's fine, but you have no idea what I do all day and you aren't interested and for all you know I could be racing around Funchal all day naked ..."

Rory grinned. "Oh, I think someone would have been quick to tell me that!"

"Rory! You're not *hearing* me!"

"I am, I am."

"Oh hell, Rory, if you don't have time to listen to me, if you're so engrossed with church stuff, then it really doesn't matter, because ... because at least I can talk to Bértrand – at least *he's* interested in my work, my research ... I just wish you could summon up a grain of interest, too ..."

She'd mopped up her tears and blown her nose before she realised that Rory was staring at her.

"Bértrand?"

"Yes," she said wearily. "He's on the board of the museum. He's the one who invited us ...both of us, note! ... to walk the levada to the Curral da Freiras ... only you were too busy ... *as usual* ..."

"Oh, him. Right. I see. Hey, so that's why you're at the museum all the time?"

"I'm not at the museum *all* the time. And no, that's not the reason. And are you jealous, because ..."

"Why? Should I be?" He was smiling. She grabbed another tissue, but he moved towards her and wrapped his arms around her. "Darling, this is such a silly argument. You're still emotional and strung-up, d'you think?"

She pulled back away from him. "Oh, so I'm hormonal, that's presumably what you mean! Haven't you heard a word I've been saying?"

"I have. I've taken it all in. And I promise I'll do better." He reached out to try to stroke her arm, but she stepped away. "Let's just have a quiet meal together and talk and you can tell me what you'd like me to do."

She caught a sob. "Please don't humour me. To be honest, Rory, I don't feel like anything to eat. I'm all choked up. And anyway, look, the spaghetti's ruined." She nodded towards the stove where the spaghetti had boiled dry and the sauce was burning in the pan.

Annoyed and frustrated weren't even the words for how she felt at that moment. Good God, why on earth had she burst out like that?

Although as she fled into the bedroom, she heard Rory swearing and didn't know whether to laugh or cry.

CHAPTER 15

ANA

There was little time to return to the clearing in the next few weeks, as Sir Robert, now healed, along with the cog's crew, busied themselves hewing timbers and building a group of simple wooden shelters from the trees that fringed the shore. They did not venture far inland, only close by to hunt and gather wild vegetables and roots, being wary of what might lurk in the dark places beyond. The furthest they went was to scramble up on the scrubby headland where they could see far out to sea. Ana begged Robert to let her accompany him there, so that she could see across the ocean to France, but he told her no, it was too steep in her condition and anyway they could not see that far, only a great expanse of water, never ending.

And so she contented herself on the shingle and rocks and caves of the beach. But her eyes were drawn constantly to the mountains, that reached their craggy peaks above the forests to the sky, that were often shrouded with mist and cloud, and that made her both curious and fearful. For often, as she drank them into her and her eyes blurred and her head swam, she thought she heard the trudging of feet and the swish of long thick robes brushing against rocks. She heard their voices, nuns' voices, she knew, murmuring urgently, tired and fearful. She felt their fear and she shuddered.

But mostly Ana contented herself with watching the buildings taking shape and thought that they were strangely shaped dwellings, with steep A shaped roofs that nearly swept the ground, thatched with the branches and leaves that grew in abundance around them. But Robert said that they were best like that because the storms would slide off and the inside would be safe from the hot sun. She wondered how long they were to be here, until the season of storms came again.

Yet as the little settlement rose, so did the injuries and accidents and fevers amongst the men. They had already lost three men: one who had sliced his hand half off with his axe and the wound had festered to gangrene, the other two from a strange fever. Joan and Ana had no notion where the fever had come from and only guessed they had drunk bad water, and yet the water from the mountains that gushed down to the shore, ran clear and sparkling and quick.

They began to use the front part of the hut where Ana and Robert slept as a sanatorium and Ana found it a constant battle to strew herbs and burn eucalyptus to keep the smells at bay.

Constant shouts of "help, man hurt!" brought Ana and Joan bustling with their bag of potions to salve and soothe, lance and stitch. Ana's stitching was becoming a little more proficient, as long as she gritted her teeth and held her breath, but most times she deferred to Joan to take the work.

"Another careless one for you, eh!" Will, the young deckhand who had brought her refreshment on one of the first mornings on this island, would say each time he helped a staggering fellow inside. He would shake his head with an exaggerated sigh. "I do not know what this rogue is about, my lady. Just wanting some womanly company and a draft of wine, eh, my friend?" And he would ease the poor fellow to the rough-hewn wooden bench and gently tease away the blood-soaked breeches or tunic or sleeve while Ana tried not to gasp at the depth of the wound revealed beneath.

"There!" Will would teasingly land a careful blow on his workmate's back or arm and cast a wink at Joan and a respectful bow of the head towards Ana. "Here you are, in good hands, ready for the kind ladies to kiss your forehead!"

"Thank you, Will. You make an excellent orderly in our little infirmary!" Ana would tease back, making him blush with pleasure. And he would back out of the hut clutching his bloody hands in front of him, unable to hide his grin.

Ana tried to work efficiently and quietly, calming fears and stroking hot brows against the pain. But she felt that she was awkward and often uncertain, looking to Joan.

"Is this right?" she would ask on many days, as she carefully bound a wound with eucalyptus leaves.

"Yes indeed, my lady," Joan would look across from her feverish patient and nodded. "You are doing well. I will have to be on guard when we are back that you do not take my work!"

Ana smiled. "You have taught me well. But it is you who do all the difficult tasks. The cutting and stitching."

"That is as may be. Yet you are a pleasing assistant! You are learning to renew our stock of balms and lotions while I work on the rest."

Ana felt a flush of pleasure at Joan's compliment, and had to dip her head in modesty, so as to hide her blushes.

But one day it all changed.

"I need to fetch more salve," said Joan, bustling out. "I will not be long. You will manage? These two just need calming and comforting now."

"Yes, of course."

For a few moments there was quiet and Ana began to hum a sleep-song that she remembered from her childhood at Darbey Hall in one of the rare times she had been given a nurse who was more interested in caring for her than gossiping or flirting. It was a gentle soothing tune that echoed through the hut and her patients were soon closing their eyes, lulled by the song and the copious amounts of wine she had poured down their throats against their pain.

A noise at the doorway to the little hut made Ana look up sharply.

"Quick!" It was Robert and another man struggling with a heavy bundle wrapped in a thick cloak. Ana pushed herself up from the floor and straightened her robe over her growing bump, dusting off the fragments of eucalyptus and fennel.

They lowered the bundle to the floor onto the strewn herbs and began to unwrap the figure within. The face turned and Ana saw that it was Will. His eyes were dark and wide with pain and his bloodless lips pressed together against a scream.

Ana crouched down again and reached to stroke the boy's shroud-white cheeks.

"Oh no, Will. What have you done, you silly thing?" She tried to smile but as she looked at the deep wound on his leg that was pulsing blood so horribly her heart rose to her throat.

"Blade ... slipped a bit ..." he croaked, and his mouth stretched into a mockery of a smile in his agony.

"Lucky it did not slice off his leg," murmured Robert.

But she knew that the effect was not much different.

By the look of it, she guessed that the blade was unclean. She looked up at Robert. He inclined his head.

"I know. I try to get the men to keep the tools clean. But it is difficult in these circumstances. They are moving from one task to another so quickly. I have buckets of salt water handy to wash the blades. But we need to work urgently and there is no time."

She shook her head and pressed a cloth against the wound. The blood soon soaked it, but she held on, hardly noticing the red that drenched her skirts. With one hand on the cloth she reached with the other for the wine beside her and juggled to pour as much as she could into his mouth.

Joan bustled in bearing a large bowl of seawater and a pot of salve.

"Go fetch a fresh cloth," she said as she set it down beside Ana, and stooped low, knees apart, pushing her skirts between her thighs. "And another flagon of wine."

Ana knew that the jugs of wine that they liberally poured on wounds and down the men's throats were possibly the greatest help, so that it was frightening to hear Robert whisper, "Be cautious, use this flagon sparingly. We have truly little left."

Ana shook her head and poured more wine onto Will's parched lips.

"What shall we do then?" Ana frowned.

Robert shrugged. "When we have finished the last, there is nothing we can do. Except pray to be delivered."

Ana stretched her back and winced. She brushed the sweat from her forehead. She looked down at her handiwork. She had been obliged to tear his breeches away from the wound in order to cleanse it, but now that the blood was not pooling over the flesh she could see that it was like the sheep meat she knew from the kitchens at Darbey Hall, raw and frightening. Will's wound was purple and creamed with pus, and she could see that the infection was spreading up his shin.

"What is this? How has this happened?"

Robert paused a moment before he whispered. "He had an injury before, but I thought ... it seemed to heal. This wound has perhaps hit the same spot."

Ana shook her head, unable to speak. This was very bad. She turned to Joan, but she only grimaced and hung her head too. Ana breathed in slowly and Will's smell suffused her nostrils, sour and thick and rancid. His face was contorted in pain and he cried out, still with that shrill high voice of a child.

"Oh God, Lady Ana ... I beg you, cut the pain away!"

Ana touched his hand and forced a smile. "Remember that rat or squirrel you brought me in stew when we first came here, Will?" she asked quietly. He nodded but his face was screwed up in agony. He tried to smile but it appeared more like a scowl. "Best not to know, you said. But all was well then and will be now. It will be worse before it gets better, Will. But try to bear it and I will bear it with you. This pain will be over soon, I promise you."

He grimaced. Ana saw from his glazed eyes that it was unlikely to get better. All she could do was hold his hand and be there with him until his time was come. She glanced up at Robert.

"I dream of our home in France, Robert, when we are rescued, as I dream of the home I had in England."

"I know, my love."

"I have scratched marks on our wall over there to measure the days we have been here and the days until my confinement. There are many of the former, and, I fear, not too many towards my confinement."

Robert touched her arm and sighed.

That night, in the darkness, Will, begging God to be let go from his pain, passed from this world in Ana's arms. She refused to leave him, even after he had gone, and Joan had to pull her away into Robert's arms, so that they could bury him.

∽

Despite the fire that Robert made on the hillside, and the continuous look-out he ordered, no ships came into view. Yet he refused to give up hope and stationed crew to keep watch day and night. But days and nights rolled on.

"There will be a passing ship, I know it," he assured Ana as he pulled off his boots one night, some weeks later.

"I know," she murmured, hiding her hot face from him, as she squatted before him, belly large and most uncomfortable by now, helping to ease his footwear from his swollen feet. "But it has been a long time. And my time is coming near." She pushed herself up, dizzily, from the wooden floor of the dwelling he had made in the centre of the group of huts. Her child was growing large now and she was carrying it low and well to the fore so that Joan declared it must certainly be a boy, although Ana was more concerned that her pains were increasing despite the potions, and that the wooden bed Robert had crafted was not so comfortable to birth her burden.

She winced and clutched the folds of her gown against the pain low in her abdomen. More men had a bad fever and there were fewer and fewer to keep the fires and hunt for food. Ana was glad that Robert had not had a recurrence of fever for weeks, but she herself felt weaker each day. Robert was constantly afraid that she was too close to the fevers, bending over fetid bodies, breathing in the foul vapours, touching noxious wounds. He feared that the contamination would enter her body from theirs and consume her, and the baby. He asked her over and over again to stay away, but she would not, saying she must help the sick.

That particular day she had been aching and flushed and hoped to God that a fever was not taking hold. But even as she hoped and prayed, she felt a sweat breaking out on her forehead and chest, and trickling down between her breasts, much fuller now. The walls seemed to be pressing in upon her, the room swaying and circling. She could not steady it. Her brain was juddering in her skull.

"My love?" Ana looked up to see Robert rising and holding out his arms to her, his sun-burned face creased with worry. "Are you not well? You have a look of fever in your eyes."

"It is simply that I bent down and then rose too quickly, Robert," she whispered.

But Ana felt her legs crumple beneath her, as Robert manoeuvred her to the bed and helped her to lower herself to the pillow Joan had stuffed with sweet herbs. She looked up to the rough steep A shape of the roof above her head, the dried branches and leaves like strands of unbrushed hair falling out of their coifs, reaching out to her, pressing in to her. And suddenly it felt as though they were fingers, bent and gnarled, reaching to scratch her, to tear at her belly. She saw again the dragon tree in the clearing and knew that those were the fingers that sought her.

Now, all the days, weeks, of crushing down the pain and the fear that filled her more and more, were crashing together like the jester's cymbals, mashing her brain and her body as fire consumed every cell in her body.

"I ... I feel most odd, Robert, my dear." She swept her hand over her wet forehead and felt her lank hair about her head, felt the sweat drip into her eyes with a salty sting. "Pass me my rosary, Robert my dearest."

Robert grabbed it from the bench and pressed it into her hot trembling hands. "I must fetch Joan."

Ana sensed that he had left the little dwelling but although she seemed to count the rosary beads and murmur her prayers, she did not hear him return with Joan nor feel the cool seawater that her servant dabbed across her forehead and over her cheeks. She did not hear or feel anything in that rough-hewn shelter because her mind fell back to the splendour of Darbey Hall, Edward's court and Sir Thomas, as the fever took hold of her and consumed her, and she fell into the darkness of delirium.

CHAPTER 16

VIV

The present day

"... Falling into the darkness."

Viv's mind jerked back to the present and she shuffled on the bone-hard wooden pew. She raised her eyes to the familiar figure of her husband in his priest's robes up there in the eagle-carved pulpit, delivering his sermon. He was raising his right arm as he spoke, the wide sleeves of his white surplice falling back from the black cassock beneath. A glaring beam of sunlight on this bright Sunday morning caught the gold embroidery on his green stole and the gold of his pectoral cross. So handsome in his clerical collar and communion vestments.

So familiar, yet at this moment, so distant.

She grimaced. If only she had not told him last night that she was often at the museum, if only she hadn't mentioned Bértrand. Why did she do that? Because she was uneasy about Georgina? Should she be? And why had she carried on about him being so interested in her research, and then ... oh why did she add that she wished Rory was too, and not always so engrossed elsewhere. He'd looked so hurt, trying to cover it up. If only their conversation had not descended into an unfamiliar row - he calm, firm, objective, she upset, crying, blaming. What on earth was all that about? They never rowed.

If only she had stuck to her intended subject of Ana and her visions, the strange experience at the Curral, trying to get through to him, trying to share. Why on earth had she even mentioned Bértrand? He was nothing to her, really. She hardly knew him ... and yet she remembered on their walk to the Curral, the casual hand protectively, possessively, the hand that held hers for even a brief moment. But it was all so innocent. Wasn't it? Well, she couldn't deny that his Gallic ways and sexy voice sent shivers up her spine and made her research at the museum far more interesting. But nothing had happened. Had it?

She stared up at the vaulted ceiling of the church and the balcony that circled beneath the dome, her eyes damp with regret. She blinked against the threatening tears, looking everywhere but at him. This church was certainly *different* - it had a tropical flavour with its murals of exotic flowers and palm trees, but it was not a place of soaring beauty like Rory's church back home. Every time she had sat in this church over the few weeks they had been here in Funchal, she had thought how strange it felt, how odd the architecture was. She could well believe that someone could feel that this room with its hidden crevices, its huge pillars and shadowy sanctuary, its small cramped apse, could harbour ghostly apparitions. Rory couldn't see it, but she could.

She'd read somewhere that the church had been designed not to look like a church, which seemed strange. Some nineteenth century Portuguese law, apparently, prohibited Protestant places of worship from assuming the external resemblance of a church. So the consul who designed it, decided he'd have a building that looked like a library instead. Yes, she could see that. Although hadn't she read somewhere else that one of the original architects had been influenced by some legendary incident in a Moorish church in Spain? That Moorish connection again … her eyes rested on the azulejo tiles on the walls behind the altar. An involuntary shiver shuddered through her body as if someone had touched her.

She glanced round but the people behind her were intent on listening to the sermon. She realised that she'd hardly heard a word of it.

Her eye caught Georgina sitting at the front near the eagle lectern from where she had been able to slide out easily for her reading. She was gazing intently up at Rory.

Viv became aware that Rory was pointing above the altar to the semi-dome painted deep blue and dotted with stars. It reminded her of a Moroccan restaurant they'd been to. She stared for a moment at the stars in the 'night sky' of the apse, puzzled by a fleeting thought that drifted across her mind. Then she redirected her full attention to what Rory was saying.

"We know that the stars are always there, of course, through night and day, sunshine and clouds. But we can't see them in the glare of the sun. We are blinded to them, blinded by the light. And Barbara Brown Taylor in 'Learning to Walk in the Dark' goes on to argue that the metaphor of darkness as sin, evil, ignorance and death, creates a problem for us because we then are led to think of all 'dark' things as anti-God, anti-righteous, things to be feared, reviled. Yet that light from our stars in our solar system, our galaxy, the universe, is always there. It's just that we can't see that light. And we are blinded to their light even in the darkness of night, because we have thrust them away in the safety of our street lamps and our electric light bulbs. We have learned to 'light the night' and drive away the fears and superstitions of the dark."

Viv bit her lip. Yes, she was afraid of the dark and *darkness* – and perhaps of Ana d'Arafet too, and what it all meant. And maybe she was struggling to make sense of the darkness and fear in her mind, that darkness of her connection to history, to lives centuries ago. Wondering how it would all pan out, what track her life would take.

Rory was talking about early man who divided the night into periods of sleep and wakefulness, rest periods of deep relaxation and meditation, when creativity became more intense, when perhaps there was deeper insight and ancient myths and legends grew out of it. "As Brown Taylor suggests, once we learned to 'light the night', maybe we lost the ability to touch the deeper insights and awareness which was familiar to early mankind."

Viv frowned. So was there a kind of light, a kind of insight, sensitivity, within those time-slips that was helping her to understand things beyond normal experience?

"And so," Rory looked up and his gaze swept towards her, "Perhaps we need to find again that faith which sees those stars, that light, even in the blinding and distracting glare of our everyday lives. Maybe we need to see beyond that glare to the truth out there, beyond our understanding. Perhaps we need to learn to walk in the dark and allow ourselves to see the stars beyond. Amen."

"Amen," murmured Viv along with the congregation around her.

The young couple and their child in front of her were shuffling and whispering, comparing the coins in their pockets, as Rory's curate announced the offertory hymn: "number 419. Lord, the light of your love is shining." She liked that hymn with its rousing refrain, with its emphatic ending of "and let there be light." Sometimes she thought that was the best thing about church.

Now, as she sang, she watched Rory move away to the altar, bowing his head then turning to face the congregation and the church wardens bearing the offertory plates. He caught her eye, and she wondered what he was thinking and how much he knew.

The preparation for the eucharist seemed to go on forever and although Viv murmured her responses automatically, she hardly heard them. Then John Waller, taking his role as church warden very solemnly, even abruptly, was indicating with a peremptory flick of his hand for her to move towards the sanctuary to receive the communion bread and wine. As she passed him, she was aware that he glared at her. She wondered what he had been arguing with Bértrand about at the museum, and what he had been doing in the church gardens that day. And she remembered the sight of him behind the Sé that time, not so long ago, but nothing had transpired from it and she wondered whether it really had been in her imagination after all, and maybe the result of stress. Neither she nor Rory had mentioned the incident again. She had a strange feeling about John; there was something definitely creepy about him. She turned towards the altar.

Because the congregation was large, Rory and his curate stood on either side to divide the group into two.

Viv chose to move to the left for the curate. As she took the bread, she noticed Rory, to her right, suddenly look distractedly behind him. She glanced over and saw him frown but continue the flow of his blessings as he administered the sacrament to the line in front of him.

She was sipping from the chalice as she saw out of the corner of her eye that he jolted forwards, as though someone had pushed him. She thrust the chalice back to the curate and turned towards Rory, stopping herself from rushing over to him. There was a communal murmur as he righted himself and steadied the salver. She saw that Georgina was directly in front of him and that she placed a hand gently on his arm, her bright red nails like blood on the white of the surplice.

∽

VIV, STANDING ON HER OWN BEHIND THE LONG TABLE IN the church garden, protected from the strong midday sun under light coloured awning, smiled as sweetly as she could as she served out the Madeira wine, coffee and pieces of honey cake to the stragglers of the congregation. Most hurried out of the Sunday service and made quickly for their refreshments. They were supposed to drop coins into the box but not all of them did, even though she looked pointedly at it. She wondered if it would be 'the done thing' to rattle the box under people's chins but decided not.

Most of them were scattered in small groups

THE DRAGON TREE

around the lawns and under the pergola. Viv could hear laughter and cheerfulness, but she herself felt anxious about Rory and what had happened during communion. She glanced over to the people sauntering slowly towards the table, willing them to hurry up so that she could clear up and get back into the apartment to make their lunch and more importantly so that she could speak to Rory. She had things to clear up and things to find out.

She was sorry for the argument last night and she was worried about him. He'd seemed evasive later that night and distant when they went to bed. Was it the obvious issues that he'd discovered at the church? Was it about Bértrand? Was it her? Or was it about Georgina?

Stragglers were stopping to chat to each other and to Rory who stood patiently on the steps outside the church door, meeting and greeting. They appeared to think they had all day.

Over the shoulders of the queue in front of her, Viv saw Georgina, who should have been helping her at the table, standing close to Rory over on the steps, her hand firmly on his arm, fingers creeping up to his shoulder. And she saw their heads bend closer as Georgina stretched up, leaned in, and pulled Rory nearer to her, whispering something in his ear. She saw Rory's gentle smile that lit up his eyes as he gazed down at her.

"Woops, sorry," she murmured as she spilt a little

wine on the cloth and handed the glass to a large red-faced man before her. He looked horribly hot and sweaty, and as soon as he had taken the Madeira wine from Viv, he pulled out a crumpled handkerchief from his pocket to mop his brow. A holiday-maker, clearly, in his walking boots and anorak. He stuffed the handkerchief back and grabbed several pieces of cake and a little pile of pastel da nata.

"Off for a walk after lunch?" asked Viv pointedly.

"Oh, I shan't bother with lunch," the man grunted. Viv raised her eyebrows.

"Well, there's more shade under the pergola, while you eat your ... snacks." She turned to the next person in the line.

She didn't know how Rory kept his patience. If these were her students, she would have lectured them about manners. Gently, of course, but firmly.

She felt prickly. And decidedly unchristian.

A light touch on her back made her swing round, almost dropping the piece of cake she was offering the tall, smart looking lady engrossed in conversation with her companion.

"Georgina!"

"I'm *so* sorry, sweetie. I just had about a million things to do in the vestry. I knew you could manage perfectly well without me."

"Well, I ..." Viv looked at the queue, now reduced to the last few, and they didn't seem in too much of a hurry. She looked over to the church door and saw

Rory, frowning, shake hands with John and begin to make his way down the path towards her.

Georgina took the coffee that Viv had just poured out and handed it carefully to the old lady next in line. "How *are* you, my dear? So good to see you. How was the operation? Recovering well, I take it?"

"Yes, thank you. Mmm, your coffee is always so lovely and welcome, Georgina." The old lady nodded and smiled. She turned to stare at Viv. "And who is this, Georgina? I haven't met her before."

Viv opened her mouth to introduce herself, but Georgina jumped in. "Well, you haven't been to communion for a while, my dear, since your little op. Oh, this is Dr DuLac. Our dear Father Rory's wife."

"His wife? Well," the old lady stared at Viv a moment. "You have a very handsome husband. Where on earth did you meet him?"

She might as well have said 'how on earth did you snag such a treasure?' But Viv stretched a smile. "That is a *very* long story. But do please try some of my honey cake."

"Oh, I do love the bolo de mel from Pingo Doce, don't you?" Georgina said. "Although I generally make my own."

The old lady sniffed at the plate of cake and slipped a large piece onto her saucer, spilling a dash of coffee onto it in the process. "So," she looked hard at Viv. "DuLac? Why have you got a different name, then?"

Viv bristled. "I'm afraid that's a long story, too."

Rory arrived at her side and she felt him slide his arm around her waist. "Sorry about that. Everything OK?" he whispered. Viv nodded.

"It will be when this is done. And you?" she whispered back but Rory just smiled vaguely.

∽

"What on earth happened in communion, Rory?" They had finally managed to retreat to the apartment. Viv slipped on her oven gloves and slid out the chicken casserole that she'd popped into the oven before church.

Rory paused as he poured the vino verde. "Was it very obvious?"

"Yes, of course it was! You looked as if someone pushed you from behind."

"That's exactly how it felt." He put down the bottle on the counter top. "Well, no. It was more like someone tapping me on the back to get my attention. It wasn't violent. It didn't feel malevolent. Don't worry about that. But of course, there was nobody there. Very odd."

They stared at each other for a long moment and Viv felt a shudder rise up her back and the heat pool at her neck. In silence, she served out the chicken and green beans and they each took a plate out onto the balcony. Rory went back for the glasses of wine and set them on the table by the basket of garlicky bolo de caco. Viv sighed and stared at her plate. Rory cleared his throat.

"Viv, I'm ..."

"Rory, I shouldn't have ..." They laughed and each signalled for the other to go on.

"Look, I'm sorry about last night." He balanced his fork on the side of his plate and ran his hand through his thick curly hair. It was a gesture that sent shivers down Viv's spine. Even now. "I shouldn't have reacted the way I did. It was unfair. I've a lot on my mind. But that's no excuse."

"Well, I understand that, and I shouldn't have been so touchy. But ... Rory, please stop pushing me away."

He shook his head, and reached across the table to touch her hand, a vicar's comforting pat. "Don't worry. I guess I need to follow my own preaching, see things differently. The church. It's not helping ... us. And you. I don't know, you seem different somehow and I can't figure out why."

She felt the familiar ache in her abdomen where she was scarred but didn't lower her hand to it. She didn't want him to think she was calling for sympathy. That she was weak. She speared a piece of chicken without much enthusiasm. She seemed to have lost her appetite at the moment.

"God, Rory, I'm confused about so much at the moment. Your sermon this morning about walking in the dark, about seeing things more clearly when we're not blinded by the light, it made me think ..."

"Well, hopefully that's what it's supposed to do!"

"Yes, but listen, Rory. The thing is, I didn't get to explain to you that I've been having these ... not slips, but sort of visions, is the best way I can describe them. And that's why I wanted to go to the museum and find out as much as I could about the history of this place. Because I think it's all somehow bound up together, past and present."

"O-kaaay." Rory frowned and looked down at his dinner that was in danger of getting cold. He picked up his knife and fork again.

"You talked before, when the slips happened before I mean, about the theories of quantum mechanics, worm holes, that touching of other times, other worlds. That bridge between the past and the present where sometimes worlds, lives, collide."

"Yes, the Einstein-Rosen Bridge theory of time." He looked across to her. Viv could hear the gulls screeching high above the garden, the deep sound of a ship's horn in the harbour. "Oh no. Do you mean that other things have happened since that incident at the rectory with those feelings about the volcano and the fossil? Is it about your mother and the excavation at Machico? It's to do with John Waller, isn't it? The church? Oh God, Viv, what have you been holding back?"

"Well. I suppose it all started at the Capela do Corpo Santo ... and then after lunch with Georgina ..."

"Georgina?"

"Please, Rory. Let me just tell you, factually, what's been happening." This had to end and maybe he would now have some common ground with her, after what he'd experienced during communion. "So ... in the Capela ..."

He listened patiently to what Viv had to say. And then he said quietly, "But what does she want of you, this Ana d'Arafet, and how can she be connected to the Curral?"

CHAPTER 17

ANA

As she tossed and turned on the rough-hewn attempt at a bed, pushing away the coarse scratchy cover, she was so feverish she could have sworn she had tumbled into hell itself.

Ana saw, in her delirium, her father standing over her prostrate body. His bulk in the heavy velvet robes blotted out the meagre light from the window in her chamber. His hand was raised to her. Yet his body was shimmering, unreal.

"Get up, daughter!" he shouted, "Get dressed and do your duty. You are not at Darbey Hall now amongst kith and kin, but here at court. And Edward the king will not be waiting for the likes of you!"

"She is unwell," she could hear her maid say, as if from a distance, and her voice was thin and trembling.

"She is not unwell, wretch. She is feigning." His voice seemed to be rolling through her brain, then fading away, like a tempest at sea. Waves high and her room pitching.

Ana could not feel her body at all, although she tried to touch her breast, her stomach. Yet her hand felt a fine silk coverlet and she knew that under it her breast was empty and her stomach flat. A wave of dizziness and confusion sent her spiralling downwards.

She felt someone touch her head, and a cloth, cool and damp. An arm, rough but plump, strong, around her shoulders, easing her up from the coarse scratchy covers – what? where was the silk? – to bend, nauseous, over a bowl, and stroke her head as she retched and vomited violently into it, her body racked with spasms.

"Get up, get up!" He was there again in her vision, looming before her in his rich fur lined, fur trimmed robes, red angry face, spittle flying from his contorted mouth. His outline seemed hazy: there and yet not there.

Oh, now someone gently lowering her to the rough mattress again.

Loud noises crashing into her consciousness, heavy wooden doors banging, voices shouting, so close, her head echoing with movement and brain-hurting cacophony. Incoherent ravings. Waves of sound crashing over her.

"Who is it? Who is there?"

But someone was tenderly stroking her forehead.

Someone whispering, "Lady Ana, Lady Ana, 'tis Joan," over and over again until she closed her hot eyelids, and all went dark and quiet.

And then she remembered. Her vision cleared as she re-lived that day.

She was hurrying down a long passageway. She could hear the rumble of conversation ahead in the royal banqueting hall.

"Lady Ana," the voice startled her. She turned, feeling her floor-length bejewelled court overgown with its lavish braiding and ermine trim swinging heavily as she moved on the stone tiled floor. Her maid, Alys, was hurrying to catch up her. A flash of searing pain crossed her temples.

"Alys? Where is Joan?"

"Joan? Why, she is back at Darbey Hall of course. In the kitchens as usual or making her potions or some such." She frowned at Ana. "Why would you think she was here at the royal court?"

Ana shook her head to clear her tangled thoughts. "I ... yes, of course. She finished her duties some days past, tending me for that short time while you were away at your mother's side. I ... I am sorry ...I am all a-jumble at present."

"No need to be confused, my lady. I expect we all seem alike to you. Your father was so good to allow me time as my mother slipped from this world. But never fear, I am back in attendance to you now." Alys glanced sideways at her. "And of course, it was I who dressed you for tonight's court banquet."

"Indeed." Ana inclined her head, and something jarred in her skull.

"It is such an occasion, my lady! Your first time at Edward the king's full court." She amended the drape of Ana's kirtle and robe as they reached the great studded doors, tweaking the triangular gores in the wide skirt to reveal the gold silk that matched those of the long sleeves. Ana wriggled her wrists to push the sleeves off her hands a little; they irritated her when she could feel them over her palms. It made her feel constrained. "One moment, my lady." Alys stepped in front of her and adjusted the drape of the caul over her tight braids and the jewelled circlet that held it in place. Then she stood back to admire her work. "Feet?"

Obediently, Ana poked her pointed turnshoe out from the hem of her gown and Alys again sucked in her breath at the lavish design on the soft kidskin leather.

"I do not know why my father Sir Henri paid so much coin for shoes that will be hidden beneath my gown."

Alys looked up to her mistress's down-turned mouth. "You know perfectly well, my lady, that Sir Henri needs for you to make an impression upon the king and his favourite courtier Sir Thomas."

"I know it. And I know also that favourites change from one week to the next."

Alys gasped. "My lady!" And she inclined her head towards the guards at the great wooden door of the hall. "Ssshhh, please my lady, I beg of you."

Ana, mouth set firmly, whisked the skirt of her robe and marched forwards, Alys falling in behind.

She was accompanied through the noisy hall, noblemen and their ladies talking and laughing loudly to each other, towards her place as a guest of honour to the king. As she swept past the lower tables, she became aware that someone was watching her particularly intensely. She glanced to the side and her eyes met those of Sir Robert Machym, whom she had befriended on his visits with the king to Darbey Hall. She thought of their secret meetings and affectionate talks. The tentative touch of their hands in the shadows of the gardens and the passageways. Now, their smiles reached out to each other across the clusters of loud, red-faced nobles. He mouthed her name and she nodded, a flush of excitement suffusing her body. But she was guided away only too abruptly.

She only just had time to find her seat at the high table, and dismiss Alys's ministrations, before the musicians in the gallery trumpeted the arrival of the king and his queen, Philippa of Hainault, and everyone rose. Even Ana, caught in the moment, gasped at the lavishness of their robes, matching red velvet embroidered with gold and pearl eagles, clouds of silver stitching tumbling through the rich nap of the fabric. Ana raised her hand to her own simple caul and circlet as she noted the queen's crespine with its mesh of filigree gold and jeweller's artwork.

As they sat, Ana leaned forward as far as she dared, and sneaked a glance at the queen. She saw that she gave the sign of the cross and bowed her head as the carvers placed meat onto her platter, and that she nodded, smiling, and thanked them. Ana was thinking that the queen's face was kind and gentle when she realised that Queen Philippa was looking at her. Ana bowed her head and saw the queen smile graciously and nod her head in return before resuming her straight-backed stance and begin to pick delicately at her food.

She wondered if the queen was aware that Ana's father Sir Henri had sent her to court, at Edward the king's behest, in hopes that she would become his favourite mistress and hence enhance his own preferment. Or that at the very least she would become betrothed to Sir Thomas, sitting now at his side, and hers, and laughing loudly at his jokes. At best, for Sir Henri at least, both at the same time. She looked at her food and at the stuffed and twisted swan waiting on the platter in front of the king, its beady eyes staring, and felt nauseous. How could this sweet, serene queen stand it?

A vulgar guffaw made Ana look up from her roasted suckling pig and delicate quince tart and look across to the king. Edward was already red-faced and sweating in the heat of the hall with its huge fireplace.

He tossed his head and beads of sweat flew from his long hair, drooping moustache, and forked beard. Although she knew that he had been married to Queen Philippa from France for nearly seventeen long years since he was sixteen and she thirteen, and had six surviving children on her, he appeared to ignore her. She saw him swipe his hand across his high forehead that jutted out like a jettied overhang above his glaring eyes and abruptly dismiss a comment from his queen wife with a peremptory flick of his hand. Like an irritating fly that annoyed him. Ana wondered if the public gossip about his mistresses was true, although some said that he was privately devoted to Queen Philippa. She could not tell.

Sir Thomas turned at last to Ana and thrust his fat red wrinkled face in hers. His lavishly pleated chaperon had slipped askew on his head so that Ana could see that beneath it he sported almost no hair. His chin was likewise hairless, save for a few carefully combed strands. She tried to stop herself staring at him as she pondered on what nature of disease or heredity had denied him the full beard and flowing locks of his kind.

As he chewed, open-mouthed, the wheat bread on his platter, his spittle flew onto her cheeks. She reached for the shallow bowl of rose-scented water and dipped the corner of the little linen towel into it, dabbing her cheek. Sir Thomas continued, unperturbed, with his inventory of his many talents.

Ana's eyes swept the hall unsuccessfully for Sir Robert, but Sir Thomas abruptly grabbed the flagon of wine in front of him and filled her drinking cup to the brim, slopping much of it onto the table as his stubby red hand shook.

"Lady Ana, I am most glad to see you at court at last. Our meetings during your father's generous hospitality have been delightful." Ana could not remember them at all. He was one of many overbearing drunken guests at Darbey Hall. "I have waited for this for a long time. And I understand that your father is not averse to my ... er ... admiring you."

His voice droned across Ana's mind as he pontificated, in great and minute detail, about the intricacies of his king's recent proposal to re-establish an age of chivalry to rival that of the legendary King Arthur, with tournaments and a round table of knights.

"Including myself, naturally," he rumbled on, inclining his head, eyes closed as if in humility.

"Naturally," echoed Ana but Sir Thomas neglected to catch the irony in her voice and leaned drunkenly towards her over-enthusiastically, managing to displace her caul which she then was obliged to straighten. Blood rushed to her cheeks.

Ana knew from overhearing murmured talk in her father's chambers that the new Round Table was yet only an idea, but it sounded rather romantic to her. She learned a lot through the walls of the chambers in the hall, snuggled up with her books. She couldn't tell whether her father was admiring or concerned when he talked to his fellows about the king reaching far in his ambition, what with the ongoing war with the French, despite his wife's French family, and indeed his own antecedents. And she did wonder how he would pay for it all, along with the mounting debt that they also spoke of in anxious tones, and this new overhaul of parliament.

And yet despite the whispered talk, her father still seemed to desire more than anything for her to simper to the king and Sir Thomas.

As Sir Thomas leaned closer and closer to her and talked on and on, not about the nature of the proposed Arthurian court, which would have claimed her interest and full attention, but about his own prowess, he crept his hand onto her thigh under the table. She shuffled away but his grip remained firm. He clutched her flesh through the velvet of her robe, and his fingers began to crawl higher like a stalking rat. She shivered and made to push away his exploring fingers, whispering "please no!" but he only gripped more tightly. She wanted to shake him off and run from the hall. She made to move, but he held her down.

Desperately Ana's eyes swept the hall again. This time she found Sir Robert and grimaced an appeal across to him. Sir Thomas caught her look and his expression changed. Fury and spite sparked from his narrowed eyes. At the same time, the king clapped his hands and called for the musicians and dancing - in the middle of the feasting, no less! But thankfully Sir Thomas loosened his grip and moved his hand away to acknowledge the king.

The king rose, swaying frighteningly, and took the queen's hand to lead her to the middle of the room and other nobles followed suit with their own ladies to join them. Ana noticed that the queen's mouth was set firmly in downturn and her gait rigid. Edward the king was looking everywhere but at his lady, although he held her hand tightly.

Sir Thomas grabbed Ana's arm and abruptly pulled rather than guided her across the hall. At least dancing would keep him at arm's length from her for a while.

But he did not stop at the dancing groups; he clearly had no intention of joining them and stay in public view. Ana shook at the sight of his sweating determined face. She tried to shake his hand from her arm but to no avail. She tried to pull away. What *was* he doing? Would he slap her, as her father often did when she displeased him? Surely someone must see and rescue her? Her father? Sir Robert? But they were all too distracted with the dancing and the music to notice her red face and struggling body.

Despite her protestations, he thrust her out through the door, past the guards and into the shadows of the passageway. There he pushed her against the wall. He swivelled round only to signal the door guards to turn away from them.

"I cannot wait," he growled spittle into her face. "We shall be betrothed properly on the morrow. I saw you exchange those simpering looks with that knave, but you can forget *him*. Your father has promised you to *me*. And *now* ..." He grabbed at her skirts and pushed them up. She shrieked "no!" but knew amidst her tears that nobody would hear her, such was the raucous noise in the hall. Her hands clutched the heavy tapestries that hung on the wall behind her, but she could find no purchase with which to beat off Sir Thomas's strength against her. For a man so old and fat and slobbery, he seemed to possess a mighty power. Her skirts were around her waist and she felt the man's hot hard flesh against her.

She could not believe that this was what her father intended! She scratched his face and beat his shoulders, but it seemed to only arouse him the more.

Surely Sir Robert had seen them leave the hall and would come after her? Surely *someone* would save her? A sharp searing pain in her groin as he thrust into her stopped all thoughts in her head. Horror consumed her and she could not think or feel any more.

His sour mouth was on her lips, her cheek, her neck, and he growled angrily in her ear. She had no idea what he said. His pumping ceased and he grunted loudly like a stuck pig. She could feel something slippery slide out of her and a wetness drip down her thighs. But she could feel nothing else; her mind and body were numb, her brain uncomprehending.

"Now you are mine," he breathed his reeking breath into her face, "and we are as good as betrothed. We ask the king tomorrow for the blessing." He tugged her clothing down to cover her again as she stood immobile, frozen. He adjusted his breeches, and as he glanced at her face from under his hooded eyes, his expression was one of disgust. "For God's sake, make yourself respectable before you return to the hall and the king."

He turned from her, mouth twisted in a sneer, and left her slumped against the wall tapestries. With no backward glance, he pushed the doors open and marched back into the hall.

Numbly Ana saw the guards slinking back to their positions at the door, but they carefully averted their eyes from her.

She had no idea what had happened, only that this frightening man had been rough and violent with her. He had attacked her, violated her. He had touched her brutally in her most private place. What it signified she did not know. Yet her pounding heart told her that no-one else should know and that she must forget it ever happened. She must blot it out from her consciousness. She must numb her mind and body to it.

She had never been in this passageway with Sir

Thomas. He had never touched her there. It had never happened …

Her brain wrenched itself back to the present. She pulled in her rough rasping breath and tried to steady her shaking, but her body was racked with violent painful spasms.

Someone touched her head, a cloth, cool and damp. An arm, rough but plump, strong, around her shoulders, easing her up from the coarse scratchy covers.

"My lady," a voice split her mind. "Lady Ana. Come back to us."

She opened her eyes, but her head was spinning, the room, the thatched roof above her, was swinging and juddering. She felt more sick than she had ever felt before, except for early the morn after the attack when Sir Thomas dragged her numb body to the king and he blessed their betrothal, while she watched as if from above, outside herself. It was then, standing in dumb horror before the king, that she had felt a sharp tug low in her abdomen.

CHAPTER 18

ANA

"Come back to us." The shrill voice echoed across her head. She pulled herself back to the present. Ana knew it was Joan, her maidservant, and yet her mind was rent in two, almost unable to distinguish past from present. Her body shuddered beneath the rough cover and the hard wooden planks beneath her ground into her bones.

Yet a strange feeling rose from her belly to her breast, a warm comfort of soft words and sweet kisses, of yearning and safety. Tenderness and wanting, desiring and craving, caressed her. That other time ... Sir Robert, not knowing, at last finding her, cleaned and silent, in the king's garden the next noontide, holding her against him. And later lifting her onto his horse in front of him, pressing her tenderly to his hard chest. Galloping away, over the desolate moors to Bristol, then the cog, the Wayfayre, bound for France, far from Edward the king's fury at being thwarted and Sir Thomas's spite, and her father's angry raving. Yes, she had lain with Sir Robert since then, properly lain with him, in mutual love and wanting, so far from the savage moments with Sir Thomas in that passageway. So far, so very far, and so different, that she had pushed the horror from her mind as if it had never been. She had not spoken of it to him, or to anyone, and never would, even if her life depended upon it. Instead she filled her mind with the gentle caresses of her true love.

"Lady Ana, 'tis Joan." She opened her eyes and Joan's round face slid into focus.

Ana's fingers sought her rosary, but it had slipped from her hand in her delirium. Instead she touched her treasures nestling under the covers beside her, her stone with the creature curled inside it, and her piece of blue and white tile, so like one of her sweet dead mother's treasures at Darbey Hall. She raised her face to Joan's. "These ... what ...?"

Joan patted the bed covers. "You called for your treasures, in your fever."

Ana held her stone and tile, clutching them to her breast. Her fingers traced the strange markings on the tile. It seemed to give her comfort.

"I think your fever is breaking, my lady." Joan whispered, pressing the cool wet cloth onto her forehead again. "I prayed that you would pull out of it.

For the sake of us all, and of course of your baby inside."

"Yes, I thank you for your ministrations and your prayers, Joan." But Ana's voice was weak and breaking, and she could barely move her mouth, let alone her limbs.

She felt Joan's arm around her shoulders, easing her up, and a cup of wine touch her lips. She tried to swallow but the pain was great, and she fell back. Still she clutched the stone and the tile in her hands as if she would never let them go.

She became aware that another figure moved towards her. Joan turned, murmured words low, and rose to step away from the bed and make way for another. Through her hot dry eyes, Ana saw Robert kneel at her side and stretch his arm across her. He stroked her cheeks so softly that she could barely feel his touch. His face looked strange to her, his cheeks wet with tears she had never seen before, mouth twisted in pain.

"My love. I have barely left your side these days. And yet you awake the moment I turn away! But you are here, and I do detect the bloom of roses on your cheeks. Do you not see, Joan?" He swivelled round to the maid, and Ana heard her say, "yes, yes, I am sure of it, my lord," but Ana knew from the break in Joan's voice that the words were hiding a falsity.

As he spoke, she felt a strong wrench of pain across her abdomen and called out. Straight away, Joan pushed Robert aside and lifted the cover from Ana's belly. She felt Joan's hands pressing on her and all at once knew what was happening.

"Oh no. No. Not yet. It is not my time." The pain seared her body and she twisted her head from side to side in her agony.

"My lady, the babe is coming early."

"Oh my God!" breathed Sir Robert.

"Well, there is nothing He or you or anyone else can do about that. So, Sir Robert, it would please you to withdraw. Just oblige me by sending in some boiled water and my box of birthing herbs." Joan swivelled around. "Now, *now*, Sir!"

～

Ana's head swam and visions swept across her mind, behind her eyes.

A stone, a curled creature cowering within, a tile - a blue and white tile, but also with strange brown and purple markings like letters or symbols, a tile whole and perfect. Looking skywards, she sees above her head the branches of a strangely shaped tree that looks like a dragon and watching its purple blood dripping slowly onto the tile. Bending, picking it up, studying the intricate pattern upon it, stroking her hand gently across its smooth raised markings. Seeing on one side of the glazed upper surface, curious symbols she has never seen before, curved, and straight and dots, but on the other, the letters IHS which she knows to be ancient Christian symbols. Knowing with certainty that this was a holy relic. Her heart filling with calm, knowing above all else that this was a symbol of peace and prosperity, a talisman that would bring hope and safety after their travails.

Looking down at something in her hands, a strange little thin black box with silver buttons, hitting the button, click, click ... the magic box showing tiny pictures, then one rushing into focus. The ocean: towering waves rising up and a tumult of roaring molten rock seethed up to the surface of the sea. A mountain rising above the waves, fire spewing from its peak, gases clouding the boiling seas below She feels the burning heat fill her body, and hears the deafening fiery explosions, the sea a boiling mass of flame and smoke. Clouds of steam and ash engulfing her, and she smells the sulphur and death, and she knows the rage and is filled with terror. Behind her eyes, darkened with the blackness of the smoke and debris, there flash the colours of a fever, blood red and orange, and she sees the churning ocean spewing out explosive gases and rocks and tiny creatures, and the air is filled with fear.

Then she startles to find herself standing in blinding sun, on craggy shingle, sand, and rocks, under towering cliffs. A woman standing there before her.

∽

SHE IS THAT PERSON AND YET SHE IS OUTSIDE OF HER, *observing, unable to move. Turning towards her and for a moment staring into each other's eyes. A searing pain passing between them. Pain, loss, emptiness.*

A fragment of rock, a strange tile. In her hands yet distant.

She sees Robert lift her son onto a cog and watches him as he stares back at the island, receding slowly into the distance. She wants to cry out "do not leave me!" but she cannot.

Ana feels the ages pass as she lies, cold, in the darkness of her crypt. She sees a great man leap from his boat on her shore, stride across her rocky shingle, touch her shelter with his questing hand. How dare he violate what is hers? She sees him turn to his men behind him and, looking up to the stormy heavens, begin to speak. But she cannot understand his words.

Sounds of voices rise and fall like a tide on the shore. A dark place, a crypt, full of shadows and silence. A man, a stranger yet familiar. Like her. Her son – a grown man. Or his son, his son's son, she cannot tell. Moving around her as she lies, reaching for her treasures, touching them, his fingers searching, groping. She can see him in his heavy cloak and strange soft headgear, staring at her, then turning away, in his haste to leave the chamber, stumbling over the broken bones that lie on the floor around her.

Lying there, unable to move, screaming without any sound, her body frozen.

"Help me! Help me!" An echo, away to another time, another place, swirling through worlds, and then back to her again.

THE DRAGON TREE

Yet she sees a man, the man in her crypt as she sleeps, who took her treasures, her son, or her son's son ... and she sees the twist of his mouth and the cruelty in his eyes.

She sees a great religious edifice rise up in the hills, like the abbeys she knows, but so much bigger, grander. Women she knows, somehow, are nuns, in their black robes and wimples, moving quietly through the corridors and halls. A peace fills her heart. One of the women, no more than a girl, slips her hands beneath her outer robe and Ana knows that she is stroking the stone and the tile she keeps there, hidden.

Ana senses trembling fear, shaking hands, a sweep of heavy robes, a movement and sound in the quiet of the halls. A glimpse of rough, tangled-haired men, their clothes torn and tattered, dirty, and stinking. She knows the nun, the girl, needs to run, to leave the halls and the cloister, the icons, and the precious paintings on the walls. To leave it all behind her, except for the treasures she clutches. To flee up to the towering mountains.

Images are exploding in her mind: violent storms that ruin shelters and towers by the broiling seas, stones falling and shattering on the black sand, the tumult of rivers sweeping buildings in their path, men and women and children crying for help as they are swept away by the roaring water and dashed upon the rocks.

She sees mothers weeping at the empty food stores, children thin and babies with hardly the strength to cry in their hunger.

And now, in her hand Ana feels the lump of rock and the tile worn smooth with her stroking. Her hammering heart calms and her eyes clear as she feels her fever recede. She remembers how she found each of them and how she knows that they are holy.

∽

Ana opened her mouth to speak and forced the words from her rough dry throat. "This place. Whatever happens. Famine and storms. Attacks. It must be blessed."

Robert was standing over her once more, and Joan shaking her head just behind him, holding something that looked like a bundle of rags. Through half-closed eyes, she saw Robert frown. "Indeed, my love. But how do you mean?"

All at once Ana knew. Her hands felt the treasures at her heart. The stone that held within it the beginning of time, creation, and the tile that held the Christian and Arabic inscriptions, they signified the peace of this place, the safe harbour for them and for all to come. They must be held together and never parted.

"I will do anything you want, my love," whispered Robert. "Anything at all. Just as long as you recover, and we will be strong again. Together." His tears fell onto her cheek as he bent to her and kissed her lips.

She saw Joan slip to Robert's side and hold out the bundle she held. "Here, my lady." But why was her voice so thin and her eyes so red? "Your son."

Ana looked down at the tiny red creature, a slip of a thing, like a slippery puppy, wrinkled, bloodied, and hairless, that Joan placed gently onto her chest. He seemed to return her gaze from under his hooded eyes. His little mouth twisted strangely, and he moved his tiny fist towards her.

"Alive, a miracle," she whispered. But she searched his features in vain to find a resemblance to her dear husband's. She tried to look up at Robert but somehow she could not move.

She was cold, so very cold.

∽

SIR ROBERT STUMBLED WITH HIS BURDEN UP THE CLIFF against the winds drawing in from the sea below. He did not hear the roar of the waves, nor feel the spray on his face. There was no heat or sunshine that day, as befitted the task he had to fulfil. He searched the headland before him and trudged onwards until he found what he was looking for. The cave. The dragon tree, her last words to him.

He signalled to his men who followed in his footsteps with their heavy loads: their tools and wood.

They worked in silence, only the thump of the digging and the banging of the planks in place, while the wind swept the wilderness around them. Only when the burial chamber was finished did he register that the wind had ceased, and the sun had risen in the sky above.

His men were sweating in the heat of labour now, but he was cold. He had lain the shrouded shape of his wife beneath the dragon tree while he had joined his men in their dreadful task. Now, he lifted her gently and took her to her rest in the chamber. As his men raised the wooden cross on to the rough roof, he fumbled in his pouch at his belt and pulled out the strange stone and puzzling tile. He slipped them under the shroud, onto her breast. One of his men handed him the wooden box with all the rest of her treasures, her jewellery, sparse as it was, and the cloth that had swaddled her baby son the moment he was born, the moment before she had passed from this world to the next.

He made the sign of the cross and began to make his way back down the cliff to his tiny son.

He shuddered as he stumbled down the steep hillside, but he did not see the ripple in the air, a rising of the wind, a murmur of time, of worlds, as Ana's spirit rose into the air above the island they had thought was their haven from the storms.

CHAPTER 19

VIV

Viv shuddered. She felt a chill rising through her body. As her grandmother used to say, 'someone stepped on my grave.' More certainly than ever, she knew that something was very wrong with Ana d'Arafet. She'd felt her cold, her suffocation, her isolation. And those voices were still there, elusive, in the back of her head, if only she could grasp them.

She picked at her chicken casserole.

"But what does she want of you, this Ana d'Arafet?" Rory ate quickly but nodded towards Viv. "Don't let your lunch go cold."

"I'm not entirely sure. But I think it's something to do with the fossil ammonite that my parents found in the dig at Machico. And something else too. An azulejo."

"Those blue and white Madeiran tiles you see everywhere?"

"Yes, but there's one connected to Ana d'Arafet that's different. And somehow it had great significance for her. I need to find out more about that. And there seems to be something important connected to the history of the island."

"So, how is all this to do with the church? With those odd events?"

"I don't know. But there was something I saw in the museum about a legend of a lost azulejo tile bearing both Christian and Arabic symbols intertwined. And I had a strange feeling, a memory even, about Ana d'Arafet puzzling over a shrine of some kind and exactly that sort of tile she found there."

"How strange." Rory frowned. "What would that signify?"

"I'm not sure. But also, in the museum there was an information board about Ana d'Arafet and Robert Machym. And, Rory, her name is spelled with one 'n'..."

"Like our Ana?"

"Yes."

"But you thought that the name might have come from some distant ancestor?" Rory shook his head.

"I know. But maybe that was not the reason why I thought of that name, that spelling."

Rory nodded vaguely and Viv knew that he was thinking things through. "And, wait a minute ... didn't you just say the name 'Robert Machym'? Georgina's name ..." Viv's heart quickened at the sound of her name on his lips, "her surname is Machin, surely? Is that the modern equivalent of Machym, do you think?"

"Oh God," Viv inhaled sharply. "Yes, the maître d' at the Golden Gate called her Madam Machin. I didn't really register it at the time, when we were having lunch. But, yes, I must have taken that in, at the back of my mind. And I think she said her husband ..."

"Late husband ..."

"OK, late husband, was from a shipping family. Something like that anyway. That's odd. Hmm, is that odd? Or just a coincidence? God, I don't know any more. Am I seeing connections that aren't there?"

Rory reached across the table and rested his hand on hers. "I don't know. But let's just recap. The 'slips' ... all this isn't quite like before, is it? This strikes me as being bigger, somehow. Before, when you slipped into 499 AD, it was about your mother's ancestors. It was kind of personal, a private quest. Resolving a mystery that your parents left behind."

Viv nodded. "Yes. It felt personal then. But this feels more ... I don't know ... public? No, that's not really what I mean. It *is* something about my parents, though, and resolving a mystery they left behind – through the fossil. It's something to do with my parents' dig in Machico because it's involving the fossil ammonite, somehow, which they found there. But this isn't just about my family, my ancestors. It's something about the island itself. The making of the island, way back to the beginning of time. And what happened to the island afterwards ..."

"And that's still happening now."

"God, Rory. Do you think Ana d'Arafet's somehow wormed her way into my head? Do you think she put the name 'Ana' into my mind? That's pretty frightening."

Viv felt Rory's hand squeeze hers, lightly but it still made her close her eyes. "But you named her Ana way before we came out here to Madeira, so how can it be to do with ...?"

"I don't know! Maybe she's been there all the time?"

"Look, Viv. We know that you're especially sensitive to ... well, whatever we want to call it that's in the air. That 'shape on the air' we talked about before. Some people just *are* sensitive to these things beyond the natural world. We know that I have a bit of that quality too – whether as a result of becoming a priest or whether it was the reason that I chose the clerical life in the first place. Who knows? But ..."

"But, before when it happened, I thought it was all tied up with my mother, her antecedents, the lady of the lake and all that. This is different."

"On a different scale, maybe. But the fossil came from your parents' – your mother's – excavations. And it seems that's the key."

"Hmm. The first thing, the first feeling, was back in

the UK, in the rectory, when I held the fossil in my hand, and you talked of coming here to Madeira."

"And when you were especially vulnerable after … after Ana …"

Viv rubbed her forehead and sighed. "But this doesn't really get us anywhere, does it? We come back to the same thing. What does Ana d'Arafet *want*?"

"The fossil? Or the azulejo you were talking about? The one you read about in the museum. The one with the symbols on it. The lost azulejo of the legend?"

"But why? And if I found it, what am I supposed to do with it?"

Viv reached into the pocket of her dress and stroked the hardness of the fossil, the ammonite worn smooth but the edges of the rock still sharp. She tried hard to focus her mind on the dreams, the visions, she'd had, and bit her lip in concentration. She closed her eyes tightly. "OK. Let me think …There is a woman, Ana d'Arafet I guess, and there is a clearing under the cliff by the shore. And I'm standing beside her. There's my fossil – but it's in *her* hand, not mine … and at her feet, an azulejo." Viv shivered. "She thinks it's strange, bewildering. Yet somehow she thinks it's a sign of hope, a treasure. It's holy, special. It's blue and white, brown and purple. She runs her fingers over it. There are markings on it that she can't understand. Arabic. Moorish symbols, as well as Christian, IHS. That's what's puzzling her. And filling her with a lightness, a calmness. No, an excitement. And …"

Her head felt as though her thoughts were stretched across it as she frowned with the effort of remembering fleeting insubstantial wisps of memories.

"… And there is a dragon tree."

Rory leaned forwards. "What? Like the one in the garden here?"

"Yes, but all around is desolate. A parched landscape, rocks, storm-blown. On the shore? Or is it on a clifftop? I don't know." Viv reached for a gulp of her red wine. "I just don't remember clearly enough. It's a blur."

"OK. Don't force it. I'm just thinking that the lost azulejo with the Christian and Moorish or Arabic symbols suggests something to do with the church maybe. Plus, these odd events in the church. So maybe it's lost somewhere here in the church."

"But how could it be? The fossil was found at my parents' dig in Machico, miles eastwards along the coast. And I think that's where Ana d'Arafet and Robert Machym were washed up. So that makes sense that the fossil should be found there. And presumably that's where Ana d'Arafet found the unusual azulejo too, in some area by the undercliff. Through a crevice in the rock that opened out into clearing that must have seemed magical to her in those days. Places that haven't existed for centuries, what with erosion and building development over the years."

"No, certainly nothing of that time would be left

today. It was so long ago. It's all concrete promenades and hotels now." Rory sighed.

"But my parents clearly didn't find the azulejo there in Machico with the fossil. Or at least, if they did, they didn't recover it. And how could it be anything to do with this church, so far along the coast? It said on the board in the museum that it was in 1344. But the island was deserted, undiscovered, covered in a wilderness of forest."

"So, in the same vein, what *was* this piece of azulejo that Ana found in 1344 doing at the location that eventually became Machico - a tile with inscriptions that suggest people had already discovered the island? Moors, not only Christians. Madeira wasn't actually discovered, explored, and settled until 1419. Zarco."

"I wonder ...?" Viv stared through the cut glass of her goblet of red wine and the balcony wall behind it looked distorted. A tiny gecko ran across her vision, misty and misshapen. There was something she had read about Zarco being blown in a tempest off course to a small island he named Porto Santo, holy harbour, and seeing through 'strange clouds', like the 'vapours rising from the mouth of hell', another larger island nearby, Madeira, that he was compelled to claim for his master.

"Yes, but there's something odd about its discovery. You get the feeling it was an eerie place – that there was some kind of mystery about it." She frowned. Had the explorers sensed that others had been there before, that they were not the first to find it? "Hmm. Zarco, Teixeira and Perestrello. Sent by Prince Henry the Navigator. Zarco was given the captaincy of Funchal, the most important settlement and therefore he became the most important person in Madeira – although Teixeira was given the captaincy of Machico and the eastern side of the island. I looked it all up on the internet after I'd been to the museum the first time. It appears they were sent on a kind of Christian mission or crusade against the Moors as well as to open trade routes for the Portuguese. Well, I guess those were much the same thing at the time. Prince Henry was the Grand Master of the Order of Christ ..."

"Ah, yes, I've heard of that. It came into my research too." Rory smiled across at her. "You're not the only researcher hereabouts! But it was a while ago for me. Let me think. The Order of Christ. Yes, one of the military religious orders that was involved in expelling the Moors from Portuguese territory in the fifteenth century."

"Yes. The thinking at the time was that maritime expansion was a great way to wage religious war against the Moors – or rather, to continue it and hopefully win. Double whammy." Viv pushed her plate away, although she hadn't eaten all her meal. "And I have a feeling I've read somewhere that the red cross on the Madeiran regional flag represents the cross of the Order of Christ."

"So." Rory leaned back and steepled his hands

together. "So, what if the Moors had got here first? The Christian Portuguese prince and the Order of Christ wouldn't be too keen on a history where it was the Moors who first discovered the island."

"Not the first time in history that's happened, with one country or another. They say history is written by the victors."

"And of course it *was* the Portuguese explorers who cleared and settled the island – and made it so important for trade and discovery further south."

"Oh yes, you can easily see why Prince Henry claimed it for his own. And his development of the island was incredibly significant. But we're back to the idea that it was known of and maybe effectively discovered, even partially settled, way before 1419 and Zarco. And, it seems, even before my Ana d'Arafet and Robert Machym."

Rory pulled his iphone out of his pocket and began to work his fingers rapidly over the buttons.

"Rory, I can tell you right now that I found at the museum and afterwards on the internet, that there are ancient references in text to what appears to be Madeira, going back to first century Pliny. And there are also map references going back to the twelfth century."

"Ah, found it!" He read in silence for a few moments while Viv drained her wine glass. Perhaps she'd gulped a little too quickly because she felt quite light-headed and dizzy. "Well, that's extraordinary. A real forgotten history."

Viv closed her eyes and lifted her face to the afternoon sun. All she could hear were the cries of the gulls as they swooped overhead and the singing of the birds in the trees below them in the garden. A gecko scuttled over her foot and she jumped, opening her eyes to the lush greenery of the church grounds, the palm trees, and the jewel-bright flowers. The dragon tree, reaching its bony arms towards her.

As she talked to Rory, it was like it used to be with them, sharing ideas. She realised that her belly wasn't sore and that as she thought about Ana d'Arafet and her – their – Ana, she felt the absence of pain. A peace beginning to fill her. No longer the heavy weight of loss. It was there, but not pressing her down. For the first time in ages, she felt a lightening.

"So, firstly, Rory," Viv said sleepily, "where is the lost azulejo? And secondly how to explain the story that it has both Arabic and Christian symbols? How can both groups have been here at the same time, long before Ana d'Arafet and Robert Machym? And what has it all to do with the church and John Waller? We come back to the same things, Rory."

"Hmmm, well, when I was doing my doctoral research," Rory said slowly as he put his iphone onto the table and began to drum his fingers on the ironwork beside his empty plate, "and looking at early medieval religious iconography, I didn't find any artefacts with both symbols intertwined. It appears like a time of religious warfare but what if there were sailors here prior to that, in a more united world, marking their religious peace?"

"Interesting," murmured Viv. She was feeling very sleepy. Not the exhaustion of stress, but a gentle drift of, what, something more akin to contentment? A doze here in the warming sunshine overlooking the peaceful garden would be so welcome. "I just want to know what Ana d'Arafet wants of me."

"What about having a chat to someone about the stories of the island? Maybe Georgina – is the Machin name significant? And anyway, she knows a lot about the island's history. She's remarkably interesting, a really lovely person."

Viv's eyes snapped open. Did she imagine that softening of his voice, swollen with affection – or with something more? She remembered those bright red nails of Georgina's against the white of his surplice, the way she pulled him towards her and his gentle smile as he gazed down at her.

CHAPTER 20

VIV

Viv balanced a box of gooey lemon gateau that she had bought from Pingo Doce, as she reached for the knocker on the huge studded wooden door. Georgina's house was at the very top of the Rua de Santa Maria in the old town. She'd been invited to afternoon tea. They both had, but Rory had an unforeseen emergency meeting and had to pull out at the last minute. Georgina had sounded disappointed. So had Rory.

Viv felt oddly compelled to find out more about her and perhaps more dangerously fascinated to put out tentative feelers about her suspicions somehow. She had a strange feeling that she was up to something. She couldn't very well ask either of them outright; that would be crass and if she was completely wrong, make her sound paranoid. But could she detect any 'vibes' with regard to Rory? Was she even slightly a

THE DRAGON TREE

threat? There was only one way to find out and only one way to scupper any designs Georgina may have been harbouring.

As Viv had struggled with her large tote bag and the box up the steep hill from the museum, past the painted doors of the lower part of the street, she tried not to focus too clearly on the paintings that had affected her so much that day of her first visit to the museum.

The house was evidently recently renovated to its former glory. Sideways on to the road, it was a large sprawling French-grey building with immaculately restored white architraves and cornices on its frontage, great doors and windows, freshly painted green shutters open to the beating sun. Viv could make out, behind the high garden walls, the top of a pergola covered in bright bougainvillea. It held a commanding position overlooking the ocean. What a wonderful garden to sit in, with its view of the sea and the waves rolling in to the shore.

She was impressed. Georgina had been complimentary about their little apartment but what must she have really thought?

"Oh sweetie, you made it. Here, let me take that box," Georgina cried as she opened the door wide to reveal a cool tiled hallway. She lifted the lid of the cake box and her eyes lit up. "Mmm, yummy. Well, come along in."

Viv followed her through to a large airy room at the

back of the house with huge plate-glass patio doors overlooking the wonderful lush gardens, with their manicured lawns and neat shrubberies. "What a fabulous house."

Georgina slid the cake box onto a wide pine side table and lifted the cake onto a china plate, next to a platter of sandwiches and scones and a huge teapot. "Thank you. It was getting run-down and quite neglected, so I thought I'd do it up a bit. It had been in my husband's family for many years, even though they lived in Lisbon. But then we came over and lived in Machico for years, and it was let out and I suppose we just let it go. When he died, I decided to have a change, come back to Funchal, and restore the old family place. Most people seem to think it's far too big and beautiful and grand for just me."

She gestured for Viv to sit in one of the well upholstered armchairs that faced the windows, handed her a pretty china tea plate, and offered the serving platter of sandwiches. "Take this plate and help yourself while I pour the tea."

Viv sneaked a glance around the room. She had expected Georgina to live in a small apartment as she was on her own. But this was magnificent. The walls were a subtle French grey like the exterior, the floor beautiful gleaming oak, and the furniture was modern classic: two pale blue fabric chesterfield sofas and armchairs in blue tartan. The lamps looked like something straight from a design catalogue. In fact, the whole room could have been featured in a 'beautiful homes' magazine. Georgina looked across at her.

"Yes, I know what you're thinking, Viv. But I dabbled a bit in interior design in my teens, just as a hobby, and although I wondered at one time about taking it up as a career – well, life intruded and took me on a different course. But I've never lost the knack."

"You certainly have flair." Georgina was very stylish, in every way. Her dress, in French grey to match the room, was slim, fitted, and sleek, and she wore a fine silver scarf draped around her neck and over her shoulders, photograph-ready.

They chatted for a while about nothing in particular, Viv wondering if there was an ulterior motive for the invitation to tea, but nothing was obvious. Although Georgina looked at her once or twice with sharp knowing eyes, she couldn't detect anything that might seem either worrying or, on the other hand, reassuring.

Georgina leaned forwards. "Rory was telling me that you are doing some research into the island's history?"

Viv finished her sandwich and frowned. Right. Here goes. "Well yes, but there are a number of mysteries. Perhaps the major one is about the legend of Lady Ana d'Arafet and Sir Robert Machym."

Georgina adjusted her scarf and exhaled as if she had been expecting a different response. "I see. OK. Right back to that. Well, the stories of the island tell that they were shipwrecked here, probably in Machico in the fourteenth century." She picked at her gateau with a silver cake fork. "There's little hard evidence to back that up, although it's survived in oral history since then. I remember a poem written by a chap called … oh … John Bird, I think his name was … early nineteenth century rings a bell. All Victorian florid language. Romantic style. You know, "romantic glades and verdant dales". Not really like Madeira – and certainly not in the fourteenth century. Not my sort of thing!"

"No, not mine either! John Bird, you say. OK, I need to look that up. But you seem to know quite a bit about it?"

"Oh, didn't I say? I was a bit of a poet myself at one point."

"Goodness, a lady of many talents – poet, interior designer! I didn't know. I thought you said you didn't do anything."

"Oh," she shook her head, "I never had a job, or a proper education really. Just a boarding school and then a Swiss finishing school. Learning how to be a socialite wife in those days. Not like you with your academic career. But I've got quite a good memory, especially for things I learned off by heart."

"I'd certainly be interested to hear what you know about Ana and Robert."

"Well, the poem says that Ana dies, and Robert buries her at the foot of an altar under a lofty tree and sets a wooden cross to mark the place. And that Robert leaves a message to say that if any Christians find the burial place, they should build a church on the spot."

"Oh, right. So, was it ever found, the burial place? And was there a church built there?"

"Not that survived. But of course, it would have been wooden and therefore perished long since. The poem does say that when Zarco arrived on the island he found the cross and cut down the tree and built a small wooden chapel with the timber, intersecting the pavement of the choir with Ana's bones. But all that might well be poetic licence. Just make believe."

"Oh." Viv stared at her plate. How sad. Of course, she knew that Ana d'Arafet was dead – she'd lived hundreds of years ago. But the thought that she never made it to safety in France filled her with a strange melancholy. Yet she somehow knew that was the outcome. So it looked as though she never established her court, never became a proper family with Robert. A wisp of memory floated across her mind. "Georgina, Ana was expecting a child, wasn't she? What happened?"

"A child? I don't think that comes into the poem but I have heard vague stories that have it that she gave birth to a son who survived and was taken away from the island by his father Robert, probably to mainland Portugal."

"And then?"

"Well, all I know is that my husband's family name

is possibly a corruption of Machym and that they are from Portugal. So, I suppose if the legend's true – and it's a big 'if' – we may be descendants of the couple in the shipwreck legend. But I don't know any more than that."

"Oh, that's a shame. I thought I was on to something, but it looks like it was a red herring." She stared at her plate thoughtfully. "But there is something else. The legend of the lost azulejo that I read about in the museum."

Georgina folded her mouth into a moue. "*That!*"

"You see, nobody seems to want to talk about it. Everyone avoids the subject. Why?"

"Ah, well. You see, people won't want to talk about its significance, the Christian and Moorish symbols on it. But again, there's another legend. It's said to have been found by Ana d'Arafet at Machico and kept as her treasure. For some reason it was precious to her and she asked for it to be buried along with her body. The story goes that right at the end her last request was for Sir Robert to place two treasures on her breast. I assume that one was the azulejo, but it's not known what the other one was."

But *I* know. Viv drew in her breath. And I know it's true. It's the fossil that my parents found during the dig at Machico. "I see," she said. "But the thing is, there's often truth in legend, or so I believe anyway."

"Maybe so. Some grain of truth at least. But stories are elaborated by word of mouth, in the retelling, and over the years they become something quite different. And the lost azulejo … well, that's a difficult one."

"But suppose the legend has a grain of truth in it. The azulejo wasn't ever found in or around Ana d'Arafet's burial place. According to legend, I mean?"

"No. I don't think anyone knows exactly where the burial place of the legend was supposed to be. There have been a couple of minor excavations in the general area of Machico, but nothing was ever found."

And my parents didn't find it a couple of decades ago, either. They may have found a burial place – but unlikely, and they could have found the fossil anywhere – and not the azulejo. Viv frowned and bit her lip. They would probably have known about the legend of the lost azulejo and if they had found it, they would have passed it on to her along with the fossil. So, it appears that it was moved, or stolen, or taken away by someone *before* my parents' dig. But who and why?

It was so quiet in the room that Viv had a fancy that she could hear Georgina's soft breathing. Viv looked up and saw that she was leaning towards her, a puzzled expression on her face.

"But, sweetie, I do remember that there was a strange story my husband told me that was from his childhood. About a rock, with something in it. Something from the beginning of time, they said, apparently." She laughed. "Well, that's what they always called it. But it may have been from the beginning of the island. What was in it he didn't know.

As a child, he said he always thought it was gold. Something precious. Childish imaginations conjure up something magical, don't they, and probably gold was the nearest thing he could think of to magic. Like pirates' gold." Georgina leaned back into the armchair and smiled wistfully. "He used to talk about wanting to find it. Sometimes he went off stomping around Machico. But he never found anything." She frowned. "But you've made me think, maybe that had something to do with Ana d'Arafet's other treasure." Her voice echoed across the room and faded.

Viv's head swam and her vision blurred. The 'other treasure', the rock from the beginning of time, was her fossil. She was sure of it. She thought about Ana d'Arafet lying cold in her grave with her treasures on her breast and it was as though she could see it there across the room, under the window, hazy in a shaft of sunlight yet enclosed in thick darkness. Her hand pressed her own chest and it felt cold, although the air was warm, close even. A waft of memory floated across her mind: someone, a man with cruel eyes, searching, groping in the dark. She shuddered.

"Are you all right, Viv?"

"Help me! Help me!" An echo, away to another time, another place, swirling across the worlds, across the centuries. Crying in the dark.

Her mind clutched at Rory's words about seeing things clearly when you're not blinded by the light. Walking in the dark.

All at once she knew what it was that Ana d'Arafet wanted of her. The fossil and the special 'lost' azulejo somehow must be reunited before Ana's spirit could rest and the haunting cease.

And she so much wanted the haunting to cease. If she could rid herself of that burden that was weighing her down, she could have the strength to cope with everything else. A drift of air lifted itself up around Viv, as if she had found something of importance and her heart floated. Seeing clearly now. The feelings she had at the Curral, the sense of clerical robes, nuns' robes.

"Viv?" Georgina was leaning forward and touching Viv's hand.

She shook her head, trying to clear the images there. "Georgina, do you know anything, anything at all ... can you remember *anything* your husband told you about any stories of descendants of Ana d'Arafet and the son who was possibly taken to mainland Portugal after her death? Anyone further in the line? Anything about a ...nun?"

"Well, as I said, it's all legend, oral stories, folk tales. Nothing concrete. Nothing true. But ..." she frowned in concentration. "But I do remember something that was said about a girl who was sent to the Santa Clara monastery as a nun, who was said to be a long distant relative of Ana or Robert Machym. Some connection with Zarco too – you know, the discoverer of Madeira. And, oh, something about a child born in the convent

… but it's all gossip and rumour. Who knows what the truth is now."

"The Santa Clara convent?" A waft of recognition drifted across Viv's mind.

… a great religious edifice rising up, like the abbeys she knows, but so much bigger, grander. Women she knows, somehow, are nuns, in their black robes and wimples, moving quietly through the corridors and halls. A peace fills her heart. One of the women, no more than a girl, slips her hands beneath her outer robe and she knows that she is stroking the stone and the tile she keeps there, hidden.

Where had that feeling come from? And Ana's voice whispering through her mind. So, she needed to investigate the Santa Clara convent or monastery, or whatever it was called now. Did the fossil and the azulejo make their way there for some reason?

But Viv had the fossil. It was right here in her bag at her feet. Always with her, wherever she went. She'd have had it in her pocket, had there been pockets in this dress. Did Ana d'Arafet want it again? But Viv would never let it go. What if Ana wanted it not only reunited with the azulejo but both of them somehow *returned* to her?

No, that was never going to happen. The fossil was her mother, her lost parents, her own lost baby Ana, her grief. She could never let it go.

She would find the lost azulejo because it intrigued her. It was almost like a fascinating quest into history, just like that strange time before when she touched the life of Lady Vivianne in the late fifth century and their lives became entangled. That, too, was a quest. Yet this was not the same. This was no time slip, no inhabiting another body in another age. This was just a glancing brush with time, a graze. An interest. An obsession, maybe.

She wouldn't be drawn in to any demands, however persistent Ana d'Arafet might be. She would keep control, call the shots. She would bring them back together again and keep them somewhere safe. Then maybe Ana d'Arafet would stop the haunting.

But where on earth was the lost azulejo? Someone, somewhere, must know something.

Later, as she made her way back down the steep street from Georgina's house, she realised that she had been so absorbed by the legend that she had not managed to discover anything at all about her suspicions regarding Georgina's designs on Rory.

CHAPTER 21

VIV

The cobbled street up to the Santa Clara convent was so steep that Viv had to stop half way up to catch her breath. As she turned to look back the way she had come, she felt she could have toppled over and rolled back down again.

She fumbled for a tissue from her bag and wiped her brow and the back of her neck. It was mid-morning and the sun was searing overhead. The houses close on either side of the street were in sharp relief and even the view right down towards the ocean was exceptionally clear. She could make out the sea sparkling between the buildings down below.

She was glad to make it to the huge wooden gates of the convent. Set in high white stone walls she could barely see through a chink in the wood. She tugged at the old bell-pull and a voice emanated from the small box she hadn't noticed at the side. The gates began to open and through them she could see the cool shade of a garden and hear the sound of splashing water, a fountain in the courtyard beyond perhaps. She had read that the convent was of the Franciscan Sisters of St Clare. Were these the Poor Clare nuns she'd heard of, she wondered, as she saw the statue of the saint set into a niche on the wall above the entrance across the courtyard. Santa Clara was dressed in dark vestments, robe and cloak held with a simple rope around her waist, a white wimple and black hood on her head. In her left hand she carried what looked to Viv like a shepherd's staff topped with gold, and in her right a strange round object rather like a barometer face.

Viv breathed in the cool sanctuary of the outer courtyard, all white stone walls, potted flowering plants and trees. She could imagine the nuns sitting quietly on the raised stands at the base of the walls, in the shade of the trees, heads bowed over their religious books.

"*Bom dia. Posso te'ajudar?*" Good morning. May I help you?

Viv turned to see a nun, small and slim, fresh pink-faced, with delicate features, hands crossed demurely in front of her waist.

"Oh, thank you. I'm English. I'm afraid I don't speak Portuguese – not much anyway."

"*Claro*. Of course. My English is good. We are all taught well in school. Because of the tourists."

"You were taught in a ... er ... normal school? I mean, not here in the convent?"

"I came here after school. But we have classes here too. We are no longer the closed order of St Clare. Not since two hundred years. But your purpose today?"

"I'm Dr Viv DuLac and I'm doing some research into a young nun, maybe a novice, who lived here in the convent many centuries ago. Possibly early on in its history. I'm sorry, I'm being vague, but I have little to go on. I think she may have been a descendant of – or had some personal connection to – Zarco."

"Zarco? I see. Well, we have no records way back because much of the early convent building was destroyed in the pirate attack of the mid sixteenth century. But the person who had the convent built was indeed João Gonçalves de Câmara, Zarco's grandson. That was in 1496."

"Ah, that's disappointing about the lack of records. I'd hoped there might be something ... But maybe if I could get some idea of the feel of the place? Particularly the older parts of the convent."

The nun smiled. "Look, let me show you round."

"That'd be great."

"I'm Sister Clare, obviously named for our founder. Follow me."

Viv was led through cool cloisters, heavily roofed with dark wooden beams, and partly decorated with the familiar blue, white and gold tiles. She peered at them but knew that there would be no way she could

THE DRAGON TREE

identify a single special one. It had to be on its own hidden somewhere, surely? "Oh, these Moorish tiles again!"

"Yes, they decorate most of our churches and public buildings. Originally Arabic I know but now so common throughout Portugal that they are simply regarded as part of the traditional culture, almost European. In all our Catholic churches."

"We're Anglican."

"Ah. But in your English church too."

"Yes, indeed. Behind the altar. My husband is the interregnum priest."

"I see. Yes. I've heard many things about him." She caught Viv's glance. "All good."

Sister Clare walked quickly but steadily along the cloistered walkways and Viv followed in her wake, feeling like a pupil following her master. Through the steeped arches and colonnades, she saw the inner courtyard, lush and verdant with fruit trees and vegetable bushes.

"The nuns grow their own food?"

Sister Clare paused and turned. "Yes, as much as we can. But to be accurate," she winked, "we are quite a rich order. Land and sugar mills and rents. We are not so poor. And from the start, the order took in only the daughters of wealthy noble families who brought their dowry for the order. Apart from one or two charity cases."

Viv raised her eyebrows, thinking that she had

always associated nuns with vows of poverty. Perhaps not the Poor Clare's order. But maybe the order gave away their wealth? She needed to do some research into it.

The only sound was the swish of Sister Clare's robe that swept the floor in front of Viv as they walked through the peaceful cloisters, turning corners until Viv wasn't sure which way they had come. There was not even the noise of distant traffic or birds in the courtyard. Viv could well believe that the nuns who lived here now and for centuries before felt themselves in a place far removed from the outside world. She knew that they ran some kind of nursery but today there was no sound of children playing and Viv could hardly imagine that there ever could be, so deep was the silence.

Sister Clare stopped suddenly, and Viv nearly barrelled into her. "This might interest you. It is what is left of the sixteenth century reredos rescued from one of our chapels that was destroyed in the pirate attack in 1566."

She stood aside and Viv stared at the huge old faded triptych that had clearly once been brightly gilded. It was characteristically ornate and beautifully carved and topped with detailed angels bending down over the central panel. Viv saw that the central image appeared to be of Mary and the visitation of the angel Gabriel. But her eyes were drawn to the panel to the side. It seemed to depict a rural Madeiran scene with

THE DRAGON TREE

three figures, one a young woman. She felt lured in to the face of the girl, pale, serious, slightly frowning, even resentful, and a cold shiver ran up her body and the silence of the cloister seemed to enfold her. A frisson of recognition. Yet she did not know who it was.

Sister Clare's voice gently slipped into Viv's consciousness. "We believe the girl in the painting might have been one of the novices at the convent at the time. The face is not the usual image for our religious icons. It is strange. Because a reredos, you might know, is the altar-piece, the large painting that hangs behind the altar. It is normally a piece that draws the eye for contemplation, for meditation. Yet this looks like a depiction of a loved one. Sometimes artists did use their family members in their paintings. Clearly this was someone special. But come ..."

The nun set off again along the walkway and Viv hurried to follow but looked back to the reredos. The eyes of the girl seemed to follow her, and the feeling of recognition remained with her as she processed further into the depths of the convent.

"This is the oldest part of the building," said the nun and her voice was barely more than a whisper. She paused in front of double doors, wooden and arched, lying open onto a tiny chapel. "The azulejo floor is protected. It is the remainder of the sixteenth century."

Viv peered inside, hesitating on the threshold, as the incongruous sound of a mobile ringtone pierced the silence. Sister Clare delved into the folds of her robe and pulled out an iphone.

"I apologise. I must take this. Please to walk around further. I will catch up to you shortly. I must ..." and she flapped her hand vaguely and scurried away back through the cloisters.

Viv turned back to the little chapel. The altar and highly gilded reredos over it looked hugely disproportionate to the tiny room. Small as the chapel was, the azulejo tiles swept not only the whole floor but also the walls from floor to ceiling in a dazzling profusion of patterns. Her chest tightened and she clutched the door jamb as the room seemed to sway and judder. Her other hand crept into the pocket of her jeans and met the fossil nestling there.

A sense of claustrophobia took away her breath. A dreadful feeling of being enclosed, trapped, enveloped her. Her eyes darted desperately around her but there seemed to be no escape. Behind her were the same hypnotising azulejo, merging and separating. Then as she looked back towards the altar and the reredos, she thought she saw a figure, dark, heavy-robed, standing before it. The figure turned and moved softly towards her.

"Ana?" Viv's voice hardly made an imprint on the air. But as the face raised and the eyes met hers, she realised it was not the Ana who haunted her dreams, but the face from the triptych. And the eyes were full of appeal.

The figure moved past and through the cloisters. Viv had no choice but to follow as she had followed Sister Clare, although she could no longer see the figure clearly in front of her, only a faint shadow.

How she found herself in the nuns' choir she had no idea. The choir stalls set around the plain room seemed to stare back at her, dark chestnut wood, stark and bare, with an angel's face above each one, wings picked out in gold paint. All exactly the same, anonymous. Except for a large bishop's throne to the side and a misericordia, high backed and topped with a gold crown, which Viv somehow knew was the stall of the Mother Superior. It held her gaze and her heart began to palpitate.

She turned. Her eyes blurred and she found herself staring through an iron grille, thick wooden doors on either side. She heard the soft swish of heavy robes sweep the floor near her and the sense of many women gathered around her, yet not touching, feeling isolated in this crowd: no reaching out to her, no sympathy emanating from the other hearts that beat here. Cold, alone.

She could see, through the small wider gap in the centre of the grille, an opening out into a large chapel, a vast ornate gold altar and reredos before her at the far end of the nave. Like the tiny nuns' chapel, this one too was decorated with a confusion of patterned azulejo, from floor to ceiling. Looking up, she saw the coffered ceiling, dark beamed and painted with flowers and there, coming into focus, a boat, a cog. A sweep of white before her and she felt compelled to lower her eyes. A stone set in the floor and an inscription carved into it. She could only make out some of the words, but a name stood out above the others. João Gonçalves Zarco de Câmara.

Viv's hand slipped into her pocket again. A chill swept through her body and the familiar zigzags of a migraine pierced the side of her right eye. The grille shuddered.

The rustle of robes pressed in upon her and she felt trapped, struggling to breathe. Whispers, impatient, annoyed, a name "Sister Agnes! Sister Agnes! Take the eucharist and move aside!"

But my name is not Sister Agnes. It is Anja-Filipa and my uncle is João Gonçalves Zarco who built this island. She turned crossly to the novice behind her and hissed. And my grandmother is Lady Ana d'Arafet who discovered it.

CHAPTER 22

ANJA-FILIPA

1566

"Oh, Novice Sister Agnes, your uncle is *not* Zarco the great explorer and your grandmother is *not* some great noblewoman called Lady d'Arafet. Neither did anyone of that name discover this island." Mother Superior sat, barely concealing her quivering flesh, behind her huge cedar desk in her huge cedar panelled study and looked at Anja-Filipa from under long dark lashes. "As abbess of this convent, I must ask you, no, demand of you, that you stop this fantasising." She sighed with a long exaggerated exhaling of air.

Anja-Filipa caught the odour of onions and fennel wafting over towards her. She sat dutifully on the hard bench to which she had been guided for the second time this week. Dutifully, but with hands clenched out of sight under her scapular. And I am not even a proper novice sister, she pouted silently, her frown nearly meeting her down-turned mouth. Dare she speak?

"I am indeed a descendant!" Her words spurted out.

"My dear, you are not any relative of the great Dom Zarco." Mother Superior leaned forwards ledging her ample bosom on the desktop. Anja-Filipa noticed that she had a smear of paint on her cheek and guessed that the abbess had been working the portrait that was propped up under the window. "Please get this clear in your mind, once and for all. Your distant relative came over with João Gonçalves Zarco in his ship. You know the story. You have been told of it so many times. He was some ..." Mother Superior shook her head "... some cabin boy, one of the crew, or some such. A hundred and fifty years ago! Dom Zarco could not be your uncle. And as for this Lady Ana ..."

"But my mother told me the stories of my family," Anja-Filipa retorted. "And she did not *lie*."

"Sister Agnes! Please! Enough of this disobedience. Off to your cell and three Hail Marys for penitence." She took a long deep breath and closed her eyes a moment. "Be pleased to be back in the chapel for compline in a calmer frame of mind. Before I despair of you."

Anja-Filipa had barely reached the door before Mother Superior spoke again in a weary voice. "Oh, my dear Anja-Filipa. Your dear mother, despite her condition when she arrived here, was so sweet and kind, she would have been filled with sorrow to hear you now. Her beloved child without a father, yet so well loved, despite the making of you. And yet I cannot let you go. You have a great mind and readiness for book learning ... when it is not filled with stories." Her voice softened. "You must control this crossness. I am trying so hard, with God's grace, to be patient, and I know that at some point the Lord will reward my patience with a gentler humbler member of our convent. And I trust He will in time make you a good nun, as your gentle mother was." She shook her head slowly. "You are my trial and my future salvation. But now, Novice Sister Agnes, go and think upon your sins."

Anja-Filipa wiped her sweating palms on her novice's robe and bowed her head, as much as anything to conceal her smile. Despite it all, she liked Mother Superior, if only because she knew that she had doted on her mother and helped her in her birthing. And she knew that even in her high position as head of the convent she had, for some unaccountable reason, a deep affection for her wayward novice. She was only *a little* afraid of her.

"In fact," Mother Superior's voice rang out again. "As I saw that smile, you will say your rosary in full, five decades and on each give thought to the Joyful Mysteries, with particular contemplation on humility, purity of mind, and detachment of the things of the world. Go now."

The cloisters were quiet as she made her way back to her cell, the others had returned to their tiny rooms for silent contemplation before their tasks and then compline. She opened the arched wooden door and felt the breeze from the open window at the far side of the bare stone cell. Oh dear, she had forgotten to close it again and the shards of azulejo that her mother had given her, had been blown to the stone floor, smashed into tiny pieces of blue and white and brown-gold.

Reflexively her hand went to the folds of her robe and inside the thick rough fabric of her scapular she found her mother's little leather pouch. Inside the thin worn material, she could feel the two treasures her mother had left her: the precious stone with the curled creature within it and the strange azulejo, unlike any she had seen covering the convent walls. Her fingers traced the raised letters I and H and S, then the markings like ancient runes below. Always with her. Safe.

She bent to brush up the shards by the window and looked out at the courtyard garden. She loved to stand there on the tiny balcony as if she could watch the leaves unfurl and the flowers break open their buds. More than that, she loved to work in the garden between her studies and the canonical hours that marked the day into divisions.

Anja-Filipa picked up her worn leather-bound

breviary, her little Book of Hours that sped the time through to the night, when, after compline, she could lie on her hard wooden bed and read by her single tallow candle, imagining her ancestors and playing out the stories her mother used to tell her. Now, she sat on the edge of her bed and opened the old book, the only other thing left to her by her mother and the only item allowed by the convent, the other treasures being kept hidden and secret always within her robes.

It was so beautifully illuminated, with reds and blues and bright clear gold pictures decorating the script, the margins and every first letter on every page. Her mother had told her it was very precious, extremely valuable, and that Mother Superior only allowed her to keep it because it came from someone particularly important and special whom she could not deny. She liked to think it had belonged to her father, whoever he was. Her mother had told her so little of her immediate beginnings, only about her ancestors.

The page she liked best was the one with a strange shaped tree, all stretching branches like the claws of a dragon, and dripping blood that merged with the capital O of the first letter of the page. She liked to imagine the tree marking the burial place of her ancestor, as her mother had told her. Lady Ana d'Arafet. Even her name sounded romantic on Anja-Filipa's lips. As she traced with her finger the image on the page, she shaped in her mind the old story, her mother's sweet soft voice caressing her. How wonderful to have such a husband as Sir Robert Machym, who loved her so much that he was heart-broken when she died in childbirth. Anja-Filipa's heart fluttered as she thought of that dear man and of how even more heart-broken he would have been had he known that his own relative, his son or his son's son, she couldn't remember, had stolen the precious treasures that he had buried with her, the strange stone and the unusual azulejo. She screwed up her mouth as she tried to recall ... was that the Filipe she was named for? Yet why would she be named for a thief? But she knew with absolute certainty that she and her ancestral line were named also for Ana d'Arafet, all save her mother who was named Maria for the kin of João Gonçalves Zarco de Câmara. *That* Maria, along with her sister and cousins, had founded the convent that Zarco built many long years ago, when she was sent away in disgrace because she bore a child without the sacrament of marriage. Just like her own dear mother, who had come in the same condition to Santa Clara, belly full with child, and been embraced by Mother Superior.

A soft knock on her door rent Anja-Filipa's dreams and she heard the quiet voice of Mother Superior whispering,

"Have you completed your rosary, Novice Sister Agnes?"

THE DRAGON TREE

Oh, Lord! "Oh, yes, Mother," Anja-Filipa called, crossing herself against the lie.

"That is good, child, and God's grace be with you in silent contemplation until the compline bell."

She held her breath until she heard the abbess's footsteps retreat down the cloisters. Then, the breviary still open on her lap, she quickly tugged at the pins that held her black veil in place and pulled it off, thrusting it beside her on the bed cover. But as she unpinned her wimple from the filet, she felt a sharp stab and realised that she had, in her haste, pricked her finger. Gasping, she watched as the bright red droplets of her blood fell onto the breviary page, merging with the blood of the dragon tree. She sucked her finger. Only a little had smeared the white of the wimple and filet, and she decided that she could easily wrap it back under her veil so that it did not show. As long as she was careful to bow her head in a semblance of meekness ... not, perhaps, a bad thing today.

Her cropped hair felt itchy and she scratched her scalp. She would never get a husband like Sir Robert Machym with this hair! But then she frowned. Obviously not. Not confined to the convent, seeing only the fishermen at a distance when they came to the main door with the market women on Thursdays when she was tending the garden. And anyway, a man like Sir Robert would hardly be a fisherman, would he?

She frowned, turned the page of the breviary to the liturgy and untangled her rosary from her belt. It was her mother's rosary that she had inherited, and she had always told her when, as a small child, she had allowed her to play with the beads, that they were gold because it was most precious and passed down the female line from Lady Ana d'Arafet. She knew that it was not like the simple plain beads of the novices' rosaries. As she began to tell the beads, one by one, and soundlessly mouth the Pater Noster and Gloria Patri before her five decades of the Ave Maria, she did not notice that a drop of her blood had also smeared the gold.

When she got to the contemplation on humility, she decided to humbly reflect for a moment on her lie to Mother Superior a few moments before, but certainly not on the declarations about her family that the abbess had said were lies. She knew that they were not.

~

ANJA-FILIPA WRIGGLED ON HER HARD WOODEN STALL IN the nuns' choir. She was trying hard to keep her head bowed so that the blood on her filet did not show and Mother Superior smiled at her and nodded. But she raised her eyes carefully from under her long dark lashes, as she looked across at the novice opposite, Sister Margaret, her friend. Margaret was much more pious than her, chin low to her chest, but somehow she sensed Anja-Filipa's look and flicked up her glance and they exchanged a smile.

"Phew," she mimed, puffing her breath upwards and briefly rolling her eyes to the heavy-beamed and painted ceiling. Margaret had walked slowly through the cloisters to the nuns' choir, holding up the novices behind her so that Anja-Filipa had time to catch up the end of the line, late as usual.

The gilded wooden angel with outstretched wings carved above each stall looked to Anja-Filipa as though it was sitting on Margaret's head and she suppressed a giggle. Mother Superior was rising to begin compline and the giggle was, thankfully, drowned out by the opening prayer. Obediently, she mouthed the liturgy but the hymns and sung responses she shared with gusto. She loved the singing and felt her heart soar.

~

IT WAS A FEW DAYS LATER THAT SHE SAW HIM. Something made her look up from her hoeing around the fennel plants in the garden. He was standing at the edge of the cloisters by the main door, across the garden, and he was staring at her as she straightened up. Her hand went quickly up to adjust her wimple and coif that had slipped almost over her eyes. Normally she had no care that her soil-dirtied fingers might have left a mark on her cheeks, but now she bit her lip and tweaked her scapular over her gown.

He was the most handsome, comely man she had ever seen. Well, of the very few men she had ever seen, if truth were known. The bishop, the only man she saw regularly, was fat and his jowls wobbled as he spoke at mass. But this man was tall, slim, strong-looking and muscular, and his face was kind and generous, with a long noble nose, a high forehead and large bright smiling eyes. How was it that she could register each of his fine features from the far side of the garden? It was as though he was in sharp focus. How was it that she could know for certain that she would never ever again see such a creature?

He smiled at her. And of course she smiled back. It would surely be rude not to, would it not? But even so, her smile was tentative as if she were trying it out for the first time.

It was a Thursday, the day she knew that the old wizened fishermen and plump market women came to the convent with their wares but his features looked like those of a nobleman, though his drab tunic, hose and boots marked him out as a fisherman. Yet she had no doubt that she had never seen this man before. He had dark thick hair and as she watched him, fascinated, he raked his hand through his curls. And her heart stopped. She clutched hard onto the hoe to stop herself falling, for she thought she would faint clean away. A rush of heat swept down her body from her face, pooling at the top of her thighs.

He raised his hand and moved as though to approach her through the garden. She stood still, hardly daring to breath. What would he say to her? How would she reply? But there was a murmur of voices back along the cloisters and he turned away to greet the nun who was supervising the kitchen that day. As he was led away, he glanced back towards her.

It took a few moments for her to breathe normally again. She had never felt like that before, except perhaps a little at night when she dreamed of Sir Robert Machym and the story of his great love for his Ana.

Dazed, she became aware of a movement in the cloisters above her and the mist cleared from her eyes to show Mother Superior, one hand on the balcony rail and the other gesturing for Sister Margaret to come down the steep stone steps to the garden. Anja-Filipa realised that it was now time for Margaret to take her turn with the hoe. She finished jabbing the soil in front of her and handed the hoe to her friend.

"It is so peaceful down here ..." Sister Margaret began, breathing in, and Anja-Filipa knew that she smelled the earthy scent of the fennel and carrots and beans, as she did.

"Margaret! Margaret! I have had a revelation!" Anja-Filipa whispered urgently.

Sister Margaret straightened up, her hand planted

firmly on her chest, and smiled, eyes bright with hope. "Sister Agnes, you have seen the saints? The light of God at last?"

Her friend turned down her mouth and her shoulders sagged as she expelled a short sharp sigh of impatient breath. "No, of course not. For goodness sake! But I saw ..." She shook her head in wonderment. "I saw a man the very image of a God."

Sister Margaret clutched her friend's sleeve and tugged it roughly. "*Please* ... Sister Agnes," she hissed low under her breath, "that is blasphemy!"

"No, no, I did not mean ... I would not put you in such a position, Margaret, to hear blasphemy, believe me. You have been such a friend to me, especially since my dear sweet mother passed from this world to be with the Lord." She crossed herself quickly. "I simply mean that I saw a man, young and ... and oh so comely and fine and noble, and, oh, he smiled at me ..."

As Anja-Filipa told of her experience, Sister Margaret's hand relaxed and she stroked her friend's arm gently. For a few moments she did not respond but nodded softly and Anja-Filipa knew that she was choosing her words carefully as usual.

"I would guess that this young man is a fisherman from the eastern quarter of Funchal, the street they call Rua Santa Maria, where the new Capela do Corpo Santo was built in the square. I remember the little fishermen's cottages there when I was a small child before I came to the convent." She lowered her head and Anja-Filipa waited for her to speak again. "Indeed, my lost father and mother lived there when I was a baby. God rest their souls."

"Your father was one of the fishermen?"

"Yes. My grandfather and father helped to build the capela and my older brothers worked on the azulejo decorations there."

Anja-Filipa frowned. "I did not know anything about your family."

"No. Nor I yours. But we should not be talking of them," Sister Margaret admonished, smoothing her scapular and robe nervously. "Our vow is to put aside our worldly family when we are brought into the family of Christ here in the convent. We have vowed to keep nothing of our past lives in our hearts, but only to keep truly to Christ."

"Well, yes I know that." Anja-Filipa also knew that was why Mother Superior dismissed her talk of her ancestors and only allowed mention of her mother Maria, because she too was a nun and so of the family of Christ. That was permissible. "But you know also that I did not take my vows properly as a novice but only the most basic simple vow of poverty, chastity and obedience, so that Mother Superior could in all conscience let me wear the habit from my mother."

"But, "Margaret protested quietly, "that was four years ago when you were twelve, and you have spent your whole life here ... you were born here. So you must keep to the vows and ways of the convent."

"I know it is wise to do so. But it is so hard. I am not pure and pious and *good*, as you are, my dear Margaret." She sighed. "I wish I were. My life would be so much easier."

Sister Margaret laughed, then stopped and looked around guiltily. "Sister Agnes, it is not so easy to be a good novice. And the religious life here is not easy. But we must also be thankful that we are not across the oceans in England where I am told the young queen Elizabeth has little mercy on those of the old faith and continues her father's work to destroy all the monasteries and nunneries. If we were indeed there, over the seas, we would be thankful to have such a life as we have here, even though it is not an easy one."

Anja-Filipa's mind flickered with images of gardening and cleaning the refectory, of cooking and scrubbing the kitchens, sewing … oh, all those habits to repair that were wearing thin… and, goodness, all those prayers, eight daily sessions. But most of all the silent times and the contemplations. "No. You are right. It is not an easy life. And certainly not when you are faithful to your vows." She smiled at her friend, looking so serious, so earnest. "You are my rock and my best friend."

She saw Sister Margaret's mouth open to say something and wondered if she would say "your *only* friend!" but she did not. Instead she stretched her lips into a down-turned smile and briefly touched Anja-Filipa's arm.

Back in her cell, she looked through the window to see Sister Margaret hoeing the vegetable garden energetically, bowed over at the waist intent upon her task. The bell rang out and she knew that it would soon be time for Sext, the sixth hour of prayer and after that, thankfully, midday dinner in the refectory. In response to the thought, her stomach grumbled loudly and to distract herself she sat on the bed with her breviary.

Thinking back to her whispered conversation with Sister Margaret, she turned to the first page and squinted at the swirling signature there. The words were written by a confident hand, a triumphant flourish with elaborate curlicues, and difficult to read. They drifted in and out of focus, but she was sure that the final word was 'Zarco'.

CHAPTER 23

ANJA-FILIPA

1566

Anja-Filipa raised her eyes to silently thank the serving novice who was laying a dish carefully and quietly in front of each nun in the refectory. She sniffed at the steam arising from her bowl and knew that it was onion soup again, but also that the hens had been laying well once more because there was a small poached egg on the top. Another server offered her a platter of thick bread hunks and her mouth watered at the thought of the rich salty butter fresh from the convent dairy that she would soon be smearing, as thickly as she could manage without Mother Superior noticing in her elevated position up at the top trestle table.

She could not get the image of the beautiful young man out of her mind as Mother Superior said the Latin grace, and her hand trembled a little when she picked up her spoon. Yet she felt an unusual sense of peace fill her soul as her mind dwelled upon him. It was as though she had found something of immense importance to her, although she had no idea what it could be. Her heart, that was always so much in turmoil, felt more at peace than she ever remembered since her mother died. She felt happy. And hopeful because she just *knew* that something wonderful was in store for her. Perhaps something outside the confines of the convent. Maybe. Head bent, she smiled to herself.

There was a clatter of spoons against bowls and she looked up, startled from her reverie. A moment of silent alarm. Then voices rising to a babble of shock and fear. She turned to Sister Margaret at her side.

"What is happening?"

Sister Margaret's mouth dropped open and she gasped as she looked wildly between Mother Superior and the refectory doors opposite through which two priests and the bishop stumbled, their robes awry and faces red with exertion.

Mother Superior was standing, white faced, supporting herself with her hands on the table top. "What is the meaning of this intrusion at table ... your Grace," she added with a nod to the bishop.

"Abbess! Terrible news has reached me." He drew to a halt in front of the top table but from her position at the side table Anja-Filipa could see his jowls shaking and his hands trembling violently. "You must all leave. At once."

He bent towards Mother Superior and spoke low but by his tone Anja-Filipa could tell his words were urgent. The older nun before him nodded and responded quietly. He and the priests bowed and moved back towards the door. Mother Superior waited a moment in thought before she spoke, but her voice was strong and clear.

"My dear Sisters of Santa Clara, we must be calm and assured in the hope and protection of the Lord. But the word is that a ship of corsairs from France has landed at the cove to the west." She paused and looked slowly around the refectory. Anja-Filipa also let her gaze sweep the nuns. They looked stunned and frightened.

"What is the problem with sailors from France?" she whispered to Margaret.

"The problem, my dear friend … is that corsairs are pirates." Sister Margaret's hands were clutching at her scapular, fists full of fabric crumpling in her palms. "I knew of such invaders, pirates, from my father when I was a small child. I have feared them ever since. They are brutal."

Anja-Filipa turned back to Mother Superior. She was continuing and her hands were trembling visibly at her crucifix, although her voice was soft and calm as the nuns' voices grew more and more agitated, echoing across the hall.

"Dear Sisters, I deem it wise to leave the convent for a while and repair to somewhere safe and quiet until all this trouble has receded." She attempted a small smile. "It will be like a … a retreat. A temporary retreat."

"Mother," called out one of the older nuns, "may I ask how temporary?"

"I do not know. But until the danger is abated. Dear Sisters, think of it as a storm at sea, but soon it will be calm waters again." She took a deep breath and Anja-Filipa's heart began to pound as the significance of the news swept through her. Leave the convent? She had never left before; she had never known the world outside. She was torn between fear of the unknown world out there and the fear of such men. And a rising sense of excitement.

"Sisters, we need to go now. Right now. They approach Funchal. Fighting delays them but they are still possibly just a day or two away. The bishop and his priests have come to help us. We go further up the hill and across the tracks to Eiro da Serrado. Return quickly to your cells and gather only small items of religious value. Take only what you truly need for our simple life to continue." The nuns' murmurings grew louder. "We must be gone and the convent closed by None, the ninth hour."

Eiro da Serrado! Into the mountains! Anja-Filipa knew that there was a wide deep valley up there in the midst of the mountains, where the volcano had made a cauldron. Her mother had told her the tales of the beginning of the island, thousands, no, millions of years ago when it had risen up from under the waves and built the mountains.

Suddenly everything became a rush of activity and noise. The serving nuns ran to collect the dishes and the remains of the food, dropping bowls onto the wooden floor in their haste, bumping into each other as they sped back to the kitchens.

A quick calculation told Anja-Filipa that she had time to gather her few possessions from her cell. Her precious stone and azulejo were always in her pouch at her waist and now she fumbled under her scapular to reassure herself that they were safe. But she must take her rosary and her treasured breviary and ... what else did she have? Nothing.

She and Sister Margaret clung on to each other's arm as they hurried along the cloisters to their respective cells. The walkways were no longer quiet but full of agitated voices and she heard snatches of frightened words: pillage, destroying houses, rape ...

Unsure what some of these meant, she felt the voices in her brain as nightmarish jumbles of terror, but one name seemed to grow large and clear as the other words fell away.

"Peyrot de Monluc!"

THE DRAGON TREE

THE TRACKS INTO THE MOUNTAINS WERE STEEP AND although the air was warm, Anja-Filipa shivered at the sight of the misty clouds that lay across the rise of the rocks above them. She stopped a moment to catch her breath. She could see the tops of the towering mountains above the clouds; they looked magical and daunting. As she moved on, she stumbled on the rocky track.

"I think that we will soon be taking the track downwards into the valley." Sister Margaret reached out for Anja-Filipa's elbow and wound her arm through her friend's.

It was not as hot up here as in the convent garden, and there was a slight breeze, but Anja-Filipa was aware of the sweat that ran down from under her arms and from her neck to between her breasts. Her heavy robes did not help. They were not for climbing mountain tracks. She could feel her linen shift beneath her gown sticking to her legs as she walked. And her wimple and filet were tight on her skin. Irritated she pushed her veil back from her shoulders, wishing she could pull the whole thing off. Wishing, in truth, that she could pull the whole habit off.

A wild goat bounded across the track and up the steep rocky crag to the side. Anja-Filipa wished that she were free to run up the hill, leaping over the rocks like the mountain goat ... if she only wore her linen shift.

"The priests are struggling," whispered Sister

Margaret, leaning in towards her friend. She glanced behind her. "Look."

Anja-Filipa turned to see the bishop and his assistant clerics hot and sweating profusely under their burdens. Gold framed paintings, icons, boxes of chalices and gold jewelled crosses. Behind them thin gnarled men pulled simple carts laden with what looked like crates, some filled with books, some with treasures of gold and silver glinting in the bright sunshine. So much wealth. Yet the nuns each individually possessed nothing. Did Mother Superior have any belongings of her own? She could not see her in the line of nuns on the narrow track.

"Do not stare so long," mumbled Margaret, pulling Anja-Filipa onwards.

Well, maybe she was the only one with precious treasures, hidden away in her pouch. Yet they may only be precious to herself and not of worldly value. She had no idea. And it did not matter, for they were her mother's and therefore beyond price. If ever she had a daughter of her own, she would pass them on to her too.

Although as long as she remained in the convent that was not likely to happen.

And then the image of the handsome man across the garden swept into her mind. Her fear and excitement gave way to a new realisation. What chance did she have of ever seeing him again when she would spend maybe years trapped in the mountains, in the middle of nowhere? This was even worse than being trapped in the convent for the rest of her life.

By the time they began their downward trudge into the valley, Anja-Filipa's calves were aching beyond anything she had ever felt before. She clutched Sister Margaret's arm even more firmly.

"I don't think I can make it!" she cried, eyes dramatically turned upwards to the sky.

Sister Margaret smiled and shook her head indulgently. "The dear Lord bless you. You must be one of the most fit and healthy of us all, with all your enthusiastic sessions in the convent garden." She patted her friend's arm. "Think of the poor elderly nuns with their arthritic legs and weak hearts."

Anja-Filipa stopped in her tracks and turned to look behind. The procession was by now very spread out along the track and she could barely see the end of the line. There were, indeed, many struggling, staggering to walk on stiff painful limbs, and a few sitting by the wayside to rest and take water.

"Yes, you are right. I am a selfish pig!"

"No, no. Do not say that. But sometimes, perhaps, you need to give your heart a little more to your sisters and their needs."

"Oh Margaret, you are too sensible and patient and good to be the best friend of such as I. Anyone would think you were as old as Mother Superior and not only a year or so my senior."

"We have had that conversation too many times

before, so I refuse to engage with it again." Margaret urged them on round the next bend in the track. "And look! Sister Agnes – see the great Eiro da Serrado ahead!"

Anja-Filipa let go of Margaret's arm and ran to the edge of the path. Looking down between the gnarled trees to the steep craggy drop to their side, grassy rocky scrubland that tumbled down to the wide valley below, she caught her breath. It was indeed like a huge cauldron just as her mother had described, the massive cliffs of the mountains rising up all around, pressing in upon her.

Her vision blurred and she felt light-headed. For a moment she thought she saw an ocean there before her in the cauldron of the mountains, a boiling ocean, and slowly a mountain rising above the waves, fire spewing from its peak, plumes of gases clouding the angry seas below, rocks flung away from the fiery explosions, and then coming into clear focus and hurtling towards her, a fragment of rock with a curled creature within it. She staggered, dizzy, and felt Margaret clutch her arm and pull her away from the edge.

"Care, Sister Agnes! You stand too close to the edge of the path! Come away."

"Yes, yes, I do not know what I was thinking. I almost fainted. Such a ... oh ..." she rubbed her eyes and her forehead. The other nuns in the line were sweeping past them, their long thick robes brushing the rocks and the fallen branches as they pushed themselves on.

She fumbled for the rock in the pouch hidden beneath her scapular. And as she did so, she felt the hot breath of someone right behind her, almost on top of her, inside her. And yet somehow it was a comforting presence. Her fingers curled around her precious rock and her breathing stilled.

"Oh, I do not know what came upon me then."

Sister Margaret patted her arm. "It is not good to look down from such a height. It makes your head sway. Are you well now, to continue down the path?"

"Yes. I am well now. But as I looked down I saw … what are those … are they buildings down in the valley? People live there?" She squinted at the path ahead but did not turn to look down into the cauldron again.

"Those are the shelters of the people, who live in this remote place. It is a small village. They farm the land here and are able to be mainly self-sufficient. It is fertile, the land of the volcano, with rich black soil, and so productive that they bring their excess produce down to Funchal for the market every so often. Had you not wondered who had made the tracks we are walking upon?"

"No, I did not think about it." Suddenly she shivered. "So … what are they like, these people? Are they dangerous?"

Sister Margaret laughed gently. "They are not

dangerous as you say. My father told me long ago that they are folk who came here to the mountains for safety and peace, a simple life. Rather like our convent. They are called the Escondidos, the hidden ones, but they welcome others who need protection. And there is a large shelter, a hall, where we can make our retreat."

"I see. That is good ... but, like us, they have little contact with the outside world?" Anja-Filipa's thoughts flickered to the beautiful young man.

"That is so. Do not be afraid. We will be safe from the corsairs here. It is too hard a journey into the mountains and they will not think to look. It is too isolated. Certainly, they will not imagine that there is anything of value here. Their efforts will be in Funchal where there are riches to be found easily."

"I am not ..." she began. She could not say that she was not afraid of the corsairs discovering their hiding place, but that her handsome young man might never find her there.

CHAPTER 24

VIV

Present day

"Oh, there you are!"

Viv turned dizzily away from the grille to see Sister Clare hurrying towards her through the nuns' choir, thrusting her iphone back into the folds of her habit. The names Sister Agnes and Anja-Filipa echoed in her head, the convent as it had been, the flight across the mountains to Eiro da Serrado. The 'treasures' that she carried with her which Viv knew were the fossil, *her* fossil, and the azulejo that she'd yet to find. And, yes, there was something else too, hovering behind her brain, if only she could clear her foggy mind.

"I was just ..." Viv did not know why she felt so guilty, embarrassed, like an intruder. Although in truth her strange feelings about a novice who lived here so long ago made her mind conflicted: an intruder into the convent's past, yet someone very much at home here, as Anja-Filipa had been. She knew without doubt that this Sister Agnes, Anja-Filipa, whose life her mind had played with, was the novice Georgina had spoken about, albeit vaguely. That she was somehow related to Ana d'Arafet and that she had possessed the fossil and azulejo at some point.

Sister Clare waved away her stutterings. "It is fine. I apologise for my absence. So rude of me. But I was expecting the call from the bishop." She smiled a little sheepishly. "Important business."

"Of course." Viv composed herself quickly. "I was thinking about the evacuation of the convent to Eiro da Serrado, to the village of the Escondidos ..." Where had that name come from? "During the pirate attack on Funchal."

Sister Clare looked startled. "Oh. The Escondidos? In English, er ... the Hidden, I think. I have not heard that name. It is possible that the peasants of the Eiro da Serrado were called that centuries ago." She frowned. "Where did you hear that from?"

Viv shook her head. "I ... I don't know ..."

"Ah well. Anyway, the area is now called the Valley of the Nuns. Curral das Freiras. That's where they fled to as the pirates invaded Funchal, looting and firing everything in their path. They reached as far as the São Laurenço Fortress."

"But the nuns were safe?"

"Yes. Of course, eventually they returned here to the convent and repaired the damage as well as they could. Monastic life continued. As you see." Sister Clare spread her arms wide.

So, if the nuns were safe and in time returned here to the convent, then Sister Agnes, Anja-Filipa, must have brought the fossil and azulejo back here with her. So where was the azulejo now? And what happened to it in the centuries since then?

Her mystery was not yet solved. But at least she had moved on a pace or two. If she could just go back into the nun's mind, and find out what happened ... Yet she knew that there seemed to be no way of creating a time-slip back again, there appeared to be no intentional trigger on her part, as far as she could tell. And that was happening in the sixteenth century; Sister Clare had told her that the pirate attack was in 1566 – and she herself had read that too. In the museum. Yes, there was a tableau of the pirates, she remembered, and she heard again Ana d'Arafet's voice in her mind: Ana in that dark cold empty place, seeing the future that would befall her precious island of safety ...

... a sweep of heavy robes, a movement and sound in the quiet of the halls. A glimpse of rough, tangled-haired men, their clothes torn and tattered, dirty, and stinking ... the nun, the girl, needs to run, to leave the halls and the cloister, the icons, and the precious paintings on the walls. To leave it all behind her, except for the treasures she clutches.

Viv frowned. Anja-Filipa hadn't actually seen the pirates, the tangle-haired men in their torn and tattered clothes, but her ancestor Ana had known them, even from her burial chamber.

She shuddered.

"Dr DuLac? Are you well?"

Viv shook her head. "Oh, I'm sorry. I was miles away there! My imagination sometimes gets the better of me. I guess it's all so atmospheric here. The history almost literally comes to life."

"It certainly does. But I'm afraid that I need to escort you back to the door, as I have the kindergarten children coming soon and I must prepare. I think we're making the saint's festive ... oh what do you call it in English? ... bunting?"

"Then I'll be on my way, and thank you for showing me around, Sister Clare."

⁓

SOMETHING WAS PREYING ON VIV'S MIND. A WISP OF A thought, just out of reach. It was as she made her way back down the steep Calçada Santa Clara that Viv, deep in thought about what she had experienced back at the convent and mulling over every detail about Anja-Filipa, remembered something. She stopped in her tracks. Amidst the confusion and fear of the nuns hearing Mother Superior's words and hurrying through the cloisters to their cells to grab their meagre belongings, a name ... *Peyrot de Monluc*. The leader of the pirate invaders.

She pulled out her iphone and googled the name. Website after website. Nothing. As she grimaced at the screen, passers-by shouted, and a car screeched its horn for her to move to the side of the street. Jabbing her finger at her mobile, making errors in her haste, she felt the frustration consume her. Then, at last, a possibility.

Yes, oh God. Peyrot de Monluc, captain of a French expedition exploring the north African coast, it said, attacked Madeira in 1566 at the cove now called Praia de Formosa ... He was also known as Bértrand de Montluc.

∽

SHE COULDN'T FIND BÉRTRAND AT THE MUSEUM. BUT Carlos was on duty at the desk and told her that he was probably having his coffee at the café down the street.

Bértrand looked up as Viv approached. He was sitting, long legs spread out, commanding the space around him, one arm casually draped across the back of the chair next to him. He wore his trademark well-cut dark suit and a crisp white shirt, open at the neck to reveal dark chest hairs and a tantalising suggestion of a muscular torso beneath. Viv noticed that the lighter hairs on his tanned hands that held a coffee cup, caught the sunlight and glinted. A couple of female tourists nearby flicked glances towards him from under their long mascara-ed lashes.

But he was looking only at her and a warm smile spread across his face. She noticed that his blue eyes crinkled in a rather attractive way. Her heart fluttered in a most unwelcome manner. She tried to hide her awkwardness with a cough. He stood up and gave a little Gallic bow. Viv couldn't help but smile in return. He gestured to the other chair at his table.

"Come. Sit with me. How fantastic to see you here. I did not expect. But I had been sitting here thinking about you, you know?"

"Me?"

"Of course. Why not? Such a beautiful and interesting lady. Coffee?" Without waiting for her reply, he gestured to the waiter and ordered her favourite Americano with hot milk, and another espresso for himself.

"So," Bértrand began, slowly inclining his head towards her. "I hope that you did not have a problem, but that you were searching for me to spend a little ... what? ... *quality time* with me?"

Viv felt herself flush. What was it about this man? It was ridiculous; he was so obviously flirting with her. Yet somehow the attention and clear attraction was strangely pleasing. Even his words and his gestures, which she would normally have dismissed as unsubtle, were calling to something within her, some need. She tried to suppress the quivering feeling in her stomach.

"Well, nice as it is to see you, I actually have a puzzle and you just may be able to help." She realised that her hands were clutched tightly in her lap. She didn't want to blurt out her suspicions in a gauche way, but at the same time she didn't want to prevaricate when this was uppermost in her mind.

"Of course." Bértrand nodded, and leaned in. "So, what is troubling you?" She could smell his heady earthy cologne.

"I've just been to the convent – Santa Clara. And I learned about the pirate attack in 1566, when the nuns fled into the mountains."

"Yes, yes. The Curral das Freiras." His smile turned to a slight frown.

"And I see that the leader of the attack was a captain, possibly a mercenary, called Bértrand de Montluc."

"Ah."

Just at that moment the waiter approached their table bringing the coffees.

"Obrigado." Bértrand spoke to him in fluent Portuguese for a few minutes and Viv shuffled on her wicker chair, wondering if he was deliberately distracting her. She poured the hot milk from the tiny jug and stirred her coffee. She frowned.

The waiter left and Bértrand composed his expression to a wistful smile, reached over and caught her hand. "Oh, my dear, lovely Vivienne. I guess we all have something in our past to hide, no?" He sighed.

"So you *are* related to this man who ... who attacked the island and pillaged and raped and forced the nuns to flee their safe lives at the convent?" Viv pulled her hand away from his and squeezed her fists together under the table, her fingernails pressing into the flesh of her palms. She wasn't sure why she was suddenly consumed with such anger but for some reason she felt personally violated. An image of nuns fleeing into the mountains flashed across her brain.

Bértrand leaned in and carefully touched her arm, then finding that she didn't brush him off, gently stroked her skin. Viv shook her head, trying to dislodge the fear that had so abruptly and unaccountably struck her heart and made it pound with dread. And as she calmed, she realised that her fear was not so much of the idea of the corsairs but of the consequences of their attack: that she would never see her beloved again. Her beloved? Rory? No, someone else. A young man who she'd never spoken to, whose name she didn't even know. Anja-Filipa's young man in the convent garden. Viv gasped. Her hands were trembling.

"Oh, my dear. It was so long ago." Bértrand sighed again. "I am so sorry that this hurts you so much. It was a disgraceful family history. But I cannot apologise enough." He withdrew his hand from her arm and took a slow draft of his espresso. "My family suffered from the disgrace for generations. But in the end, we found ways to compensate the people of Madeira, in little ways over the centuries. This was why I myself came here and made no attempt to hide my name. But I helped to promote the proud history and heritage of the island. Maybe by doing that I could ... what is the word? ... ameliorate the actions of my ancestor."

"I see." Viv took a deep breath and calmed herself. Her heart stopped pounding and stilled. "Well, I'm sure that nobody can be held accountable for the awful things their long past ancestors did, however dreadful."

Bértrand looked deep into her eyes for a moment, then slowly, as if allowing her time to pull away, reached across again and gently brushed his fingertips down her cheek.

"Viv, it wasn't *me*."

Viv shook her head, and all she could see was this man with the deep blue eyes that she was drowning in, holding her completely, her whole vision, her body and soul.

"I know," she whispered. "I don't know what got into me just then. I felt consumed with the past, as though it filled me and ... and almost ... I don't know ... devoured me."

"I think something is possessing you." Bértrand gave her a rueful smile as she shuddered.

Possessing her? She couldn't help thinking of the medieval fears of people being 'possessed' by evil forces. That was horrible. He caught her expression.

"I think that is the wrong word," Bértrand said with

a grimace. "I am sorry. I am not sure of the correct English word. I mean that something is troubling your soul and we say that you are maybe obsessed? Or maybe that is not the correct word either. Oh dear!"

"It's OK. I don't think there is a word for it, actually. Empathy, maybe?"

"Ah yes, you are very empathetic. Perhaps you are feeling strongly the stories that you saw in the museum, the one about the lovers and the one about the pirate attack. The models. They are very realistic, yes? And I think that you are a little … vulnerable at the moment."

Viv looked down at her coffee cup and dare not answer, but she heard Bértrand lean back in his chair and drape his arm across the back of the adjacent chair again.

"So," he said. "I think you need a little distraction."

Viv looked up quickly, aware of what his words might mean.

"You must come with me on my boat. Oh, don't worry! I guess it will be of interest to you as an historian. As it was to me when I built it."

"You built a boat?"

"Yes, well, clearly not on my own. I had a team to help with the work, but it was to my specification after my research. You see, I too am fascinated by the events on this island over the centuries. I built a boat to replicate the caravel that the captains Zarco, Perestrelo and Teixeira first sailed to Madeira." He shook his head sadly. "It was also to be a business project, for tourists to enjoy sailing round the coastline like the discoverers. But unfortunately, we were too slow and somebody else completed a similar one, well, a carrack, before we were ready – they called it the Santa Maria."

"Oh, yes. I've seen the tourists' 'pirate ship' in the harbour."

"Ah well. It was not to be. But I had my replica for myself. And if you would like, I can show you how it feels to be under sail. The movement of the wooden planks and the breeze in the canvas. It is soothing and sleepy. It is like going back into history."

Viv shivered. She could hear the creaking timbers and the sailcloth catching the wind, and felt the movement of the cog, gentle at first, then beginning to heave in the mounting waves. Rain lashing her face, an awful echo of splintering wood and the rush of water as the sea battered the craft, smashing and pounding the timbers. She clutched at the hard reality of the café table edge and took a deep breath.

"Do come. We can sip the Madeira wine and eat the bolo de mel and forget all the troubles."

Something within her was whispering a soft 'yes', an echo across her mind and across the centuries, yes, you must go.

She nodded. "Yes, thank you. I'd like that."

CHAPTER 25

ANJA-FILIPA

1566

"Yes." The soft whisper drifted across Anja-Filipa's mind as she paused in her task of helping to unwrap some of the icons that they had brought with them here to the retreat. They had kept some of them, including this one, wrapped for weeks until they were sure that they would not have to run again. She felt strangely compelled to unveil this one, and yet a frisson of fear rippled up her spine. She let the linen fall back onto the figure on the canvas that she had begun to reveal.

These strange whispers in her head seemed to be increasing and they made her feel uneasy. She stood, straightened her back and gazed out of the window to the mountains beyond. Every day they seemed to creep nearer to her. She wondered whether at some point she would wake to find that they had closed in upon them and that she would be unable to breathe any more. Sometimes she felt the same at the convent in Funchal, although the cloisters and her cell were airy. It was more a feeling in her heart, a tightness, that at times threatened her next breath.

Yet the air was fresh and sweet here in the curral. She had eagerly offered to make the kitchen garden for the displaced convent and spent most of the past weeks outdoors digging and planting.

She looked out at the freshly turned earth, so dark and rich, so fertile. They would have a good harvest.

"Sister Agnes," came a voice behind her and she turned from the window to see Mother Superior. "Have you forgotten what you are supposed to be doing?"

"Oh, of course not, Mother Superior. I was just releasing my back a little." She bent down again to squat in front of the huge reredos she was revealing from its linen wrappings. "Oh!"

The face stared back at her, serious, almost glowering from inside its brightly gilded frame. It was the triptych from the nuns' chapel at the convent. The image of the girl on the right-hand panel was different. She had not seen this one above the altar in the chapel, she was sure. If she had, she would have known that face anywhere.

It was herself. She shivered.

"What is this?" she breathed, swivelling round to look up at Mother Superior.

The abbess was staring at the painting, her hand on her ample bosom. "Yes, my dear, it is a portrait of you. It began as a memento of your sweet mother but then, after her passing into the next world, I changed the eyes and the mouth just a little and it became you."

Anja-Filipa reached out to touch the face on the panel, as if she would test if the paint were still wet. It was dry but she kept her hand on the face because it was not only herself but her mother that she could see. She had never realised before how alike they were.

"But why? Why did you paint my mother's portrait in the first place?" She squinted at the background scene behind the figure and knew that it was a local site. "This should be the Madeiran Madonna."

"Of course. It was. That's how I painted it originally. But as I looked at the face of the Madonna, I felt more and more that it was a likeness of your dear mother." Her voice was soft like the caress of the summer breeze upon the trees in the garden. "And so I ... adjusted it a little."

"You painted over the Madonna?" Anja-Filipa gasped. Was not that blasphemy? She was not sure, but maybe it could be, in the eyes of the church. "And why my mother ... and me?"

"Sister Ag ... Anja-Filipa, your mother was like the daughter I never had – no," she turned her eyed upwards to the heavens, "no, the daughter I had to give away. And so you are like the granddaughter I should have had."

Anja-Filipa's eye prickled and she swiped away the tears that threatened to fall. The tiny shiver of fear that she had always felt for Mother Superior, behind her liking, fell away from her, and she saw beneath the austere habit and the stature of authority, a real person with feelings, a history, a sadness that would never truly disappear. We are all of us here only normal people with dashed hopes and broken loves and sad histories, she thought. We wear the robes and wimple and veil that protect us from what might have been. Yet we hold on to what might have been, in the depths of our hearts. I am not so different, after all.

"This frowning expression on the face, Mother Superior ... so serious," she said, "but perhaps also resentful?"

The abbess smiled sadly. "Indeed. And so like you."

Anja-Filipa stood and rubbed her back. She glanced out of the window. "I would like it here if I did not feel so enclosed."

"I know. But we are safe here and it will not be for ever. We will return to Funchal, to our convent when all the danger is passed. And our cloistered life will continue."

"Exactly!" Anja-Filipa exploded and Mother Superior looked startled. "I know how well I am looked after and cosseted here and at the convent. But I want something more. I do not know what life is like out there! I want to see for myself!"

"Oh dear," the older nun touched the large golden cross that nestled on her bosom. "I had hoped that you were a little more settled in this life by now. I understand, truly I do. But ... certainly, you do not know what life is like 'out there'. It is not freedom and doing whatever you want. It is often harsh, and there is suffering and coldness and daily struggle for many. Here, even here in the stark mountains, you have beauty and warmth and you have food to eat and rest times. You have comfort and gentle companionship. Outside there is ugliness and poverty, cruelty and disgrace. I have seen it, and I have experienced it." She inhaled deeply and pulled herself up to her full height. "Believe me, Sister Agnes, you do not want to be out there in a friendless world."

Anja-Filipa wondered exactly what had happened to her before she became the abbess, what kind of cold isolated world she had inhabited. And who had made her feel so. Had she never had a love? Yet she had spoken of a daughter she had to give away. Who had made her do such a thing? A lover? Goodness, Mother Superior with a lover! She could not even imagine such a thing! But surely a man could not be so cruel as to betray his lady and his child?

The stories her mother had told her spoke of chivalrous lovers and romantic love. The tale of her ancestor Ana d'Arafet and her Robert were of a love beyond death. Her own mother's story, although never detailed, never naming, were of a love that survived enforced separation, and resulted in the grace of a much-loved child.

"Well. I must go." Mother Superior turned quickly and left the hall, an aura of unease and regret left with her, and hanging in the air, a knowledge of words that should not have been spoken.

Anja-Filipa turned back to the reredos and pulled at the remaining covering. It was, after all, a typical altar-piece for contemplation. If you looked at it from a distance it was nothing special.

"Oh, there you are!"

She turned dizzily away from the reredos to see Sister Margaret hurrying towards her across the hall, straightening the folds of her habit. She lowered her voice.

"I see your young fisherman has found us, Sister Agnes."

The room seemed to sway and Anja-Filipa's head felt so light it could almost have floated away from her body. Yet her body flushed and her heart pounded.

"F ... fisherman?" she stuttered.

Sister Margaret knelt down beside her friend. "That young man you saw in the garden at the convent. At least I think it is him. He looks as you described him – on numerous occasions! And all the others are old men, shrivelled with age, so I cannot imagine that they would have drawn your attention so well."

Anja-Filipa stood and pulled Sister Margaret up with her. "Where? Where is he?" she gasped.

"At the kitchen doorway. Where he should be. Proffering a basket of espada to Sister Leonor. I thought you might like to know."

"Yes, yes!" Anja-Filipa turned but before she reached the doorway she began to tremble. What if this man was not as she had dreamed so many times? What if he looked at her with disdain? She knew that she had no idea what to expect of him. Surely he would not have been dreaming of her as she had of him. She must calm herself and be realistic.

She composed herself and tried to straighten her scapular and wimple before she reached the kitchens, Sister Margaret following close behind.

She barely registered the elderly Sister Leonor examining the fish in a huge basket that was ledged on the kitchen table. The figure who turned at her breathy entrance held her whole vision. He was just as tall and muscular as she remembered him and as he had inhabited all her dreams for weeks, and his face was just as sweet with such a generous mouth. His large gentle eyes were turned to her and did not falter as he looked upon her disarray, clutching her hand to her breast and struggling to draw air into her lungs. He smiled.

Smiled! At her! Again – as he had done in the convent garden! Did he remember her?

Anja-Filipa tried to still her shaking hands and

calm her pounding heart. As she paused in the doorway, trying to regain some equanimity and look serene as she thought a nun should look, she took stock of him. He was clearly a fisherman, in the rough-spun tunic and pointed hat of the rank. Yet his face bore noble features and his tunic and trousers were clean white, his boots tanned leather. He pulled off his cap as he nodded to her and ruffled his thick dark curls. His eyes were smiling at her and his mouth was full, his fleshy lips parted.

"We met, I think." His voice was deep and resonant so that her heart twisted, and she felt dizzy. "In the convent garden."

Sister Leonor gasped, ready to reprimand, and her old forehead wrinkled even deeper into a frown of horror.

The fisherman caught the look and hurriedly added, "I mean that I saw you working in the garden. I saw you across the fennel plants."

Anja-Filipa bowed her head and felt her filet slip. Under her lashes she glanced up at Sister Leonor. "Possibly, sir. I am often in the garden. I mean, I was. I still am, here ..." She drew an unsteady breath. "I like gardening."

"Novice Sister Agnes! What, in fact, have you come to the kitchens for, precisely?" The elderly nun waved the black shiny espada in her hand, face red with anger at the presumptuous novice before her.

"I ... er ..." Anja-Filipa pressed her lips together

and squinted. "I wondered if you wanted any … any long beans from the garden to go with the fish?"

The fisherman smiled.

Sister Leonor shook her head and spoke through clenched teeth. "Yes, indeed we shall. But I *thought* you were unpacking the icons in the hall? I, at least," she threw a furious glance at the fisherman, "did not have the pleasure of seeing you in the kitchen garden."

Anja-Filipa felt the grip of Sister Margaret's hand on her arm. "No, Sister, it was I who wanted to know. I am just about to go to pick the vegetables for our meal."

"So. Indeed I see that you are both incapable of using your brains to choose our vittles. I think our dear Mother Superior would demand six Hail Marys for your stupidity. Go, go!"

As she turned to go, Anja-Filipa threw a glance over her shoulder and called out clearly, "Of course, Sister. But I shall help Sister Margaret with the bean picking for a few minutes before I return to the unpacking. In the kitchen garden at the southwest side." She raised an eyebrow at her friend who was intent on ushering her quickly out of the kitchen. Sister Margaret shrugged her shoulders and muttered under her breath.

"I should not be aiding this encounter," whispered Sister Margaret, as they made for the side doorway and the kitchen garden.

"Then why are you?"

"I have no idea!" She grumbled and picked up a willow trug from the store and made her way along the line of bean plants that wound themselves up the laurel poles in neat, regimented rows.

Anja-Filipa waited at the end of the first line; it was nearest the kitchen door yet out of sight of the windows. Presently the door opened, and the fisherman sauntered out, carrying the huge empty basket.

"Thankfully Sister Leonor bought all the catch. I think she wanted to get rid of me out of her domain. She is always uncomfortable with me. I think she is afraid of men."

He dropped the basket onto the ground and studied her for a moment. Anja-Filipa was, for once, lost for words. But only for a short while, as the warning bell for Terce rang out.

"I am Anja-Filipa. I mean Sister Agnes," she said quickly. "I am a novice nun here."

The man grinned. "Yes, I gathered that much!"

"Oh, I ... er ... well. And you, may I ask?"

"You may indeed. I am João Moniz, from the Old Town. Originally my family came from Machico." He made a little bow. "I am pleased to make your acquaintance."

"And I yours. But how did you find me ... *us*... here?"

João laughed, a deep throaty laugh. "The whole town knows where you fled, Sister Agnes. Although we kept your secret from the corsairs. Their leader is dead, and it is now safe for us to come up here without revealing your retreat. But I must leave, and I think your bell means that you have prayers?"

"It is only the warning bell." Anja-Filipa flapped her hand dismissively, but Sister Margaret appeared out of the lines of beans and raised her eyebrows at her friend.

"We must go indoors, Sister, and prepare ourselves for Terce. You will need to return to finish your unpacking after chapel and midday meal. Come now."

Anja-Filipa gave a smile of regret towards João Moniz and turned to follow Sister Margaret.

"I will be here tomorrow at the same time," he called at her retreating back.

She buried her chin in her wimple to hide her smile.

"Oh, he is so comely," breathed Anja-Filipa in the chapel, pulling her wimple across her mouth to deaden her words.

"I am sure he would be regarded as such by many," whispered Sister Margaret out of the side of her mouth. "But you must take care. And I will not be a go-between."

"You enabled our meeting this morning," Anja-Filipa protested.

"Only to stay your mind. Only once. You must remember your vows, Sister Agnes."

"Oh, my *vows*."

"Yes, indeed. Your vows of chastity and obedience." Sister Margaret carefully straightened her robe across her knees.

"You imagine that one glimpse, one word, with such a man would stay my mind? You have begun a turmoil!"

"Shush. Do not raise your voice."

"*Pater Noster ...*"

Anja-Filipa tugged at her rosary, then grimaced. She did not want her beads to go scattering across the wooden floor of the chapel. She looked up at the reredos above the altar and realised that it was *her* reredos, the one she had not finished unwrapping, and that Mother Superior must have unveiled it and ordered it to be set up above the table with its ornate gold cross and its golden embroidered cloth. She stared at the altar cloth. The delicate stitching made patterns that looked very much like fish swirling and intertwined.

∾

JOÃO DID COME THE NEXT DAY, AND THE NEXT, AND FOR many days after that. And always Anja-Filipa managed somehow to be there in the kitchen garden to see him. She knew that Sister Margaret was uneasy even though she had been at least partly responsible for setting the train of events on its journey. She thought that maybe her friend was feeling guilty for leading her astray against her vows, so she avoided her as much as she could, and even sat away from her at table and at chapel.

Partly, the distance that grew between the friends was also because Anja-Filipa felt so different. She had always felt that she did not fit in with the monastic life as well as the other nuns. But despite Sister Margaret's ability to fit in, with her devotions and keenness to obey the rules of the convent, Anja-Filipa had known that her friend was somehow not as rigid as most of the community. Or at least she was perhaps more open and willing to listen, even though she did not approve.

But she also knew increasingly that nothing, absolutely nothing, come hell or excommunication, could stop her finding stolen moments with João. She knew that she could not live without those wonderful hopeful moments, those glimpses of another world, another life out there.

"Tell me about your family," she would say over and over to João, as they whispered behind the bean rows far from the kitchen doors, "As I have told you about my ancestors." João would smile indulgently, as though he was not entirely sure that the stories of Lady Ana d'Arafet and Sir Robert Machym, and João Gonçalves Zarco de Câmara were truly real and not just the magical tales of a fond mother.

"Today I will tell you about my father and grandfather who taught me how to decorate the capela floor and walls," he said one day, as he brushed away a tendril from the bean plants behind his head. "They were the great experts on tiling."

"Tiling?"

"Yes, with the azulejo. Making the most beautiful patterns of blue and white. And sometimes brown or gold. And they would make the pictures on the tiles, sometimes of scenes from home that they knew. The villages and the life they used to have up in the mountains."

"They came from the mountains? I thought you said they - you - were from Machico? On the coast?"

"Yes, but two or three generations ago my father's family farmed a little patch of land on the steep slope of the Eira. They made terraces of the earth in order to grow vegetables and fruit, and many vines. They should have grown sugar beet and then they would have become rich!"

"So why did they come down to Machico to fish?"

"That was my mother's family who fished. My father's ancestor was the third son and he was not going to inherit the land so when he met my mother's ancestor at the farmers' market he came down to the coast with her and became a fisherman and a maker of the tiles."

Anja-Filipa clasped her hands together. "Oh, that is so lovely. How romantic!"

"Well, perhaps not so romantic as your family stories." He smiled fondly at her and she wondered if he would be so bold as to touch her sleeve. She hoped so.

She sighed. "I wish that I lived by the coast. I wish that I lived in Machico and went out every day on a fishing boat and smelled the sea air and felt the wind on my face." She thought of the stories her mother had told her of Ana and Robert, and the journey they had made across the seas to escape to be together. She could almost hear the creaking timbers and the sailcloth catching the wind, although she had never been on a boat in her whole life. Yet she felt the movement of the cog, gentle at first, then beginning to heave in the mounting waves. She heard the creaking of the timbers and the slap of the breeze on the canvas.

Something made her shiver. Cold fingers crept up her spine and she brushed her hand across her face, feeling something covering her eyes, her mouth, pushing away the veil she felt upon her: a cloth, a shroud?

She slipped her hand inside her scapular and felt the leather pouch hidden there. As her fingers touched the azulejo, she shuddered. A chill seemed to slip across the mountainside, and stroke her body, and she felt a ripple in the air, a rising of the wind, a murmur of time, of worlds, as a spirit drew itself from her and rose into the air. *Ana.*

"Are you well?" João's voice cut through her

dizziness. He was gripping her arm and stroking her face.

"I ... felt faint for a moment." She felt even fainter now that she flushed with his touch.

He pulled his hand away. "Oh, I am so sorry. I did not mean ... You are a nun, even though we are friends now, but I know that you have vows and ... I am so sorry I touched you. How presumptuous of me."

She could not help but laugh at his shocked expression. "Oh, João. If you only knew!"

"You are not angry with me? We can still be friends and meet and talk?"

"With all my heart I hope so."

He gazed at her for a moment and then, as she knew he was breathing in her smile and glowing eyes and the way she seemed to be leaning in towards him, he tentatively bent and gently, briefly, kissed her lips.

"*Sister Agnes*! What *do* you think you are doing?"

CHAPTER 26

VIV

Present day

What do you think you're doing? A voice echoed through Viv's mind as she took Bértrand's hand to clamber aboard his boat.

"Welcome to my little private domain," he smiled as he helped her from the gangway.

She dropped his hand and looked around at the gleaming wood and brass fittings, the towering masts, and furled sails. "Goodness, this is remarkable."

"Yes." Bértrand said proudly. "It is. This is like a fifteenth century caravel. The other one is like the Santa Maria, Christopher Columbus's boat. That is later. My boat is the one that Zarco arrived here in, to discover the island and settle. It is carvel-built, that is, with timbers edge to edge. Look." He pointed up to the three tall masts. "Lateen rigged. That is, triangular sails. And look. The raised deck at the aft, with the cabin under."

"I see. How interesting." Viv turned to look around her, not sure what she was supposed to see.

"But Portuguese caravels used some features that were exploited later on with the carracks."

"So, I'm confused. You're saying that the Santa Maria is a later version?"

"Larger, square rigged."

"I have the word 'cog' going round my head. What would that have been like?" Viv frowned. She felt a desire to feel as Ana d'Arafet had felt on their cog, the Welfayre. But without the storms, of course; the feeling that she must have had when she boarded with Robert to sail to freedom.

"The cog is earlier, more simple. It is clinker-built. That is to say, the timbers are overlapping. And a single mast."

"So, would that have been a usual boat in, say, the middle of the fourteenth century?"

Bértrand stared at her for a moment, and she wondered what was going around his head. "Yes. Indeed. I guess it would have been more fragile. A single mast would have been critical enough in the Mediterranean but in an ocean like the Atlantic, for example, it would have been a faster sail but more unsafe. But," he shrugged, "it was what they used."

Viv dragged her hand across the timbers of the cabin with its little door, beneath the raised deck. She took in the benches along the length of the hull and the tall masts with the tiny crow's nest perched near the top.

"And this one is just like the boat Zarco arrived in here in Madeira? In Machico?" She felt as though she had slipped back in time to the fifteenth century.

"Look at this." Bértrand held open a book and in it were photos of the different stages of building the boat. It was so detailed, with close ups of the timbers and the sails, that Viv couldn't really take in, not knowing enough about the techniques of ship-building. But there was also an image that purported to be a likeness of Zarco himself.

Viv blinked at it as it seemed to blur and tremble in front of her eyes. Underneath the image Bértrand had scrawled the name 'João Gonçalves Zarco', a swirling signature. She heard words as though they were thoughts spoken inside her head: drifting in and out of focus, a triumphant flourish with elaborate curlicues. She peered short-sightedly as though the signature was difficult to read. A soft determined voice echoed through her foggy mind, 'Zarco'. But that name was in a breviary, and she could see a dragon tree with blood dripping onto the page.

She juddered, startled. "Oh."

"Is everything alright?"

Viv looked up from the book as Bértrand snapped it shut and rubbed her forehead. "Um, I just went a little dizzy. Headache. Sorry."

"No, no. You are faint, no? Please sit down here on the bench and I will fetch you some poncha and cake."

She gathered herself as quickly as she could. "Poncha might make my head worse!" She laughed, knowing that the traditional drink that was made of white rum, lemon, and honey, was quite potent.

"Ah, we say that it is the cure for everything – colds, fever, headache, hang-over!"

He disappeared into the little cabin under the raised deck and returned with a couple of glasses bunched in one hand and a basket of bolo de mel in the other. He kicked the door shut behind him and sat beside her. "Here, this will make you feel better. Or knock you out, one or the other!" He laughed his deep throaty laugh as he handed her a glass and proffered the basket.

Viv became aware that another man had jumped lightly onto the boat and was starting up the engine. She looked quizzically at Bértrand.

"My crew," he waved his hand and Viv saw that there was a second person releasing the mooring ropes on the quay, hurling them onto the deck before leaping after them.

"So this boat has an engine? Not, I think, like Zarco's in the fifteenth century?"

"Of course not! But necessary these days. We will be under sail as we return along the coast. The wind is right. And it is a wonderful experience, with the breeze in the sails. Very relaxing." He leaned closer to her.

"And do not worry about the crew. They do not disturb."

~

They did not sail far, hugging the coast from the marina to Ponta da Cruz, the bay of the cross, where Bértrand pointed out the old cross on the headland, and a short way beyond past Praia de Formosa.

"So that is where your ancestor landed to attack the island?" Viv felt a chill rise up her spine. Yet as she looked at the hotels that now guarded the bay, she could not imagine it. In the clear sunshine it was hardly possible to credit such an invasion. She squinted at the figures sunbathing on the beach, stretched out, relaxing in the heat. All so peaceful.

"Sadly, yes. But so long ago. Forgive me." Bértrand bowed his head, and Viv found herself giggling strangely. She peered blindly at her glass. He had filled it up again with poncha and to say she was lightheaded and silly was no exaggeration. Surely she had only drunk a couple of glasses. Three? No, surely not. She leant forwards to peer at the flagon on the deck at Bértrand's feet but there was no label to tell her the percentage of alcohol in the rum. She guessed it was high. Her head was swimming and the far side of the boat shuddering. She leant back against the gunwale and tried to close her eyes against the dizziness, but her head still spun nauseatingly, and it was almost better to keep them open. She focused on trying to still the movement in her head.

By the time they had turned about and the crew had unfurled the sails, Viv, lulled by the poncha and the gentle movement of the boat as it rolled smoothly with the waves and the breeze in the sails, felt her eyes drift close.

She was vaguely aware of Bértrand moving nearer to her on the bench, his body hot and muscular against her, his tanned thighs in his linen shorts touching hers. Once, it was like that with Rory. She could almost believe that the image of masculinity beside her was in fact the Rory she had first met. The gorgeous man in the black shirt and stark white clerical collar with his lopsided smile and dark deep eyes that only embraced hers. His strong arms and thighs, tanned from his daily running down the lanes. She could almost smell his signature bergamot cologne. His arm, once resting on the gunwale, slipped across her shoulders and she felt her head nestle on his broad shoulder.

"My dear Viv, is this OK?" he whispered softly in her ear, blowing on her hair.

She found herself murmuring "yes" as she snuggled into him.

This was a feeling she had not experienced for some time. A sense of being truly wanted and valued. A shiver that formed itself, behind her eyes, into Georgina and Rory threatened the warmth she felt right now. If only ...

She was only partly aware that it was Bértrand beside her.

He was asking her more about her research, the most recent developments, what had she found out about the fossil, the azulejo – was he asking her that or was it her imagination? Her thoughts were adrift, her usual sharpness scrambled.

She was aware that she told him about some of her research but not about her visions. That was too personal, too close to speak of. Only Rory knew about that. There was no way she could share that with Bértrand, or anyone else. Rory understood her and her strange visions; didn't think it was too weird because he had experienced something similar too.

Her eyes opened and she saw with intense clarity the wooden edges of the gunwale opposite, the blue of the sea beyond, the sharp outlines of the print on the sails that snapped on the wind above her. Her head was snuggled into Bértrand's shoulder.

What *was* she doing?

She gasped and jumped away from him.

CHAPTER 27

ANJA-FILIPA

1566

Startled, they jumped apart.

"Mother Superior!"

Anja-Filipa, still dazed from João's kiss and the deep longing she felt, gasped at the abbess, at first not understanding what on earth she was doing in the garden. She could not seem to compose her mind that was wracked in turmoil. Her body ached for João, his beautiful mouth on hers and his strong hard torso against her softness and she did not know what was happening to her. Her strange emotions were pulling her heart and mind apart.

She felt João's hand which had fallen away from her slip around her waist, pulling the thick, rough cloth of the scapular and robe into her curves. His fingers found the leather belt that held her mother's pouch beneath, and he stroked it, not knowing what it contained, but just because it was close to her body.

"I..." but she had no words to express the momentous feeling she had, the love that suffused her body.

She saw that Mother Superior's face was drained of blood and her eyes wide with fear. "Dom Moniz, be pleased to release my novice and leave the convent. You will not be allowed to return." As he squeezed Anja-Filipa's waist and dropped his grip on her, and began, hesitantly to step away from her, she added, "Do you have any idea what you have done?"

João glanced at Anja-Filipa's startled face and tried to smile. "What I have done," he began, "is to come to love her. Over the time I have talked to her, she has become more dear to me than life itself. I would not hurt her for anything in the world. I have hardly touched her until just now."

"That is not the point, Dom Moniz. I hope for the good Lord's sake that you have not touched her before, nor that you have hurt her in any way. But the fact is that she has made her vows to God, of chastity and obedience. And that means not looking upon any man with ... with *feelings*. Please leave us."

With one last look at Anja-Filipa, he hesitantly moved away, and she watched as he slowly made his way out of the garden and onto the path down the mountain.

Mother Superior was trembling, yet Anja-Filipa

felt a calmness suffuse her. He loved her. She was more dear to him than life itself!

"Who has helped you in these assignations?" she asked, gripping her novice's arm.

Anja-Filipa saw Sister Margaret's face flit across her mind. "No-one." She bowed her head.

"I sincerely hope that is the truth. Oh, Sister Agnes, oh dear, oh dear. You must come to my room but first go up to your cell and pray your penitence and for forgiveness. You must cleanse yourself of the impure thoughts you have manifested. Say your hail Marys. Wash yourself, your face, your mouth. Then come to me and I will take you to prostrate yourself before God in the chapel."

Anja-Filipa felt the vibrations of the abbess's wrath and she peered up through her downturned eyelashes to see the quivering flesh before her. She saw fear and she knew that Mother Superior would not easily forgive her. Because something had been breached that she thought was solid and it had shaken her to the core. She knew that the abbess was not completely condemning of sin because she had looked kindly on her mother, and others, but this was something else. Perhaps it was not simply trust, but a real fear of what her novice had opened herself up to.

Head still bowed, she moved slowly along the path to the doorway, hearing the swish of Mother Superior's robe behind her.

∽

Only Sister Margaret spoke to her, and that in low whispers and with furtive glances around her. Word had scurried around that Anja-Filipa had disgraced herself with the fisherman and all the nuns avoided her eye and her person, as if, unless they scurried away from her, they would themselves become tainted by her sin.

She was given duties on her own, gardening which she did not mind doing alone as it provided her with time to think and dream, and she had often done so in the past. But an elderly nun was always sitting on the bench at the side under the shade of the eucalyptus, keeping watch over her in the remote possibility that João might return, although he was banned entry to the convent. After a while she began to invent games to play on the nun: looking up suddenly from her hoeing or pruning with a huge smile on her face and uttering a breathless "oh!" to the empty archway that formed the entrance into the retreat. The nun would startle and jump up ready to accost the knave and defend the novice's honour. But soon she would be shaking her head and muttering at Anja-Filipa.

At sewing she had always been able to whisper rumours and gossip, but now she was positioned on her own at the far side of the chamber and the other nuns turned their bodies slightly away from her so that she saw only their back or shoulder. She could not compare her stitching with theirs and therefore compliment herself on her neatness or frown if someone else displayed greater skill. She simply sat there quietly, looking demure but thinking about the man who brought a rush of blood to her cheeks and a flush of heat to rise up her spine. She tried not to sigh in case it might reveal the fact that she was not praying in her silence, but imagining João coming up the mountain to rescue her and take her back to his cottage in Machico where she could hear the gentle rush of the waves on the shingle.

At mealtimes she ate alone, except for Margaret bringing her food and sitting briefly beside her until Mother Superior signalled her to move away.

But if the abbess hoped that isolation would smother the feelings she had, then she was mistaken. For Anja-Filipa raised her head and held it high, unbeaten. She was loved by a man, and the world opened up before her.

"I know that you did not betray me," she murmured to Margaret as her friend quietly filled her water cup with a shaking hand.

"I would not," Sister Margaret touched her arm gently. "Mother Superior has asked me what I knew of you and João, but I would not speak. It is not mine to tell."

"Nor I you. You helped us but I would never disclose that." She was aware that Sister Margaret raised her hand to brush away a tear from her cheek. "I do not wish for you to be punished for your kindness to me."

But as time plodded on, she found herself turning from hope to frustration and despair. She refused to renounce João.

"You must promise never to see him again," Mother Superior said.

"I cannot."

"But in fact, you will *not* see him again because he will never be allowed back to the convent. So your promise is simply to confirm to me and to God that you have rejected sin and are truly penitent. Why can you not do this?"

"Because I cannot say that I do not love him any more or that I do not believe he loves me any more."

Mother Superior sighed loudly and her shoulders slumped. "Oh, Sister Agnes, why are you so stubborn? In practice it makes no difference at all. Just promise and that is the end of it, we will never speak of it again."

"How can I say what I do not believe? How can I tell you – and God – that I will never see him again when that is the one thing that I truly want more than anything else?"

The abbess shook her head and flicked her hand to dismiss her unruly novice.

She had been told to say the rosary in full again for all of the fifteen mysteries, every day for three weeks. She had to meditate particularly on the purity of mind

THE DRAGON TREE

and body and contemplate the importance of obedience. Yet again. She hardly needed her breviary; she could almost recite all this by heart.

She was given more cleaning, scrubbing floors, and polishing the benches than she ever remembered anyone doing. But no cooking as she was kept far away from the kitchen in case any of the fishermen came to the door. She laughed when she was told, because why on earth would she want to see the wizened old fishermen who brought their baskets of espada and seabream and prawns. João was not going to come. They would stop him even if he tried.

It took all her strength not to fling her breviary across her cell as she cried and trembled at the unfairness of it all. Then she would take a deep breath and hold her precious stone and her azulejo to her breast and whisper her heart out to her long-dead mother.

"What is João doing now? Is he crying too? Or has he forgotten me?"

And her mother would whisper back. "Do not cry, my love. One day ... one day."

~

SHE COULD BEAR IT NO LONGER. HER NECK WAS STIFF with holding her head high when her throat was choked. There were no proper cloisters here but a shaded passageway that stretched the length of the main hall. She had taken to drifting slowly along it, muttering her rosaries under her breath, with only half her mind. The other half was rapidly engorging itself with righteous indignation. She tugged at her rosary and spat out her words.

She sensed rather than saw the other nuns pass her from time to time, their heavy robes sweeping the tiled floor, and she wondered if they could tell that her hands were clenched on her beads and her breathing so raw. She became aware that someone had paused ahead of her. She looked up and saw Sister Margaret hovering there against the wall.

"Sister Agnes," she whispered, looking around. "I wish I could talk to you properly, but I am prevented. Are you well? When will Mother Superior release you?"

"Never," Anja-Filipa snorted. "I will be walking this passageway for ever! When I am dead you will see my spirit here, muttering the rosary!"

"Oh, dear Sister Agnes," she giggled. "I miss you. I know that I should not even think of undermining Mother Superior's commands, but I wish there was something I could do to lighten your burden."

Anja-Filipa inhaled quickly and her eyes flicked behind her. "There is, my friend. But it is much to ask, and I do not know if ..." then in a rush she said rapidly, "But can I endanger you once more to ask if you could take a note to the kitchen when the fishermen come again and maybe they could take it to him?"

She gasped with the enormity of what she had just asked for, and clutched her rosary to her breast, searching her friend's face. The serene expression before her did not waver. But Sister Margaret did not speak for a few moments and Anja-Filipa hopped from one foot to the other.

"That is much to demand. And much to ask of a sister nun. I am mindful of my vows of obedience. I do not like this. I wish that I could stop you. I fear for you. I fear that your course is unwise and that you will suffer." She shook her head and turned to retreat down the passageway. "I ... I am also mindful of compassion and love. I must pray for the right path to take." She swept away.

That evening after vespers, when Anja-Filipa returned to her cell, she tore a page from the back of her breviary and scrawled a message to João, then brought it to her lips and slipped it into her pouch. Even if it never reached him, she would know that she had tried. And perhaps he would somehow know it too.

The following day at time to break the fast after Prime, when Anja-Filipa sat alone at the far table of the refectory, she watched as Sister Margaret approached, offering the water jug to the older nuns nearby. She raised her eyebrows as she filled Anja-Filipa's cup, although the sadness in her eyes was clear.

"Do you have it?" she hissed as she bent beside her.

Anja-Filipa slipped her hand into her pouch and

pulled out her note, sliding it into Margaret's palm. "You prayed, then?"

"And He answered. I hope that I heard Him rightly."

∽

"Sister Agnes." Mother Superior peered at her across her desk. "I have done enough. The time of your penitence is completed. I do not believe that you are changed but perhaps you understand a little more about the consequences of your actions. And I do not think that it will gain anything more to continue with the punishment."

"Thank you, Mother Superior." Anja-Filipa bowed her head but she hid a smile that played on her lips as she thought of what was about to happen shortly at Sext, the midday contemplation.

"You may go back to your cell and reflect." She shook her head. "I am not at all sure that I can make a good nun of you."

"No, Mother Superior."

She backed out of the room to hide the bundle she carried behind her. At the door she paused. "I have had a life here that I shall always hold dear to my heart."

The last thing she saw was the abbess's puzzled frown.

Then she ran, her few precious possessions clutched to her chest. By the time she reached the outer door she was breathless. Sister Margaret stood there, her stillness and calm demeanour belied the troubled frown and glinting eyes.

"He is at the top of the path. Go round by the bean canes. I will keep watch here until you are out of sight down the path." She hugged Sister Agnes and kissed the crown of her head before squeezing her eyes shut and firmly crossing herself. "Go well and go safely. Live a good life, Anja-Filipa."

"I will try to," she said through her tears. Her hand slipped under her scapular to her leather pouch and she stroked the stone and the azulejo that nestled there together. If she had been listening, she would have heard the air seeming to rumble around the mountain cauldron like the beginning of a thunder storm. She was only half aware of the murmur in the breeze, the rising of the wind, the murmur of time, of worlds, and a spirit rising into the heavens.

Quickly, before she could change her mind, Anja-Filipa tugged Sister Agnes's wimple and veil from her head. She wound her rosary around her wrist and turned her face towards the path down the mountain. She took a deep breath.

She did not look back.

CHAPTER 28

VIV

Present day

*W*hat was she thinking!

Viv turned away from Bértrand and took a deep breath. She felt nauseous and faint. Her heart was pounding. A terrible sadness seemed to fill her body and she had no idea why. A fear of something unknown ahead of her, of something precious she was leaving behind.

She heard the soft swish of heavy robes sweep the floor near her and the sense of many women gathered around her, yet not touching, feeling isolated in this crowd: no reaching out to her, no sympathy emanating from the other hearts that beat here. Cold, alone. Viv felt strange, dizzy, disoriented.

She clutched the side of the boat to steady herself. With her right hand she felt for the fossil and azulejo in her pocket but found only the stone as her fingers touched the shape of the curled creature inside.

The breeze caught the sails so that the boat rocked a little and she staggered. Clouds were beginning to form on the far horizon. Was that a rumble of thunder she heard? She became aware that a wisp of air seemed to swirl around her and rise into the clouds. Her eyes followed it as it rose and hovered, rose and hovered, above her, pausing before it disappeared into the sky. Her heart stilled and her breathing became regular again.

Then as her mind became clearer, she felt a glimmer of hope. She was stumbling down a rocky path, holding out her hand. Another hand, warm and rough, strong and enfolding, captured hers in its grip.

"What is the matter?"

Viv startled at the grip of a hand on her arm and the visions cleared.

"Bértrand. Oh, nothing. I just felt odd for a moment."

"It is the movement of the timber hull cutting through the waves. Do not fear. It is usual. It often makes people dizzy."

He reached for her as though he would embrace her but at that moment she felt a sharp pain low in her stomach. She clutched the site of the discomfort and winced aloud. She hadn't felt anything there for a long time now and it made her shudder. *Ana.*

"Sit down again, my dear Viv. Here, have this

cushion behind your back. Let me fetch you some coffee from the galley."

"Thank you." She smiled up at him. "It's good to be looked after." As soon as she had said those words she felt guilty. It must be interpreted as a slight on Rory. But of course he looked after her. Of course he cared for her well-being. Didn't he? He helped with things in the apartment, the nitty gritty of their lives. The daily mundane things. Like …

When was the last time he had nurtured her? Well, of course he had been distracted and bereaved after their loss of Ana … She'd tried hard to be understanding to him in his grief, even as she felt consumed by her own. Yet somehow they had drifted apart. She had to acknowledge that. And now there was the matter of Georgina. Perhaps things would never be the same again.

Bértrand slid a mug into her hands. The rich aroma of coffee drifted up and she inhaled it deeply.

"Mmm, that smells good. Thank you."

"It is my pleasure to see to your comfort." He smiled and she felt the tingle up her spine. "The colour is coming back into your cheeks now. That is good. And may I say, you are extremely attractive when you smile."

Viv felt a very English desire to thank him for the compliment. But she said nothing and let it pass. She was so aware of him sitting down next to her, his arm resting casually along the gunwale behind her.

"I am wondering whether we could use your expertise in the museum," he said. "I, for one, would be most grateful for your professional eye on certain historical matters."

"Goodness, I'm sure that you already have plenty of experts in Madeiran history. I really only know about medieval England, that's all."

"You are a well-known academic. Your name on our materials would be an excellent promotion for our work."

Viv shrugged her modest deflection of her academic value. "I'm not so sure about that." She sipped her hot coffee.

"Pff. Nonsense. I have googled you. And I think your name would be valuable to us. I see that you have a strong international reputation as well as in England. People across the world like to read what you say. And certainly here in Madeira there would be a great deal of interest in a different perspective on our history. Interweaving it with our own view, of course."

"Of course. But I really don't have a 'perspective' on Madeiran history. I mean, I haven't researched it as closely as you would need for the museum. I'm sure you have people much better qualified than me in the specifics."

"I think you would be ideal." He slapped his palm down on the top of his thigh, as if to brook no argument. "I think you could use ... what should I say

... *critique*. And perhaps see beyond conventional views."

"What do you mean? New interpretations of ... what?" She thought of the novice nun, Anja-Filipa, and the flight to the mountains. "... the corsairs' attack?"

Bértrand's face flickered and she felt a frisson of guilt. Why did she have to bring that up again? "No, no. I am not wanting you to rewrite *that* history in a different way. I am just thinking you could cast your eye over what we have. Is it correct? Is it consistent? Is the message clear? Perhaps there is a different way of looking at it?"

"Look, I'm happy to help, obviously. But ..."

"But I would like your name on our brochures." His tone was firm, insistent. She recognised that he was not a man to take refusal of his demands easily.

"I'm not sure that it wouldn't be somewhat misleading! But what exactly are you wanting?" But even as she wondered what she could possibly do to help, in reality, she was also thinking of the strange visions she'd been having of Madeira's past, and how they fitted together, what they were asking of her. Did she hold some sort of key to the past?

And how could she be sure that what her strange experiences of the past were telling her, was significant? Or just some kind of haunting.

"I get the feeling," said Bértrand, "that you know more than you think. Perhaps your research is deeper than you are saying. Or maybe you are being modest about your achievements."

Or perhaps I have a connection that defies all logic, an ability to reach out to other layers of time?

She shivered.

"Let me fetch a blanket for you. You are cold. The wind is getting up and although that is good for the sails, it is not so good for the delicate English skin."

Viv gulped down the rest of the coffee in her mug and wondered whether there was some kind of ulterior motive in Bértrand's request. But yet she had no idea what it could be.

He returned from the cabin and wrapped a thick woollen rug around her shoulders, so solicitously that she was sorry for her suspicions about him. What possible motive could he have? Was he still flirting? Or was it something else? And she had to confess to herself that she was indeed flattered at his interest and his desire to use her professional capabilities. It boosted the ego that had eluded her for some time now. That he thought she was elevated enough for her name to grace the museum literature was wonderful. That he was impressed by her research and her work on the medieval world made her heart glad.

"Well, I'll certainly help all I can but ..."

"Then let me show you something I need advice on. For your first job!"

"O-ka-ay."

"I have to be able to trust you completely."

"Of course." Viv frowned.

"You see, it is something I think is especially important. It is an artefact, a special one."

CHAPTER 29

ANJA-FILIPA

1568 Machico

"Such a special one," murmured João, stroking his tiny daughter's head.

Anja-Filipa looked up wearily from her bed and smiled wanly. But her eyes were gleaming with the miracle she had been a part of. Her sister-in-law tenderly wiped a cloth across the sweat on her forehead and bushed away the strands of damp hair that stuck to her skin.

"Thank you, Catarina. You have been a wonderful midwife."

"My dear sister, you are most welcome. To see my brother so happy and contented is worth the night's efforts and exhaustion." She straightened up and stretched her back. "I have birthed several babes but this one was not easy. There were times in the dark hours when I thought ..." She shook her head. "You were feverish, and I feared the worst. You called out strangely. *Robert*, you said! I do not know who this is." She looked to João, but he shook his head with a frown.

"I do not know anyone of that name," Anja-Filipa puzzled. But then she too looked to João and knew that the same name flickered through both their minds. Her long distant ancestor, Sir Robert Machym. But why she should call his name at the moment of birth she had no idea. So neither of them spoke aloud.

And staring into her husband's eyes she heard again in her mind's memory the words that had swept across her head as she had writhed in pain: *storms, attack, blessed, must be held together and never parted ...* Who must never be parted? She and João, clearly. They had survived and made a little home together here in Machico, near to his family.

"Blessed, a miracle," she murmured, echoes weaving around her mind.

"Indeed she is," said João, planting a kiss on his daughter's crown. But Anja-Filipa knew somehow that she had not been meaning her own new child. Although of course she was both of those! "What shall we call her, my love?"

Anja-Filipa had no hesitation in speaking the only name in her head. "Ana."

"Ana. After your ancestor. Yes indeed."

THE DRAGON TREE

"Who was this?" Catarina asked, raising her eyebrows at the unusual name.

"Lady Ana d'Arafet," said Anja-Filipa firmly.

∽

Later, when Anja-Filipa had slept and the baby Ana was cradled on her breast, João said softly, "Do you ever regret leaving the convent, the quiet life of contemplation?"

She drew in a sharp breath at his sudden question and had to realign the baby to suckle. The tiny child was getting tangled in the laces of the loose chemise that was becoming yellowed and threadbare from washing. "Not ... no. At least I miss my dear friend Sister Margaret and in truth I also miss Mother Superior who became *a little bit* like a mother to me ... well, a strict mother anyway, not really like my real mother, who was soft and kind. And I am very aware that I will never see them again. I would not be *allowed* to see them again, sadly. I brought disgrace to the convent, and of course I regret that. I was so young, I did not realise."

João laughed. "So young then! It was only a year or so ago!"

"But being with you and doing the things we do," she blushed, "and giving birth to our daughter – these things have made me feel like a hundred years old!"

"Goodness, my love, I hope not! We have many more years together, I hope."

"I hope so too, João, and that we have a quiet gentle life together here with our children … there will be many more, with God's grace. I do not want to be anywhere else than this little house."

"I am only sorry that it is only a fisherman's cottage and not a rich home for you, with gildings and tapestries on the walls and tiles on the floors."

"João, I like the wooden floors and wooden walls. It is simple and beautiful. We have two rooms all for ourselves. I want for nothing else." She looked around over the baby's head at the furniture that João had made so lovingly for them; they were not richly decorated with gold and carvings and there were no paintings on the walls as the convent had, but what little there was had been hewn and polished and whittled with love. Many an evening over the past months as her belly grew large, they had sat together as she embroidered tiny clothes for the baby and he carved a cradle and toys. "We have made it all ourselves and so it is our richness, not someone else's that we have inherited!"

"We were fortunate, though, that we could take this cottage when my uncle died and make it habitable again and our own."

"Indeed, and that we have the vegetable patch just above on the hillside. What with your pick of the catch every day and my vegetables, we could not ask for

THE DRAGON TREE

more! Little Ana will grow very well here and so will any more that we are blessed with."

João smiled, but he looked troubled. She hoped that he had not seen her distant eyes, as though she saw something else, far away, and that he had not noticed her weariness and the way she rubbed her back even before the baby grew inside her. She hoped that he had not seen her looking up to the cauldron of the mountains high above the shore and to the west where now the nuns were home safely in the convent. She did not want him to know that, although she loved him and she was happy in their life together, she thought often of the convent. Not the richness of the life there, but the way that she had left. Did they hate her, despise her? She could not bear it if they did. Or maybe they had forgotten her. She forced a wave of sadness from her heart; she knew that it was not good for the baby to suckle on sadness.

She straightened her back and little Ana mewed like a kitten as her mouth lost the nipple for a moment. She took a deep breath. "So, are you out late tonight again with your brothers to fish for the espada?"

Thankfully, he was not out every night, but when he was, she liked to sit outside the cottage that overlooked the bay, in the darkness, and watch the small fishing boats sail out towards the far horizon. She would count the lights on the prows, shining like a row of jewels in the dark night sky. Catarina would come over from her cottage and sit with her and they would try to guess which one was João's. In the convent she had never imagined how the deep-sea fish were caught. They just arrived each day in a basket for the kitchen nun to choose which she wanted.

João reached out to touch her arm as it cradled the baby. He grimaced. "I am. But I need to tell you some other news. I have been delaying it for a while as I did not wish you to be distressed."

Anja-Filipa felt a chill rise up her spine and held the baby more tightly to her breast. "Oh lord, what is it?"

"My love, I have been asked to help with the new tiling in the capela in Funchal. The repairs. Now that the corsairs are long since gone and we no longer need to fear the danger of another attack, we need to make everything right again. As you know, there was some damage done, although not as much as in the new cathedral in the centre of Funchal town."

"But I thought that your father and brothers were engaged with that work?"

"Yes, my brothers are, but my father is not as agile as he used to be, nor as accurate in his tiling work. He can manage the fishing but the delicate work of decorating the tiles is beyond him now, I fear. My older brothers have had to take over his tiling. My younger brothers are helping on the boat."

"So why do they need you?" Anja-Filipa pouted in dismay. Funchal was a distance west along the coast and he would surely need to stay there while he worked in the capela in the fishermen's quarter. She would be here on her own. And with a tiny baby.

"My youngest brother is old enough to take my place on the boat, but he is not careful enough yet to work on the azulejo. I am sorry, my love, but I am needed there." He patted her arm, but she shrugged him off.

"Well. I did not imagine that I would be alone so soon." She thought of the convent where even during her periods of solitude and contemplation in her cell, she knew that in a short while she would have the company of the other nuns. And that she rarely had to be alone in her tasks unless she chose to be. There was never a time when she was aware of anything but living within a community. How would she manage now, not just for a night but for weeks, months perhaps?

"Catarina will come to sit with you in the evenings."

"Catarina has her tasks as a midwife, and she has a husband, and grown children who still come to be fed. She cannot be *here*, with me!"

"But *I* am not here with you all the time, my love."

Anja-Filipa pulled the baby from her breast and moved her round to the other side. She must have tugged at her because the tiny mouth opened to a loud wail. She thrust her onto the nipple, squashing the little face into the cushion of her breast.

"That is not ... João, when you are away from me or

the house you are not far! Only in the evenings when you are fishing for espada are you far enough from me that I cannot call you. And then I have Catarina for a few hours. But way in Funchal! What am I to do? I have a new born baby!"

"My love," João began, biting his lip, "I do not need to go to Funchal until next week."

"Next week!"

"I ... I think it is best if I leave you in peace while you feed Ana. It is not good for her to be disturbed." He stood and adjusted his tunic and belt and pulled on his boots. "I will call Catarina to sit with you while I go up to the boats to help with mending the nets."

"As you like." She frowned and pressed her lips together hard.

By the time, she heard the clump of João's boots at the doorway, she had calmed herself and slept awhile with Ana lying snuffling on her chest. She was so much more tired than she had ever been before, even with all the hard work of her convent tasks, gardening, cooking, mending worn habits and torn wimples. She had no idea that birthing a child would leave her so exhausted.

She felt so drained of life that sometimes when she looked upon her tiny daughter, she trembled with a strange fear. Of course she loved the little scrap. She was a miracle, was she not? The miracle of birth itself was to be wondered at. Certainly, at the convent they spoke of the birth of the baby Jesus as a miracle, and

THE DRAGON TREE

Mary as the mother of God. They spoke with wonder and praise. But *this* ... She had never known that her body and mind would feel so drained.

With one hand holding the baby from slipping, she reached for her rosary which she always kept by her bedside on the rough-hewn table.

She was saying the Hail Mary as João came through to the room where they slept.

"Ave Maria, gratia plena ..." she had never forgotten her rituals and often read her breviary, yet João looked at her in surprise.

"My love?"

She did not respond but completed her rosary before she looked across at him. He stood, tall and strong, raking his hand through his thick dark hair, his face tanned and rugged from the outdoor life he led. She could not help her heart trembling at the sight of him and melting a little.

"I am sorry," he murmured, almost under his breath so that Anja-Filipa had to strain to hear him. She slipped the rosary back onto the side table and wriggled to prop herself up, Ana still snuffling with sleep on her chest. "I should not have told you today. I should have waited for a better time."

She knew that there was no going back on his decision. Only perhaps a 'better time' to tell her of it. She sighed, spent. She could no longer argue or vent her feelings.

He smiled at her and she remembered how she

had fallen in love with this man and how he had loved her and made her a home with his own hands although they were often red and raw. Her mind was filled with conflict and her heart felt twisted and wrung.

She remembered her prayers for humility and obedience.

He sat on the edge of the bed and described to her what they needed to do in the capela. Some of the azulejo had been deliberately smashed and replacements needed to be made and fixed. One wall was almost completely destroyed. Perhaps he would begin a new pattern there.

"I know that this is not a good time. Again." He grimaced. "But I need to ask you something." He hung his head and she saw that there were flakes of black sand glittering on his crown. "It is a very big request, my love. But I wonder if you would let me use your precious azulejo as a pattern for the new wall in the capela? Then there would be something of you forever reflected there."

She frowned. "What do you mean? How would you use it?"

"I would need to take it to the capela. Do not fear. I would keep it safe and bring it back to you. You see, I need the tile itself, not a drawn copy, so that it is accurate. As soon as I have a copy worked onto a new tile, I can return the original to you." He stroked her arm. "I would like it to be the heart of my pattern."

Anja-Filipa began to shake her head. She did not allow her treasure out of her reach. Even now it nestled on her shift, in her pouch at her waist along with the precious stone. Even through childbirth it had remained there. She had held it and gained strength even as she strained to push Ana into the world.

Then an image drifted across her mind, of the beautiful pattern of her mother's precious tile decorating the capela walls to the glory of God, there for all to see and marvel at. Her mother enshrined in the capela in the great city of Funchal for centuries to come.

She saw someone, a lady, in strange clothes, not the long skirts, apron and cap like hers, but peculiar tiny breeches and showing her bare legs disgracefully, sitting on the wooden benches of the capela, eyes wide as she looked upon the frescos and ceiling paintings, the altar with its great mural. She felt a tightness in her chest and pressed Ana closer to her. She could see again the image of the fisherman, a bit like João, and the Portuguese cog, clinker-built with distinctive rigging. It drew her in, and she could not drag her eyes away from it. Her vision blurred and she blinked hard. *Ana*. But it was someone else's voice, one she did not recognise.

João, so near to her, an arm's length away, seemed to shimmer before her eyes.

"The heart of your pattern," she heard herself murmuring. "Well then. But you must bring it back to me as soon as you have copied it. Not at the end of your repairing work, but straightway when the copy on the new tile is done. I will only let you borrow it and then you must make the journey back here with it before you go back again to your work at the capela."

"I understand. Thank you, my love. I can never thank you enough. It will be magnificent, a monument to you and your mother."

CHAPTER 30

ANJA-FILIPA

1568 Machico

"How long has he been gone now?" Anja-Filipa paced the small room of her little cottage, jiggling the baby in her arms. The winter storm raged, the wind battering the fishermen's cottages on the cliff. She was glad that they were well above the waves crashing into the bay. She had never seen them so high and knew that no fishing boats had gone out last night nor were out today. The storms did not usually begin until the springtime, after the Christmas festivities. But this year they had come early, and nobody was hanging the flower adorned streamers across the narrow streets that normally heralded the advent of Jesus.

She bit her lip at the thought that João might be caught in the high winds, but she was quite sure that he would be protected in the little fishermen's cottages set in a square around the capela. And even in the middle of the town, the water from the high mountains would be channelled through the valleys down the new levadas, the water courses that brought the rain water from the mountains down to the farms on the hillside and finally safely out to the sea. So he would be safe. He must be.

But why had he not come back with her azulejo?

She paced another length of the house and wondered whether they felt the storms in the convent way up the steep street in Funchal. Whether they sheltered in one of the chapels and prayed for safety. Whether they had enough fresh fish or meat up there. Then she realised, of course they did. It was so far away from the coast and so high above it, that it would not be battered by the ocean waves as she was down here in Machico. They may not have fresh fish today, but they would have their salted and dried fish, meat and vegetables and there would be plenty of barrels of flour for bread. It was she who could not get up to the little vegetable patch, although in truth there would not be much at this time of year, only carrots and onions and kale, perhaps a few bulbs of fennel left in the ground after their harvest.

The torrential rain pounded on the thin roof of the one-storey cottage. Holding Ana to the side, she peered out through a gap in the shutters. The street outside looked more like a waterway than a cobbled passageway. The rainwater rushed past the house like a river in spate, cascading down the narrow alleyways to the side, making waterfalls of their steep steps. As she moved back from the window, she heard the thunder rolling round the bay and flashes of lightning echoed through the slats of the shutters.

"Where *are* you, João? Where is my azulejo?" She cried to the pink gleaming crown of Ana's head, but the baby only mewled angrily as she bounced up and down on her mother's hard bony hip.

Anja-Filipa heard the latch of the front door raise and the slam of the door against the wall as the wind blew it out of grasp and a gust rushed through the house rattling the shutters and shelves. The meagre fire guttered.

"João?" she called from the far side of the room, quickly pushing a loose hank of hair back into her close-fitting cap and smoothing the full skirts of her faded dress that brushed the reeds on the floor.

"No, it's me. Catarina." She gasped and coughed as she forced the door shut against the gale and struggled with the latch.

"Oh." Anja-Filipa could not help but show the disappointment in her voice, her heart was so anguished.

Catarina pulled off her shawl from her head and shook it although it was soaked through and needed wringing properly. Her hair had fallen out from her cap and was stuck to her cheeks and dripping down her face and back, even though she had only run a few paces from her own door.

"I will not take the baby from you, I am so wet, I do not want to give her a fever. But you look pale and exhausted. Was she awake through the night?"

"No, I am just so worried."

"Of course. But João will be fine. He is with his brothers and they look after each other. So do not fear."

"I am afraid for my azulejo ..."

"Your ...?"

"Oh, nothing, just something precious I lent to João. If he returns soon with it all will be well."

Catarina's forehead creased into a puzzled frown, but she continued with her message. "You do not know? The brothers have sent word with the ox carter that they have had to leave their work in the capela for a few days to go up to the little wooden chapel on the Rua do Quebra Costa - you know, where the burial site is. All the men have had to go up there because they say the burials are being washed up with the floods."

"Floods? Up the mountainside street? But the river water should be going down the levadas, not down the streets."

"Anja-Filipa, did the younger brother Tristão not come to tell you? He was sent with the message at daybreak! The rivers have burst their banks and the levadas are broken. But João and the brothers are safe and have joined the group at Quebra Costa. I came to tell you that the carter gave me this pouch to pass to you. I could not come across before because ..."

"Where, where?" Anja-Filipa swung Ana further over on her hip and thrust out her hand to Catarina. It must be a pouch protecting the precious azulejo. He had not forgotten after all! "Give it to me!"

"Here. But calm yourself, my dear." Catarina shook her head and fumbled beneath her over garment and pulled out a damp cloth bag.

Anja-Filipa snatched it and tugged at the grubby hemp closure, awkward with one hand securing Ana. The bag felt flatter than it should be. Fingers clumsy, she widened the opening and peered inside.

It was a piece of paper, not her tile.

"What is this?" she demanded. Catarina shrugged her shoulders.

As she drew it out of the pouch, Anja-Filipa could see that it appeared to be the pattern of her azulejo sketched carefully in detail.

"Why would he send me this pattern? Where is my azulejo?"

"I have no idea what you are talking about."

No, of course she would not, because she had sworn João to secrecy. Nobody else knew about her precious treasure.

Anja-Filipa sat down heavily, the baby jolted in her arms. She barely seemed to notice although Ana cried out, red faced and flailing limbs catching the strings of her bodice.

"Let me take Ana," Catarina said, her voice breaking. "I am drier now. And let me fetch you some poncha. I know you are shocked at the storms and with João away, but you must calm yourself. It will harm the baby if you are distressed when you feed her. Your shock and hurt and fear will enter her heart with your milk."

You do not know my fear, Anja-Filipa's heart cried out as she passed Ana into Catarina's arms. I am lost without my azulejo. *Everyone is lost. The island is lost,* the voice in her mind echoed. *They must be held together and never parted.*

She could not move. *She was cold, so very cold.*

"Here. Drink this. It will make you feel better."

A cup was pressed into her hand and she raised it to her lips, automatically taking a small sip. The depth of the white rum and the sharpness of the lemon soothed with the honey began to numb her senses.

She took a deep breath and looked across at Catarina, sitting on the bench beyond, bouncing Ana on her knee. She drank too quickly, and the room started to shimmer as she put the cup down on the stool at her side. Ana was laughing, chortling, at her aunt's exaggerated expressions - happy, while she herself was frozen with anxiety.

Anja-Filipa reached for her rosary and began to say it, fumbling with the beads in her trembling fingers.

A commotion in the rain-swept street outside

pounded in her head. Catarina leapt up with Ana still in her arms.

The door banged open again as a huge rough wet figure staggered in.

"Donna Anja-Filipa!"

She clutched at her robe and gasped, heart pounding. The baby let out a piercing shriek. Catarina jumped up just as Anja-Filipa did.

"*What*?" She felt the room swing around her, the floor unsteady beneath her feet.

The man pulled off his fisherman's cap and wrung it in his hands. "I ... I have news," he stammered. "I fear ..."

A wave of nausea rose in her gullet. "It is João, is it not? He is injured? Missing? Dead?"

And she crumpled to the floor, incapable of thought except one ... the azulejo.

∾

THEY TOLD HER THAT JOÃO HAD SLIPPED IN THE MUD AT the burial site, that he had fallen against the fragile wall under the dragon tree and that the stones had buried him, covering his face. When they had scrabbled the stones from him with bleeding fingers, they had seen his crushed head. They had seen the greyness of the matter that oozed from him and the redness of the blood that poured from the wounds into the flood waters and the mud.

She listened to their words, but they seemed to make little sense. Her body was as cold as the stones that had killed him and the mud that he lay in.

She felt hands upon her trying vainly to settle the baby in her arms.

And later she watched as if from a great distance as Catarina nursed the baby, suckling her at her dry breast.

People bustled around her, but she did not know who was there in her cottage, who arrived cautiously and who slipped out silently.

Her eyes were blurred, and her head was pounding like the thunder that had echoed around the bay and the rain that had pummelled the roof of the cottage.

Gradually as she was capable of speech again, she asked,

"Was anything found on him? Anything unusual? A pouch?"

They shook their heads. "No, nothing unusual. Only the torn clothes and the battered body ..."

"But something ... a tile? An azulejo?"

"An azulejo? No, why should there be? The tiles were all down at the capela where they had been repairing the damage and restoring the walls and floor."

"But you do not understand!" she cried, and Catarina tried to stroke her arm.

"It is all right. Please, do not distress yourself. We

are bringing him down in the ox cart and you will see him again. Please! Think of the baby."

But she could not think of the baby. She had let down her mother and her ancestors. She did not know what the task was, but somehow she knew that she had failed it.

~

Day after day she sensed Catarina attempting to press the baby into her arms and guide the little mouth to the breast. But day after day she would sigh and open her own chemise for Ana's questing lips. Anja-Filipa could see that somehow, miraculously Catarina's milk had started to flow from her, and the baby quieted. But she watched without any feeling. Just coldness and despair.

She saw João's body being brought into the cottage, his wounds covered and hidden from her eyes; she saw him being laid carefully across her bed, a cloth spread over his battered figure. She made no attempt to lift the covers from his face as she knew she should, nor to look at what horrors lay beneath, and she was aware of the puzzled frowns directed at her.

Her hand appeared to move tenderly over his body, over the little of it that was uncovered, but she hardly knew what she was doing. Half her mind was searching for something she was driven to find. But there was nothing. They had been right; there was nothing unusual there, except for the horror of the evidence of death.

She heard the anguished cries around her, Catarina wailing at the sight of her brother's prone, still figure, his mother held up by his brothers, all with tearful sobs.

Gradually her consciousness registered people talking in shocked tones around her. She recognised the voices, those Machico accents. João's family. How would she live, they asked each other? How could she raise the baby? However much they helped out, she had surely lost her mind, had she not?

She should come to Catarina's house, live there with her baby. Maybe in time she would take the baby back. But in the meantime Catarina and João's mother would look after the poor little one. Yes, that was decided. It was what João would have wanted.

Although she heard the talk, none of it seemed to relate to herself. She knew, of course, that it must be she herself they spoke of, but could not bring herself to care about any of it.

She had lost the most precious thing in her life. João, of course, her husband, although they were not properly married, in church with the priest's blessings, the father of her baby, was he not? A wisp of memory flitted across her mind: she wanted to live the rest of her life with him, had she not? This man. This beautiful man – that is how she remembered him. Yet he was not beautiful any more. He was not here, with her. He was gone. But she had known him for such a short time. And the thing that was most precious of all, that she had carried with her against her body all her life, along with the stone bearing the strange curled creature, was her mother's azulejo. And that loss broke her heart and mind in a way that nothing else could.

∼

THE STORMS OF THE PAST WEEKS HAD ABATED. The early morning sky was clear again and the waves sucked at the pebbles on the shore. She stood in her thin linen shift, looking out to sea, not aware of the old wizened fishermen mending the nets, heads bent trying not to catch her eye.

She heard a cry, but it might have been the squawk of a seagull or it might have been the wail of a baby, perhaps her baby Ana. Catarina was in her own house feeding her. She would be safe there with her. She did not need her real mother who birthed her but could not look after her.

There were no duties she needed to perform any more, no tasks, no rituals as she had at the convent. Her tortured mind flicked through the pages of memories: the quiet sounds of the cloisters, the swish of the nuns' robes, the closing her eyes before the reredos in the little chapel, the breeze through the leaves in the garden. The dragging and chopping of the hoe. The bell for Sext, the aroma of cooking drifting across from the kitchens. The peace of her cell as she read her breviary. Mother Superior's calm gentle voice. Sister Margaret's secret smile.

She pulled her rosary out from her pouch at her waist and swirled it around her wrist. As she did so, her eye caught the stain of her blood on the beads, the blood she had shed so long ago in her cell at the convent, when she had pricked her finger with the pin as she pulled off her filet and wimple. Before she first saw João.

She knew what she must do.

Turning towards the mountains, she climbed up the shingle to the street. She slipped quietly into the empty cottage and gently placed the pouch on the bed, noticing the slight bulge which marked the creature in the stone. She brought it to her lips, and then tucked it beneath the covers for baby Ana to find when she was older.

She quickly pulled on her robe and cloak and opened the door. She took nothing with her but the rosary on her wrist and her breviary tucked into her chemise. But she looked up to the mountains that rose high above Machico, as she knew they also towered above the town of Funchal.

Anja-Filipa turned her face in the direction of the convent.

CHAPTER 31

VIV

Present day

"But she never found it!" Viv said, clutching the side of the boat and staring across the expanse of sea towards the coast, the mountains, and the town of Funchal nestling in the foothills, strands of houses straggling away up the steep slopes. Her eyes sought the slash of the valley in the distance where she knew the convent stood.

"Found what? Who?" Bértrand touched her arm. She swung round startled. He was frowning at her. But in his hand he held something he had brought out from the cabin.

"Wha ... I ... I don't know!" Viv tried to shake away the visions in her mind, the images that flickered through her brain, like a film behind her eyes, or like memories that were growing clearer. She reached into the pocket of her shorts and touched the fossil that nestled there, stroking its hard core, the curled creature five million years old, asleep forever in the stone. She saw the novice nun, Anja-Filipa, her baby she named Ana, a little rough fisherman's cottage where she was happy for a time. She saw grief, loss and a frozen heart, a mind disturbed. She saw the fossil that Anja-Filipa had hidden for Ana to find, that the child would never discover. That for some reason she didn't know, was left there in the cottage, undiscovered. She saw the little house gradually falling into disrepair over the years, and finally in ruins, the timbers rotting, the bedding ravaged by rats, and the signs of life disappeared. She saw the fossil bury itself into the earth once more, forgotten.

For her parents to find, centuries later.

"Here. Look at this," said Bértrand cutting across her visions. Viv shook herself into the present. For a moment she couldn't think where she was, what she was doing on this boat with Bértrand. "This special artefact." He held something out to her, and she looked from his face to his hand.

He was holding out an azulejo. She took it from him and turned it over and over. It was blue and white with smooth raised markings. On one side of the glazed upper surface were symbols she knew were Arabic and on the other were the letters IHS, the Greek letters, iota eta sigma. IHΣ. In Latin, Jesu Hominum Salvator. Jesus Our Saviour. But there was also a brown pigment, maybe it had once been gold.

And a streak of something. It looked almost like blood, but it was a purplish kind of red.

Bértrand was saying something to her, but she could barely hear him above the clamour of her thoughts. She struggled to focus her mind on him.

"What is this?" Bértrand was asking her. "I know it is important. But I only know what is in the museum about the azulejo. This piece is different. I think that, whatever you say, you have researched into these pieces and I think you have accessed the origins and history. You said to me ... You called out ... I have to know, is it the lost azulejo?"

Viv ran her fingers gently over the markings. Her heart was beating so loudly she was sure that Bértrand could hear it. She struggled to make her voice sound as if it was not trembling. "So. Where did you get it?"

"I was asked to keep it somewhere safe and not to show it to anyone. But you are different. I think you know more than you say. And I need to know whether it is precious. For the museum."

"But who was it, who gave it to you?"

"That does not matter. I need to know whether perhaps we could sell it, to a private buyer. If it would help our developments at the museum."

"It is ... strange. And *I* need to know who gave it to you, where it came from, what its past is," Viv insisted.

Bértrand sighed. "It was given to me by John Waller, the church warden at ..."

"Yes, yes, at Holy Trinity, I know who he is. But where did he find it and why did he give it to you?"

"I understand that he discovered it when he was doing some work in the church gardens, under ancient stones, by the dragon tree that is still there."

"I see." Viv could hear the voices in her head as they told her that João had slipped in the mud at the burial site, that he had fallen against the fragile wall under the dragon tree and that the stones had buried him, covering his face. Yet of course it wasn't her but Anja-Filipa. And she remembered seeing John with a spade in the church garden under the dragon tree – although that must have been long after he found the azulejo. Perhaps he had been looking to see if there was anything else there. "But why did John Waller give it to *you*?"

"He was afraid." Bértrand grimaced. "There are markings – I know them as Arabic - as well as Christian symbols on it and he feared them."

"Feared the Arabic markings?"

"Feared what they might represent. Moorish influences. The idea that there was some link between Moorish people, Islamic maybe, and Christians. I think he holds very close the history of this island, the Christian history, the discovery by Portuguese Christian explorers. He became most agitated as he was asking me to keep the azulejo away from anyone else's eyes."

"Then why did he not destroy it? I mean, thank

God he didn't, but if he was so afraid of what it represented, why not get rid of it completely?"

"He said that he thought it held something evil, and he dare not destroy it, that it had made terrible things happen at the church whilst he kept it there."

"Like what?"

"I did not press him any further than he was willing to say. He was most agitated. He just kept on saying that he did not want it on his hands. He worried that the new priests would begin to investigate the strange happenings in the church. He spoke of ghosts, hauntings. I thought he was ..." Bértrand made a circular movement with his hand against his head. "A little crazy. So I said I would hide it away for him, to stop his ramblings. I do not know what goes on at that church. It is not mine. I do not understand what goes on in the minds of the Anglicans! When I attend communion, it is at the proper Catholic cathedral." He shrugged. "But he said he was in touch with someone who could help him ... er ... a private investigator?"

"What for?"

"He said to find out how much the priest, you, knew."

Viv shook her head. So, she *had* seen him coming out of that office, what was it? ... Jorges da Freitas?

Viv thought back to things that John Waller had said and done, and her mind began to clear. "He took on board the fear that he – and others have – of weird happenings, superstitions. And he used those very things to try to rid the church of anyone he feared might investigate and discover the azulejo with the Arabic markings. Did he fear what might be Islamic markings or maybe that they might be some kind of evil runes? Something bad for the church anyway. It's prejudiced and frankly ridiculous. Madeira does have a history way, way back."

So, John Waller had realised that she was an academic, someone who knew about the medieval world, someone who was asking questions. He probably found out that Rory also had a doctorate in ancient religious symbols. He had set out to frighten them off. She recalled Georgina's words about the previous priests during the interregnum only staying a short while. She guessed that John would never have felt safe.

Well, he wouldn't frighten them off. If Rory wanted to stay, they would. How dare John hurt other people for his own ridiculous obsessions?

"Wait a minute," she looked up from the tile at Bértrand. "So why would he give it to you? How do you know him?"

"I … he found out something that I did not want made public," Bértrand grimaced. "Something that would have damaged someone else."

She guessed. "A woman?"

He shrugged. "I had no choice. But of course, *you* …"

"Ah. You used me? To find the truth about this tile?"

"Oh, no! I was – I *am* – really very attracted to you. We would be good together."

Viv narrowed her eyes, a growing awareness bringing into focus so much of what had been happening. "Absolutely not. How dare you, Bértrand. This is all madness." She turned away from him, from his attractive eyes and soft charming voice. How could she have been so blind? Blinded by his attention and his flattery. She shook her head and drew in her breath. A sharp pain in her lower belly made her hand automatically reach down and stroke her abdomen. It felt sore again, as it had done weeks ago. "How dare you take advantage of my situation."

"No, no, that was not so. I would never take advantage." She felt his warm hand creep round her waist, tantalisingly intimate in its caress. "You are so attractive to me. I cannot resist you. Beautiful. Clever...."

Viv swung round to face him. "Don't."

He shrugged and held up his hand in a defensive gesture. "I understand your distress. This azulejo. It has some kind of hold over you perhaps? So maybe we can help each other now. Do you not think? We are friends!" He paused and smiled slyly. "And, yes, OK, maybe I thought we could be 'the friends with the benefits' – is that what you say?"

Viv sighed. "No, I don't think so. Perhaps for a moment back there I behaved ... inappropriately. You are very charming, Bértrand. I can't deny that. But, oh dear, I'm a little vulnerable at the moment, you know? And you hit a weak spot. Just think of it as a slight aberration, a mistake. I'm sorry, but I can't have an affair with you, Bértrand."

He smiled. "You know, I think you are the first woman who has ever said that to me. I am used to getting my way. But, in a strange way, I admire that."

"Really? Well, maybe it's about time, then."

"But we can be friends, beautiful Viv?"

"Of course we can be *friends*. But only if you stop trying to hit on me."

"Hit you? I would never hit you, or any lady!"

"No, hit *on* me ...it just means, well flirting."

"Oh dear, I cannot promise not to try to flirt with you."

Viv shook her head. He was incorrigible. "Well then, just understand that it won't work any more."

"So, do we shake hands now?" He stood before her, legs apart, head bent to one side, and grinned. She couldn't help smiling back and shrugging a casual affirmative.

She looked down at the azulejo in her hand, turning it over in her palm and tracing the markings gently with her fingertips, knowing that other fingers had done the same, centuries ago, Lady Ana d'Arafet seven hundred years ago, possibly Filipe her renegade descendent, Anja-Filipa the nun become mother and peasant fisherman's wife. And the last person to hold it and look kindly upon it, João, in his last moments.

"OK, but this azulejo, my dear Viv," his words cut across her thoughts. "Please help me with this, I beg you. Is this artefact valuable? Should I ... could I reveal it and sell it? There may be perhaps someone in America who might be interested in such an item. What is your professional opinion?"

Viv turned the azulejo over in her hand, making a show of peering closely at it. Who did it really belong to? John who had found it but clearly didn't want to keep it even though he couldn't destroy it. Bértrand who had been given it for safe-keeping. João who had died with it. Anja-Filipa who had inherited it from her mother, her ancestor Ana through Sir Robert's family, even the Machyms represented now by Georgina?

Or herself who was invoked to bring it to its rightful place with the fossil her parents had left her?

She could not let this go. She remembered the words that drifted through her mind. The fossil and the azulejo must be united. She was the only one who could do that.

She could keep them together in her parents' memory box, along with the story of their survival and discovery. And her own children, if she had any, would inherit them in their turn.

There was no way some dealer in America could provide the ending that Ana d'Arafet had appealed for to her, whispering in her head across the centuries.

And even if that person was a genuine collector of artefacts or religious symbols, or an historian of religion, or whatever else, there was no guarantee that the outcome would be right. Morally right, anyway.

There was only one way she could fulfil Ana d'Arafet and Anja-Filipa's desires. Viv took a deep breath.

"My professional opinion? It is a beautiful item, but objectively, no it is not financially valuable. It is worthless." Monetarily speaking that may well be true. "These markings, I think, are fake," she lied. "And see here, the purple-red stain? Look at its colour, its shape. The Arabic markings. Look, this one isn't accurate. No, I'm afraid that it is only a poor copy of the legendary lost azulejo."

Bértrand sighed and shook his head. "So it is worth nothing to the museum, either in investment or as an historic artefact. Well. I kind of guessed so. John was completely mistaken. Or he was playing with me, blackmailing me, perhaps. So, you take it as a memento of me. I may as well have a picture of it in the museum as the real thing. Why, after all, would it possibly have been buried in the Anglican church's garden, under a dragon tree?"

Viv smiled, wrapped her fingers tightly around it and hoped that he did not see the relief in her eyes. "Why indeed."

CHAPTER 32

VIV

Present day

"So what would you have done?" Viv asked Rory. She crossed her fingers that he wouldn't say that he would have given it away, to any supposed rightful owners or to the museum or wherever.

She drummed the crossed fingers against the metal of the balcony chair. She hadn't told him the full story about Bértrand and their relationship. Well, it wasn't really a relationship after all, was it? Not even a fling. Nothing happened, did it? And sometimes certain things were best kept in the past, if they had no bearing on the present, and would only cause unnecessary hurt and pain. But she had recounted to him, diplomatically, the events that had led to the discovery, at last, of Ana d'Arafet's and Anja-Filipa's azulejo.

Rory was silent for a while and Viv watched him as he frowned and ran his fingers over the tile she had laid in his hand. Then he hooked a finger over the edge of his clerical collar as if to loosen it a little. "And you're sure that this tile is the one that she lent to João for the pattern in the capela?" Viv nodded. "Then I think the right thing is to do what those voices, those shapes on the air, are telling you. In the vast scheme of things, set against the enormity of history and time, it must be right. To bury the fossil and the azulejo together in the most significant place where they will remain for eternity. Under the dragon tree."

"*Bury*?" Viv flushed and turned away from him to look over the garden, her eyes seeking out the dragon tree standing firm against the wall. She was at least thankful he hadn't suggested praying together about a solution, the right path ahead. That would have been too much. Although she was sure that he had done just that in his head.

She was also thankful that he hadn't declared that the azulejo should be given to Georgina, which was the other option she feared. Of course, if he had, he would have outlined excellent reasons why he had come to that conclusion and she would have been torn.

"So what were *you* thinking, then?"

"Well, I was going to suggest that I kept them together in my parents' memory box ..."

THE DRAGON TREE

"Er, but they aren't your memories. Or even your parents' memories since they didn't find the azulejo. May not even have known that there was one to find."

"No, but it seems appropriate that they are kept together as I'm sure I'm being called to do. And I couldn't think of a better, safer place."

Rory nodded. He placed the azulejo carefully on the table between them and they both stared at it for a few moments. "OK. I see that. But the memory box will be in the UK, far from here. And the significance is for Madeiran history."

"Oh Rory! I don't know!" Another twinge of pain flickered across her abdomen and she rubbed it. "I'm just so tired. I feel as though I could sleep for years."

Rory frowned and reached his hand across to stroke hers. "Are you OK?"

Viv grimaced. "Not really. There's been so many strange things happening lately and I guess it's been stressful. After all the stress of losing Ana and coming here and ... and everything that's come in its wake."

"I'm sorry, Viv. I shouldn't have brought you here." He raked his hand through his hair and stood up from the table to pace along the balcony. "I thought it would help. You know, distancing ourselves from what happened. But then, things went wrong. And I guess it challenged my faith a bit."

Viv caught his hand as he paced past and felt that he was shaking. "I know. I guess the miscarriage affected you more deeply than I realised. I guess it's no wonder your faith should be challenged. And you've had to sort out a lot of mess here, what with the church finances that John failed to keep an eye on..."

"I think it was more than that. I'm afraid to say it but I've gone through all the accounts and records and contracts thoroughly and it seems that he could have been ... well ... embezzling money – not a lot, but some, and I've had to bring in the church's accountant. She couldn't find anything concrete, but amounts didn't tally and it all points to one person. John's been acting as the treasurer during the whole interregnum. The books don't balance, Viv. I found discrepancies right from the start. I don't understand why the others didn't find or suspect anything. Maybe they just didn't want to look into things too carefully."

"Oh Rory, why didn't you share with me more, why didn't you involve me? I thought you were blocking me out."

"I didn't want to worry you or give you any more to stress about when I knew you were devastated after the miscarriage. And anyway, Georgina was trying to help."

"Hmm." Viv flushed.

Rory bent and kissed the top of her head. "You aren't ... *jealous*, are you?" His hands slid around her body and rested just below the swell of her breasts. She knew that he could feel her heat.

"And was there ... *is* there ... anything I should feel jealous of? You spend a lot of time holed up with her."

THE DRAGON TREE

He laughed into her hair and kissed her again. "Georgina! Of course not. Goodness, why on earth would I look at *anyone* else when I have you, my gorgeous wife? Although ..." she could hear his voice softening, "I rather like the idea of you being a bit jealous! But seriously, Viv, no, I spend a lot of time holed up with various people. Trying to sort out the issues here hasn't been easy."

"I know that."

"And anyway, what about this Bértrand fellow?"

She had the grace to blush. "Honestly, Rory, there's nothing of any importance to tell. He is no threat to us."

"But *was* he?" The uncertainty in his voice caught her breath but she knew it was all in the past now and she shook her head. "OK, I get it. Husband neglecting you." The uncertainty swerved into teasing. She'd go with that.

"Hey, don't put me on the back foot! And where's the gratitude for solving the mystery of John Waller and his little games?"

Rory pulled her up to standing and wrapped his arms around her, bending to nuzzle her neck. "I am grateful. I've already said that. And I'll show my gratitude even more tonight. Or right now if you prefer? The pew sheets can wait." He pulled her tightly to him, almost crushing her against his chest. She could feel his heart beating. "If I've seemed distant, I'm really sorry. If I've seemed to be ensconced in my study,

I'm sorry. It's all been a bit overwhelming." He stroked her hair, bending to blow the escaping tendrils that had escaped from her messy pony-tail. "Do I really have to tell you again that I love you – more than I could possibly say? That I love you more than when I met you in the bistro? More than when we got married? More each day I live with you?"

Viv buried her head in his black priest's shirt, feeling the edges of the clerical collar insert underneath it, and smiled. "Yes," she said. "Yes, you do."

～

Later, as Rory made fresh coffee for them both, Viv wandered from the bedroom into the living room of the apartment and sighed.

"Oh goodness," said Rory, "that sounded deep from the heart. What is it?"

"My fossil."

"What about it?"

"I know we were talking about burying the azulejo and my fossil here in Madeira. Under the dragon tree. But, Rory, when you said that, I really didn't want to let it go. And I still don't, deep in my heart."

He turned and took her into his arms. "The fossil is so precious to you, because it was in your parents' finds and you kept it all these years in your memory box. It's different with the azulejo. You didn't even know it

THE DRAGON TREE

existed until recently." She felt his hand soothingly stroking up and down her spine. "But the legend – and we're assuming it's true – is about both of them, and the need to keep them both together. The reality is, therefore, that they should both have been discovered by your parents in their Machico dig. That seems to have been Lady Ana d'Arafet's intention."

"My parents never found Lady Ana's tomb, or so it seems, even if it existed. But even if they had, the fossil and azulejo wouldn't have been there. They must have found the fossil somewhere around Anja-Filipa's cottage, and of course the azulejo was lost up at the site where our church is now, under our dragon tree there in the garden."

Rory drew in his breath. "Hmm. So when was the first time you had these ... visions ... about Madeira, about Lady Ana?"

Viv pulled back a little from him and looked up into his clear dark eyes. "Well, you know that it was after we'd lost baby Ana, and when you told me about the secondment to Madeira." She could still see, in her mind's eye, standing in the rectory drawing room, the French windows giving out to the rainy dank gardens, the fossil clutched in her hand. She looked down. Her nails were no longer bitten and ugly as they had been that day. They were freshly polished and smooth. She opened her palm against Rory's chest. The scars the fossil had made that day were gone; the surface of the skin healed. "When I was consumed by grief and loss."

He reached for her hand and his thumb stroked her palm, tracing where the scars had been. "We'll always feel the loss. But is it exactly the same now, for you?"

Viv thought about the way she had changed since being here on this island. She was no longer shrivelled with grief and guilt. Yes, the awful loss was still there in her heart, but it was different. Time wouldn't take away those feelings, but they were not as raw as they had been, so wounding, making her feel so vulnerable. She'd been jealous of Georgina, no doubt about it, and thought that Rory was drifting away from her, maybe to seek comfort from someone else who was not so damaged. She knew now that was her own construct and she'd drawn herself away from him in consequence.

"It's different now, I guess. A deeper feeling of loss, not so much on the surface as it was, not so much a wound that could easily be opened up again." She frowned. "I don't think about her constantly. She's always there and I do think about her every day – it'll always be like that, I guess. Little things that bring it all flooding back. But I can deal with it now. I don't feel so consumed with guilt. I understand now what you said before, about time not exactly healing but making it easier to deal with."

He was silent for a while, then he whispered softly into her neck as he drew her close. "Both of us, we've been through so much." She wondered if he had in fact been tempted by Georgina. But then she supposed she'd been tempted by Bértrand. In a way. "Viv, can we start again, do you think?"

"Start again?"

"I mean, here, on this island. The fossil, the visions, the island, Ana – they're inextricably connected, aren't they? It's almost as if they all collided somehow that day at the rectory, and then pulled you into a cycle of history. How do we break that cycle?"

"Well, there must have been many other 'Ana's over the centuries, connected with Lady Ana's family and the Machym's, Anja-Filipa and her daughter. And my family. I know it was the name of some ancestor of my mother's but ...Why me? And why did I decide on the name 'Ana' for our baby - why did that name thrust itself into my mind? As if it was meant to be? Maybe others through the centuries have been involved but never finding a resolution. And it's all come down to me, to us." Viv bit her lip, something she realised she hadn't done for ages. "It's the fossil and my grief, isn't it? Colliding with the island across time?"

"I think I understand what you're saying."

"OK. I can't let go of baby Ana. The grief is not so intense. I've let go of the way it consumed me, even though the loss is still there. So, the only other thing I can do is to let go of the fossil." A silent tear was coursing down her cheek. "It came from here, from Machico, just along the coast. Both the fossil and the azulejo originally came from the place where Lady

Ana d'Arafet lived and died. Our dragon tree was just a symbol to call to us, a cry to make us listen, to make us find the azulejo. The tile and my fossil – *the* fossil – need to go back to where they came from, in Machico. It's time."

Rory pulled her in so tightly that she thought he might crush her against him. He cleared his throat. "Are you sure?"

She took a deep breath. "Yes. I'm sure. And you think that's what we must do, don't you?"

"I do."

"The site in Machico where Lady Ana died and the crevice in the rock where she found the azulejo no longer exist. It's all under concrete promenades and shops and hotels. But I know that Sir Robert Machym buried her on the headland above the bay. I just *know* it. Rory, I think that's where we need to go."

Rory stroked her back gently and she could feel him smiling into the top of her head. "Yes. I feel that's right."

"OK. Let's do it. Before I change my mind and want hold on to my fossil for ever."

She could sense Rory nodding into her hair, and the slightest breath of his sigh. "And after that ... what will you feel about the island? Do you want to leave it and go home?"

Viv thought of the beauty of the landscape, the vegetation, the warmth, the ocean. "No. I want us to resolve this thing together and sort out the issues at the church – together this time. Something needs to be done about John Waller, for one thing, and these ridiculous superstitions. And then perhaps we can actually start to enjoy this beautiful place. What do you say?"

"I say you're the best wife and partner I could possibly have at my side."

She laughed. "What? Better than Georgina?" she teased.

Viv lifted her head enough to catch his wink.

"I don't think I need to say anything to that!"

CHAPTER 33

VIV

Machico

They struggled up the isolated rocky track on the headland above Machico and its wide bay that was fringed with modern concrete hotels. A warm breeze blew in from the sea. Rory stopped, rested his burden of long-handled planter for a moment, digging it into the earth, and held out his hand to Viv.

"OK?"

She felt in the pocket of her shorts for the shapes of the fossil and the azulejo, aware that she didn't want to prick herself with the sharp edges this time. But it was unlikely as she had wrapped them both, together, in a scrap of bubble wrap she'd found in the kitchen drawer at the apartment. In her hessian carrier bag was a cutting she'd taken from the dragon tree in their garden.

"Yes, I'll be fine." She took his hand and felt his reassuring squeeze.

Truth be told, she'd wobbled that morning and again on the drive along the coast to Machico. What if she couldn't do it at the last minute?

But then she had thought of the consequences – that the visions might never end. That it might all go on and on, after Anja-Filipa, through the centuries. She was convinced that it was all true, not only a legend, but she was only supposing that it ended with her hiding the fossil for her daughter. What if someone else had found it and the story had continued with others? She had only guessed that it was buried, undiscovered, for her parents to find it at their dig. What if that wasn't what happened at all, and that wasn't the end of the story until her parents dug up the site of the cottage? No, she must hold on to the belief that this would be the end of it all, right here, back in Machico.

"We're doing the right thing, Viv, I'm sure of it," Rory said. "I know it's hard for you."

It was, but she must remember that she had her other mementos of her parents, in her memory box. The letters, the personal things that meant so much more than this fossil.

They had to climb a narrow stony path a few metres down from the edge of the cliff top to a wide ledge. In her intensive research into Machico over the past few days since they had decided on their course of action, Viv had found a rare and unremarked geophysical image on an obscure online website. It indicated an area that could possibly have been disturbed long ago, and something, maybe a whisper, in her mind told her that this was the place. It was merely a hunch and of course she could be wrong. But somehow she knew.

They couldn't have it confirmed because they couldn't let anyone know about it. If word got out there, it was possible that someone somewhere could apply to excavate the site. Perhaps fourteenth century bones might be discovered. Or evidence of fifteenth century disturbance of the burial site. Viv knew that couldn't be allowed to happen. Lady Ana d'Arafet must be left in peace. That was, after all, what this was all about.

Anyway, there was no way she could explain how she knew about this burial. Who would believe her story of visions, voices across the centuries, the intersections of time?

But of course, everyone thought it was only a legend, didn't they? The museum designated it as such. The real history of Madeira began with its discovery by the Portuguese explorers led by João Gonçalves Zarco who were sent by Prince Henry the Navigator. The rest was largely conjecture. Wasn't it?

Viv looked up at the squat old dragon tree that

THE DRAGON TREE

grew at a strange angle nearby and stretched its branches out over the rocky slope towards the sea. So many like it all over the island. Yet this one seemed to her to weep its dark brown sap to the red soil beneath.

"Here, I think." Viv felt a strange excitement fill her and for a few moments her mind juddered.

Rory looked questioningly at her and she nodded. He began to thrust the planter into the hard earth. Then it suddenly slipped abruptly downwards, and Rory stumbled with it.

"Heavens! The soil's quite soft just a few inches below the surface. As if ..." He didn't need to finish the sentence.

Viv took a deep breath. "This is it."

When Rory had jiggled a hole wide and deep enough, he stood back and looked at Viv. She knelt down and reached for the fossil and azulejo in her pocket. She lifted the bubble wrap from around them and stared at the fossil for a while. This was one of the hardest things she had done in her life. She looked at the curled creature embedded within it and knew that this did not 'belong' to her, or to her parents before her, or to any person. It belonged to the earth, to the land of this island that had risen up from the seabed five million years ago. She touched the ammonite with her fingertips before she gently slid it along with its companion, the azulejo, into the darkness of the grave.

A mist wafted across her sight and the earth shifted, the ground beneath her knees trembling. She thought she heard a voice sighing. And she was aware of a ripple in the air, a rising of the wind, a murmur of time, of worlds, as Ana d'Arafet's spirit fell from the air above the island and settled down deep into the earth.

She did not see it, but she knew that the fossil and the azulejo sank through the soil and came to rest amongst the hidden forgotten bones that had lain there, disturbed and shifting, for so many centuries. A long receiving sigh reverberated through the earth beneath Viv's feet.

Viv exhaled, not realising that she had been holding her breath, and felt as though a physical burden had lifted from her shoulders. A sense of absolute relief filled her body and her heart soared.

She pulled the cutting out of her bag as Rory dug another hole with his planter, and there she set the new little dragon tree, ready to settle its roots and grow and spread, mingling with the ancient tree, uniting the past and the present in this place, sheltering its secrets.

"There. That's done," she whispered. "It's as it should be."

She felt Rory's arm slip around her shoulders. "Are you OK, darling?"

She nodded.

Hand in hand they made their way back down the rocky hillside towards the town below. Viv felt a pain in her lower abdomen, and it reminded her of the loss of their baby Ana. She could see the beach below, with its black sand stretching out on either side of the promenade and the jetty, and she thought of Lady Ana so long ago in that tiny rough-hewn shelter, long gone, giving birth to the son she would never see grow up.

A wisp of a memory floated across her mind, insubstantial, almost out of reach.

Thomas. Sir Thomas.

A growl. "I cannot wait." A fat red face thrust into hers. Spittle flying from his bread-filled mouth onto her cheek. Grabbing at her skirts and pushing them up. Shrieking "no!" against the raucous noise beyond. Hot sweaty flesh against hers. Scratching, beating, desperate. A thrusting and a sharp searing pain in her groin. Pumping, grunting like a stuck pig. Then, nothing ...

Viv stopped in her tracks. Rory turned to her, wide-eyed. "*What?*"

"Oh my God," she stuttered. "Lady Ana. Her baby. The son. The one from whom all the others, down to Anja-Filipa, and beyond, came. Maybe he wasn't Sir Robert's! She was raped at court by Sir Thomas."

"Sir Thomas?"

"I don't know who he was. Only that he was a courtier in King Edward's court, a favourite of the king's and of Lady Ana's father."

Rory was staring at her.

"Maybe the son was the product of the rape. In which case the line was broken. Or perhaps she felt a huge guilt."

"But that wouldn't have been her fault if she'd been raped."

"No, of course not. But did she ever tell Sir Robert? Or did she keep it to herself. Maybe hoping that he might have been Robert's. She loved him so. Did she deceive him? Or did Robert collude in the pretence, perhaps thinking it could well be his child after all?"

"Well," Rory stroked Viv's arm, "we'll never know that."

But Viv was still pondering. "I'm just wondering if it was Lady Ana's guilt about a deception that meant her spirit couldn't rest? And that the fossil and azulejo that had been buried with her in the first place were symbolic of peace and the beginning of things?"

"In any case, Lady Ana and the troubled Anja-Filipa are now at rest, aren't they? You know, Viv, I felt the earth shift as you buried the artefacts. It was strange. As though the ground, the foundations of the island were receiving them."

Viv nodded. She knew only too well.

Church bells were ringing out down in the town and Rory interlinked his fingers through hers. "Come on. Let's go. To focus on the present, I've got a meeting with John Waller shortly that I'm not looking forward to at all. And then the PCC."

"At the very least that will clear the air – and explain a few things."

"Viv, are you sure that you want to stay on here, after all this?"

Her eyes swept the vista of the bay down in Machico and she thought of the centuries of history behind them. She looked at the little chapel out on the promontory that welcomed people to the island, the shingle that swept down over the black sands to the sea, the cliffs that had sheltered Ana and Robert seven centuries ago. The old cottages where Anja-Filipa had lived simply two hundred years later as a fisherman's wife and had born her child were no longer there, but she could imagine where they had been – and where her parents had excavated and found the fossil. She looked back at the mountains that she knew rose steeply up from the promenade along the coast in Funchal, the slash of the valley that hid the Eiro da Serrado where Anja-Filipa and the nuns had sought refuge, the almost vertiginous street that led up to the convent of Santa Clara.

She couldn't see the Rua do Quebra Costas further west in Funchal and where she knew that Holy Trinity church nestled. Yet she could see in her mind the beauty of the jewel-bright bougainvillea spreading across the pergola in their garden, the pretty pink hibiscus and the scent of the oleander, the tall fragrant eucalyptus, and the jacaranda. She saw the red pantiled roofs of the whitewashed houses perched on the hillsides. She could hear the shrill cries of the gulls wheeling high above their apartment and the sweet gentle birdsong in the air. She heard the deep boom of the Porto Santo ferry early in the mornings, the crash of the ocean on the rocks. She smelled the wood smoke and the deep scent of the sea. She felt the warmth of the sun on her shoulders as she sat on their balcony working on her laptop, reading her research papers.

And she could see the strange shape of their dragon tree nestling by the stone wall in the church garden, its gnarled branches reaching downwards to cover its secrets.

Viv realised that she had repeated the designation "their" and knew that it was true. She turned and looked up at Rory.

"Yes," she said and raised her hand to smooth the frown on his forehead. "I do want to stay on here. I want us to make it all OK again, and to make the most of the rest of our time here. There's so much I want to explore. This time with you." She smiled. "Before we have to go back to our cold Derbyshire rectory!"

EPILOGUE

"How did it go?" Viv looked up from her laptop as Rory stepped out of the living room onto the balcony.

He had lost the pained frown that had darkened his face for some time, and the worried defensive expression that had clouded his eyes. Today, his eyes were bright against his tanned skin and he held out his hand to touch her upturned cheek. She noticed the golden hairs on his forearms gleaming in the hot sun and felt his long sensitive fingers gently exploring her face. He was smiling and looked as though a burden had fallen away from him.

"OK. I won't bore you with the details, but John Waller is leaving the church and the island. He flies back home to the UK next week. Not sure whether the church here will want to take it any further, but I've provided them with a copy of my findings. It's up to them to decide what they want to do with it. Georgina said she'd reluctantly stay on as church warden for a couple of weeks until two more are appointed. I don't think she was too keen, too much hassle, she said. But I don't think she ever really wanted to do it in the first place. She says she wants to take a back seat from the church and spend more of the year in mainland Portugal. I think there's some grand family property there." He grinned at Viv. "And she kept mentioning someone called 'Philip' who was apparently her late husband's business partner in Lisbon. Very wealthy, I understand."

Viv smiled. "Well, that's probably best all round, then. Do you know, Rory, I always wondered how much she actually knew about what was going on with John. I mean, how could she not have known about the mess he was making and what he was into? She must have had her suspicions if nothing else – surely? Or perhaps it was her irritating over-familiar behaviour around you that seemed so dubious. Perhaps I'm reading too much into it. And maybe I'm just cynical."

Rory shrugged. "It hardly matters any more. I'm just glad it's all resolved, thanks in no small measure to you."

He moved away from Viv and leaned against the balcony rail. She drank in his height, his broad shoulders, thick dark hair curling around his ears and the nape of his neck, and as he smiled ruefully back at her, his olive skin and deep smoky eyes, the designer stubble across his strong jawline, she remembered the man she had fallen in love with, the man she nearly lost.

"I was thinking," he said, "we need to celebrate a burden lifted. I say we book a romantic candlelit dinner tonight at that place, the Golden Gate, used to be called the Grand Café, you know, on the Avenida Arriaga, by the Zarco statue. I know it's expensive, but I think we deserve it, don't you? What do you say?"

Viv raised her eyebrows. He'd clearly not remembered that she'd been there with Georgina. "That would be great. I hear the food is lovely and the service old-fashioned and rather grand."

She winced at a slight pain in her abdomen, the discomfort of something nestling, embedding itself. She'd felt it for some time but consigned it to the backburner with all that had been happening.

"We'll break out a bottle of champagne."

"Probably not so much for me," Viv smiled. That morning, in the bathroom, she'd stared at the word on the little screen in her hand, with a mixture of joy, fear, and apprehension.

"Are you OK?"

"Well, I have a doctor's appointment this afternoon." She stroked her belly and Rory's eyes followed her hand, a glimmer of a hesitant, hopeful smile on his lips. "I think I'll have some news for you that might be another cause for celebration."

. . .

If you enjoyed *The Dragon Tree* check out Julia Ibbotson's other books at http://Author.to/JuliaIbbotsonauthor

and her website at https://juliaibbotsonauthor.com to read the latest news about her writing life and her books, as well as life in Anglo-Saxon times and a few recipes thrown in!

She would love to hear from you! You can also sign up for her newsletter from the website if you would like.

If you enjoyed the book, please consider writing a brief review on Amazon. She'd be very grateful.

Many thanks!

AFTERWORD

AUTHOR'S NOTES – HISTORY OR LEGEND? THE BACKGROUND TO THE STORY

I love stories that ask, 'what if' and play around with history, mingling conventional truth with imagination. My regular readers will already know this from ***A Shape on the Air*** (and other novels) which precedes the events of this book. I do, however, try to make it clear in my books which is which.

Although a considerable amount of this novel is based on historical truth (as we are given it), and some local legend, I have also taken a few liberties in an imaginative exploration of 'what might have been'.

So, what is 'true' and what is not? The subtropical island of Madeira is a beautiful place and the museum by the cable car exists (although not Bértrand!). The English church of Holy Trinity is there off the Quebra

AFTERWORD

do Costas, up the steep streets from the centre of Funchal, and there certainly is a Capela do Corpo Santo in a little square in the Old Town and both are much as I have described in the novel, with one or two changes for dramatic effect, of course.

The volcanic origins of the island are as accurate as I can make them geologically (I started as a geologist) and much of the background is on public view at the São Vincente lava caves and museum. The island is also rightly famous for its beautiful examples of azulejos. And so, in my mind, the story of the fossil ammonite and the legendary azulejo began.

The character of the novice nun Anja-Filipa is entirely fiction, but the convent of Santa Clara in Funchal exists and is well worth a visit. The artefacts there provided me with some fascinating material to slip into my story: the reredos for example. The nuns did flee from the convent up to Eiro do Serrado ('Nuns' Valley') in 1566 as a result of the invasion by corsairs led by Montluc. As far as I'm aware there is no descendent currently on the island ... but I guess there *could* have been.

While Machico is a town east along the coast from Funchal, as far as I know there have been no excavations of the kind I describe in my novel, nor the area of geophysical interest on the cliffside above the bay, so please don't go searching for it.

Let me also say categorically, however, that the present-day church wardens and the priests of my

AFTERWORD

story are purely the products of my creative imagination, and are not based on any real persons, living or dead. The church did experience a period of interregnum and that is when I first came by the notion (purely in my mind) of problems that could potentially arise in such a situation without the guiding eyes of a permanent priest. I am sure that the current (and past) church wardens are nothing at all like John Waller!

But I wanted to link these theoretical church problems to the history of this fascinating island. I am, by profession and personal interest, an almost obsessive researcher. And my investigation into the history of Madeira has been intriguing, not least by its hints and vaguenesses, its fascinating glimpses of possible truths and its many myths. A gift for any novelist.

So, here's the history bit. Conventional accounts of the history of the island state that Madeira was discovered by the Portuguese explorer João Gonçalves Zarco, having been blown off-course in storms in 1418 onto the nearby island of Porto Santo, and then on sighting a strange cloud formation swirling around another island nearby, he investigated, arriving in Machico, Madeira, in 1419. The following year Prince Henry ('the Navigator') sent Zarco (along with Teixeira and Perestrello) to begin the settlement and population of the islands. By 1483 the 'Ilha da Madeira' appears widely on maps.

AFTERWORD

However, my research indicated that there were references to what could well be Madeira in much earlier maps and documents: recent excavations on the Selvagens (islands off Madeira) suggest possible Bronze Age structures, and Pliny the Elder (23-79AD) refers to Madeira as the 'purple isles', possibly from the sap of the 'dragon tree' which was a precious commodity for making regal purple dyes. I found references by Moorish scholars of Arab adventurers from North Africa and the Iberian peninsula (from 8th-15th centuries), even a band of runaways from Lisbon landing on what was supposedly Madeira, 'an island populated by cattle' in 1147, and a map by the Genoese Nicoluso da Recco dated 1341. The Medici Atlas dated 1351 shows the Atlantic islands at 'the very western edge of the known world': Madeira, Porto Santo and the Desertas, and the 1375 Catalan map has Madeira named as the 'Isola de legname' (island of woods).

Then I came upon a legend and a mysterious poem which raised even more questions, and I began to really explore: what if ...? The legend and its popularised form in the poem by James Bird in 1821, which my enigmatic character Georgina discusses, tells of the romance of Robert Machym and Ana d'Arafet (there are several spellings of both these names, even within the same documents) who fled the English court of Edward III when Ana's father forced her into a betrothal to a court nobleman of higher status than Robert, and who became shipwrecked on

AFTERWORD

Madeira in 1344. The poem is full of the florid high-flown language and elaborate Romanticism of much minor Victorian poetry, but it gave me the basis of the oral legend of its origin on which to build my story. I changed the legend's conclusion and some of the details, but it was certainly my inspiration from which my imagination took flight.

Further research both on-site and online, led me to muse upon the accepted 'truth' of the discovery of the Madeiran archipelago by Zarco in 1418. What if the major motivation of Prince Henry was two-fold: (1) commercial: not only to seek out new lands for trade expansionism, but also specifically to break the Arab control of trading routes in the eastern-most Atlantic, and (2) religious: to crush the much-feared (to the Portuguese of the time) Islamic hold on North Africa and to spread Christianity instead? But what if the islands off the west coast of North Africa had already been discovered and even occupied by Arab Islamic exploration long before Henry's forays? What if there was truth in both the legend of Ana and Robert 100 years before Zarco, and in the notion that the island was not only discovered but maybe partially settled many centuries even before that, by Moorish explorers way before the conventional narrative?

These musings led me to create a story where the real discoverers were in fact the forgotten Moors from North Africa, and that Ana discovers this, whereupon her story is remembered only as a myth and a new

AFTERWORD

'historic truth' is born from the more palatable (to some) Western history of Prince Henry and Zarco.

I thought: what would the more narrow-minded and anxious church warden make of this? And so my story of present-day John's deception and Dr Viv's discoveries amidst her 'haunting' by the restless spirit of Ana d'Arafet, then Anja-Filipa, arose.

And I suppose the biggest 'what if' is about time-slip or time-resonances, the ability of someone with a highly attuned sensitivity to touch, in some way, the echoes of another time, and to reach across time and space? **A Shape on the Air**, **The Dragon Tree**, and the last in the trilogy, **The Rune Stone**, all explore this as a possibility. I'd like to think this could be true.

How do we know what is 'truth' and what nuggets of truth there are hidden in legends and folk tales? What if …?

Dr Julia Ibbotson
2021

Further reading you might like (not an extensive list, just highlights!):

Ancillo, T., Giovine, L., Hernandez, A. (2015) *Flora of Madeira* (Escudo de Oro; SA)

Bird, James (1821) *Machin or the discovery of Madeira, a poem in four cantos* (Warren; London)

Fernandes, C., Gottardo, S. et al (2015) *Madeira* (Bonechi; Florence)

Mark, O (2006) *Edward III 1312-1377* (OUP; Oxford)

Mark, O (2012) *Edward III* (Yale UP, Yale)

Munby, J., Barber & Brown (2007) *Edward III's Round Table at Windsor* (Boydell Press)

Ornelas, P (ed), translated by Blandy, R (2007) *The Madeira Story* (Lisgrafica; SA)

Regan, Lesley (2018) *Miscarriage: what every woman needs to know* (Orion; London)

Rogers, C.J. (2000) *War cruel and sharp: English strategy under Edward III 1327-1360* (Boydell Press)

Taylor, Barbara B. (2014) *Learning to walk in the dark* (Canterbury Press; London)

Ute York (ed) *Insight Madeira* (APA Publications)

ACKNOWLEDGMENTS

Acknowledgements for information:

João Spinola: a huge source of information about Madeira

The Madeira Centre, Funchal: a wonderful hands-on museum of the history and geology of Madeira

Ariel Levy: articles on the effects of miscarriage on mind and body

Geologists at Grutas e Centro do Volcanismo, Sao Vicente, Madeira: adding to my knowledge of geology and vulcanism with specific application to Madeira

ALSO BY JULIA IBBOTSON

A Shape on the Air

The Rune Stone

The Drumbeats Trilogy

The Old Rectory: Escape to a Country Kitchen

S.C.A.R.S (a children's novel)

Printed in Dunstable, United Kingdom